HARRISON'S HEIR

MEG STEVENS

Sequel to 'In Her Mother's Footsteps'

Order this book online at www.trafford.com/07-1109
or email orders@trafford.com

Most Trafford titles are also available at major online book retailers.

Note for Librarians: A cataloguing record for this book is available from Library
and Archives Canada at www.collectionscanada.ca/amicus/index-e.html

Printed in Victoria, BC, Canada.

ISBN: 978-1-4251-3054-1

*We at Trafford believe that it is the responsibility of us all, as both individuals
and corporations, to make choices that are environmentally and socially sound.
You, in turn, are supporting this responsible conduct each time you purchase a
Trafford book, or make use of our publishing services. To find out how you are
helping, please visit www.trafford.com/responsiblepublishing.html*

*Our mission is to efficiently provide the world's finest, most comprehensive
book publishing service, enabling every author to experience success.
To find out how to publish your book, your way, and have it available
worldwide, visit us online at www.trafford.com/10510*

www.trafford.com

North America & international
toll-free: 1 888 232 4444 (USA & Canada)
phone: 250 383 6864 ♦ fax: 250 383 6804
email: info@trafford.com

 gdom & Europe
ph   local rate: 0845 230 9
fa

To all those who read my first book and who gave me the encouragement to have this second one published.

PART
ONE

CHAPTER ONE

Tommie's head suddenly began to reel and he felt the colour drain from his usual rosy cheeks as he sank back in the low but comfortable armchair and exhaled a weary sigh. He couldn't believe, perhaps did not want to believe, what he had just heard and was certainly finding the matter very hard to digest. For a fleeting moment he imagined that it was the whiskey playing tricks on his mind but he knew in his heart that he wasn't drunk.

No, he had definitely heard right! This man in front of him had unexpectedly admitted that he was his biological father and was willing his big estate to him. God, it was certainly the biggest shock that he had ever received in his young life and he didn't quite know how to respond. How was he supposed to feel about it? What was he to say? It was simply impossible to come to terms with it all.

Glancing quickly across the long, polished oak desk Tommie tried to compose himself as he realised that it was indeed a sad and lonely individual who was facing him, yet he found it hard to muster up any feelings of sympathy towards him. Ken Harrison was his father by birth right only! He had had an affair with his mother many years ago and he had been born as a result. Had Jack Bordoni, the man whom he had always looked upon as his Dad, been aware of his wife's betrayal? He couldn't be certain but one thing for sure was that Rosie, his older sister, knew all about it. Harrison had told him as much! But then again Rosie seemed to know everything!

1

Tommie's mind quickly wandered back to that day, during his early childhood, when he had come home from the village in tears. His mother had only been dead about a month at the time and the boys had been teasing and punching him around. Fint Browne, from the post office, had been the cruelest of all and it was he who had actually spat into his scared little face. "Go home to your father, Mr. Ken Harrison" his eyes had been full of malice as he spoke. "Go home to Harrison and ask him if he is your father!"

"He's not my father!" Tommie had stoutly denied the allegation and supposed that Browne was mad.

"Course he's your father" Browne had continued with venom. "Sure everyone around here 'cept you seems to know that. Look at yourself, for God's sake, you're the absolute spitting image of him!"

Tommie, horrified and heart broken at the cruelty of the harsh hateful words, had tried to punch Browne but had come out the worse for the wear. Rosie, upon hearing of his plight, had held him to her bosom and persuaded him that it had all been a load of nonsense. He had believed her, in his innocence, and yet all the time she had known the truth. What an utter fool he had been! He'd certainly have to have it out with her later on and he'd make sure that she'd never pull the wool over his eyes again as long as he lived!

"Tommie, please say something." Harrison's voice suddenly broke through his thoughts and quickly brought him back to the present. "At least tell me what you are thinking." As he stared at the still, thoughtful figure his swelling heart leapt within his aging chest; he was so full of pride at the very sight of this boy whom he had finally acknowledged as his own. Tommie was indeed tall and handsome and his body strong and muscular. He had lost the unruly mop of curls that had sat on his head as a child and had grown to become a man that any father could be proud of.

"I don't know what to say!" Tommie played with the glass in front of him as he frantically tried to make sense of his thoughts and feelings. "To tell you the truth this is indeed a shock and I am finding it hard to take it in. Don't get me wrong here, I am delighted with your gift of the estate but you must realise that it will take a little time for me to adjust to the fact that you are my father. I certainly had no idea! You are sure about this, aren't you? There is no doubt at all in your mind?"

"No Tommie, I can safely assure you that there is no doubt what so ever!" Harrison was thoughtful for a moment as he scratched his shiny head. "Your mother and I were lovers for years and sure all you have to do is examine yourself closely and you will know that you are mine. You have my nose and my mouth! Your origin was kept a secret and Jack Bordoni never knew the truth. He always believed that he was your father because that was the way your mother wanted it and I respected her wishes. I hadn't planned to say anything to you today either, I was going to wait and let you find out when I am dead and gone and my will is being read, but I am weary with all the lies. In fact I am weary with life itself. I am tired of farming and all the hardships that go with it and I long to retire to a nice small cottage near a seaside. I have watched you closely over the last few months and I know that you will cherish this place just as I have done down through the years. That alone will give me peace of mind."

"Did you love her?" He needed to get it straight in his head, needed to know if he had been born out of lust or passion.

Harrison was quiet for a moment as the memories of his past warmed his soul yet again and brought a rare smile to his wrinkled, down turned lips. When he did speak his voice seemed gentle yet distant.

"Yes, Tommie, I can safely tell you that I did love her. More than anything else in this world, in fact! She meant everything to me but I couldn't have her, you see! She loved your father and wouldn't leave him. No amount of persuasion on my part could alter that! I thought that I found another love after she passed on but sadly, that too is now lost to me. I have to get away from this place before it brings me down altogether but I would like to feel that you and I could be friends before I go. Do you think that that is possible?"

Tommie's heart slowly began to mellow as he looked at the sad, aged man and noticed that he had failed a lot over the last few months. He had never really been the same since the night he had been stabbed. It had obviously taken more out of him than he had cared to admit and he was lucky to be alive at all after it. All of a sudden the pity that he had been unable to feel earlier gripped him like a bad pain and all his sympathies went out to Harrison.

What had he in his life? Oh, he had his estate and his beautiful Manor house but was that enough? Tommie didn't think so! Harrison had no one to share his ideas and aspirations with. He had no one to greet him on the hearth when he came in after a long hard day's work and no one to cheer him up when he was feeling a little down. Rosie did his housekeeping during the day but she was so moody lately that she couldn't be much company for anyone.

Yes, what did he have to lose by being friendly with him? He had never known his real father as Jack had died shortly after his birth. Then again his real father was sitting in front of him at this very moment and had just made him a landowner. He was no longer an employee! He was his own boss! He was the sole owner of two hundred of the best acres in County Laois. It was more than he could ever have hoped for and, no matter what the circumstances, he knew that he owed his gratitude to this man. Yes, he certainly had nothing to lose by being friends with him.

"Mr. Harrison." He swallowed any bitterness that had developed as he extended his right hand towards his father. "It would indeed be a great honor for me to accept your kind gift and I do think that it is important that we remain friends. I will be expecting you to show me the ropes around here so I hope that you won't be leaving straight away. I want to learn to farm this place exactly the way you have managed to do over the years. The success of Dalesport farm must be allowed to continue."

"That's what I like to hear." Harrison shook the hand vigorously and knew in that instant that he had definitely made the right decision. "We'll go into my solicitor some day early in the New Year and make this official. Oh God, I am so happy Tommie! This is the day that I have spent my entire life dreaming about but never thought that I would be alive to enjoy! Now, I know that it is a little too late in the day to expect you to call me 'Dad' but do you think that you could manage to drop the 'Mister' business and call me Ken? It's less formal."

"I'm sure that can be arranged, Ken" Tommie joked as he finished off the whiskey in his glass. "Now, I'd best get on home

4

but let me wish you a happy and a peaceful Christmas before I go. It's certainly going to be the best one that I have ever had." He hugged his father before leaving and then made his way out onto into the cold, dark December evening.

As he walked around the outhouses Tommie's mind was not on his origins now but was firmly fixed on his future. His thoughts raced ahead as he began to make ambitious plans. He had been the poor boy up until today but life had miraculously turned around. In a few years time he would be rich and he couldn't wait to see the look on Rosie's face when he told her his news. Glancing across at the winter clad fields he grinned to himself with pride as he realised that all this was now his. Allowing a whoop of delight to escape onto the frosty air he hugged himself tightly and practically skipped back to his cottage in a frenzy of excitement.

He called over to see his sister at around eight that evening and, as he had anticipated Rosie was not at all amused by Harrison's revelation. She was in fact fuming over it and Tommie failed to see why she was so concerned but he honestly didn't really care. He refused her invitation to Christmas dinner the following day and returned to his home a tired but happy man.

He opened a bottle of red wine, stroked and fed the dying embers in the old stove and sat down, immersed in his own thoughts.

Sipping the sweet claret Tommie could feel his body start to relax and, all of a sudden, he began to regret the fact that he had not known that Harrison was his father while he had been growing up. How many times, in his world of cackling women, had he longed for a male companion to confide in? And he had actually thought that he had been an orphan when his mother had passed away! Still, he'd make up for lost time now. He'd get to know the man who had been his superior all his life and maybe some day they could really be as father and son. He went to bed that night in an intoxicated state but tomorrow was Christmas Day, a day of peace and rest, so he felt no guilt. He intended to take things easy for a change. After all he was no longer an employee!

Tommie awoke the following morning with the mother of all hangovers and was not in the mood for doing anything at all. He lazed about the cottage and didn't have the will or the energy to face mass. Rosie's four children called to see him around midday and tried to persuade him to join them for dinner. Again he refused the invitation but sent them home laden with Christmas presents and they seemed to be content enough then to leave without him.

After preparing a simple meal for himself he cleaned the dishes and opened yet another bottle of wine. He seemed to be under the illusion that if he fed his hangover it might just disappear altogether! He kept meaning to wander over to the Manor to visit Harrison but it was bitter cold outside and his fire was so cosy. Anyway he felt too tired! He'd wait until tomorrow, St. Stephen's day, and maybe he might be feeling more sociable then!

He had just polished off a second bottle of wine when he heard a loud frantic banging at the door. Christ, what was wrong now? Who in the name of God was in such a panic? Rising unwillingly he made for the door and was very surprised to discover Rosie standing on his doorstep, looking like death warmed up. She was clearly agitated and what was more she refused to come inside.

"What the hell's the matter with you?" he was a little frightened by her appearance but tried to calm her down. "You're making a terrible amount of noise altogether! Is there someone out there chasing you?"

"Tommie, you have to come quick! It's Harrison. He's had a bad heart attack." She gulped in huge mouthfuls of the cold afternoon air and couldn't seem to stand still for a second. "Jesus, I think that he might be dead!"

"Christ, no, this can't be for real!" He didn't wait to see if she was following but raced across the estate through the wet December grass, his heart pounding frantically against his ribs. The icy winds hit him hard in the face and the effects of the wine caused his head to spin.

Despite all his misgivings he managed to reach the Manor in record time and entered through the open door. Quickly making his way towards the study he gasped as he discovered Harrison's body on the floor. He knew straight away that he was dead; there was no movement what so ever and no sound of breathing, but he checked for a pulse anyway, just in case.

Upon failing to find one he sadly laid pressure to the cold, staring eyes and closed them for the last time.

Tommie's heart felt heavy and his stomach sick. What a time for Harrison to depart this life just as he had confessed the sins of his heart. He had been so looking forward to getting to know him as a son should and now here it was snatched away from him again. Life was so unfair!

He couldn't understand how Harrison had suffered this heart attack so suddenly. He had seemed perfectly healthy yesterday, a little down perhaps but healthy! Rosie claimed not to know anything about the attack but she was so shaken that Tommie knew she was lying. She was a strange one that girl! He never could make her out at all!

The first of the winter snows fell on the morning that Harrison's body was laid to rest. He had chosen a plot at the back of his estate and the funeral was quiet and subdued. Tommie had not cried for a long time but the tears fell freely as he stood there, witnessing the coffin being lowered into the cold, dark depressing ground. His heart was pining for something that he never had and he was feeling vulnerable. How many people had he already lost to death? Jack Bordoni had died a young man and his mother had been taken when he was only ten. Sylvie, his sister had disappeared and nobody knew where she was and now Harrison, his biological father was gone.

His mind was disturbed as he slowly followed the crowd back to the Manor for the reading of the will. He had no interest what so ever in the will as he already knew the outcome but he longed to get it over and done with. Rosie seemed to be in a fidgety state and he wondered why. He knew that Robbie, her husband, had left on Christmas day but he assumed that he would be back. She was probably missing him, that was it!

The will opened and the crowd that had gathered let out a loud gasp upon discovering that Harrison had sired Tommie. The dark, carefully held secret was finally common knowledge and now everyone knew of his origins. Oh, to hell with it! He was gone past caring. He had his farm, his father's estate, and all these men would be working for him. Let anyone of them who dared step out of line or say the wrong thing and that would be that! He'd terminate their jobs immediately and send them packing.

What followed next, however, stunned even him. Harrison was leaving the Manor house to his other child, Dawn. But Dawn was Rosie and Robbie's daughter! Something was wrong here. He looked across at Rosie and raised his eyebrows and knew in an instant from the look on her face that nothing was wrong! Harrison had indeed been Dawn's father too! So Rosie had been the second love that he had mentioned. Jesus it was unbelievable! But how was Dawn taking the news? The tears were streaming down her young face and she was racing towards the door. Rosie was getting up to follow her but the poor child would be better off left alone for the moment to deal with the pain. Catching his sister by the arm he bade her to remain seated and she meekly obeyed.

Tommie intended to pull his sister aside after the session. He needed to find out some truths, some facts that would allow his mind to digest what had been going on but noticed that she had already left the room. There were so many questions that he needed to ask her but they would have to wait until later. After been congratulated by the farm hands on his good fortune he put the will out of his head and set about his business. He worked hard throughout the afternoon and was determined to make his dead father proud of him.

CHAPTER TWO

The snow was really pelting down as Tommie made his way back to the cottage at half past five that evening and it lay in soft, unspoiled drifts along the edges of the outhouses. Under different circumstances he might have paused for a moment to exclaim at it's sheer virginal beauty but he was tired and hungry and depressed. All he wanted to do was get inside and rest.

Pulling some logs from the tidy heap at the back door he shook the cold white particles from his coat and entered his home.

The kitchen was cold and dark and, as he walked across the grey tiles, an unnatural shiver suddenly raced down his spine. Shuddering, he felt that someone had walked all over his grave and he automatically blessed himself. He wasn't what you would call a religious man but he did have certain beliefs. Setting about lighting the fire as quickly as he could he had just put the kettle on to boil when he heard a knock at the back door.

Assuming that it was Rosie who was outside he was in no hurry to open it. She was the last person on the earth that he wanted to see right now. He had no energy to argue with her and he wasn't sure anymore if he really wanted to hear the truth about her affair with his father. He felt that ignorance was certainly bliss in this instance, for the time being anyway. However, it was in fact Kitty, his other sister, who stood there and he beckoned at her to come in, frightened by the panic in her eyes.

"Hi Tommie" she tried to smile at him but was finding it hard. "Is Rosie or Dawn here with you?"

"I'm on my own here!" Tommie nodded at her again to come inside. "I haven't seen either of them since the reading this morning. Have they not been home yet?"

"No, Rosie stuck her head in the door and said that she was going to look for Dawn. But that was ages ago and neither have been seen since. It's so cold and dark outside and I'm really worried about them at this stage. It's not like Rosie to stay out like this."

"You're right, Kitty, it is most unusual! Rosie was always one for the bit of heat. I'll tell you what, I'll go fetch Jake and we'll have a good look around. In the meantime, try not to worry, I'm sure everything will be fine."

"Oh God, I hope so but I can't help feeling that something terrible has happened. I'll wait here until you return. Try not to be too long!"

Jake took to search the fields at the back of the Manor while Tommie, for some strange reason, was automatically drawn towards the river. The snow had stopped falling for the moment but a heavy blanket lay on the ground and impeded his progress.

As he eventually approached the riverbank Tommie shone his torch ahead and thought that he could make out a distant shape near the cold banks. Quickening his pace he hurried towards the shadow and gasped as he realised that it was actually his sister. She had obviously collapsed in the snow earlier and had lain there since. Her eyes were closed and she was as still as a corpse. There was no sign of Dawn.

Wiping the tiny particles of snow from the cold, stiff body he picked it up in his arms and was grateful that she was breathing gently. It was certainly a struggle to reach the house; Rosie seemed to be getting heavier by the minute, and he silently prayed as he walked. Kitty was waiting anxiously for him and immediately telephoned for an ambulance. Both of them knew that Rosie was very ill but didn't comprehend just how bad she really was. Kitty tried to warm up her sister's body as they waited and prayed feverently that she would remain breathing. After all, where there was life there was hope!

The ambulance arrived within twenty minutes and Rosie was taken to hospital and treated for hypothermia. Kitty accompanied her while Tommie went to find Jake. They trudged back through the snows again, searching the entire estate for his missing niece. At eleven o' clock, tired, hungry and disillusioned they reluctantly gave up and made for home. Tommie had only just entered the cottage when the telephone rang. It was Kitty again and she sounded anxious.

"Tommie, is that you? Kitty here! Jesus, things are really awful! Rosie is not well at all and it looks like I am going to have to stay the night with her. Will you go over and mind the children? I don't want them left on their own any longer than is necessary."

"Of course I will. Kitty, will she be alright?"

"The doctors are not sure yet but they are hopeful. They will know more tomorrow."

"Please God, she will be okay. She's a tough nut, you know! I've searched and searched for Dawn and I can't find her anywhere. I'll don't know what to do at this stage. She could be miles away by now."

"Christ, Tommie, how can I tell you this? It's terrible!" Kitty's grief spilled towards him down the telephone line and unsettled his nerves. "From the bits I can gather it would appear that Dawn has fallen into the river. Oh Tommie, I think she is dead! Rosie is in a coma and is unable to speak but every now and again she keeps on muttering that Dawn is in the river and that she couldn't save her. It's dreadful!"

"Jesus, Kitty, are you serious? You don't think that maybe Rosie is only hallucinating?"

"No, I don't think so. I think that she saw the child fall into the river and that is what brought on her collapse. We will have to face it, Tommie, it looks like poor Dawn is dead."

"Oh Lord! This can't be happening, what are we to do?"

"Say nothing to the kids until I come home. I'll be back early in the morning and we'll talk then. I'd better go now, the doctor is coming back to Rosie and I want to be there when he arrives."

"Ok. See you tomorrow then." He replaced the receiver gently, his hand shaking uncontrollably, and wondered how much more of this grief he could actually cope with.

The snow had begun to fall again the following morning but Tommie arose early and worked around the farm. He wanted to be free when Kitty returned. She would need him when she told the children about the awful tragedy. He had informed them the previous evening that their mother was in hospital and that she would be okay. He had also told them that Dawn was with her. While he hated himself for the lie he knew that he hadn't the guts to tell them the truth. They were so young and innocent and it broke his heart when he thought of what lay ahead for them.

It was nearly half past ten by the time Kitty finally arrived. Her face seemed to have aged about ten years and there were large black circles underneath her tired eyes. Tommie put the kettle on the hob and, after a quick mug of coffee, she mustered what little courage and strength she had left and gathered the children around. She spoke slowly and softly.

"Darlings, there is something that I need to tell you all and I expect you all to listen carefully and be very brave. Your mother is in hospital and is in a coma. She will get better soon but we have to be patient."

"Can we go and see her?" Jack looked hopefully at his aunt.

"Maybe, in a couple of days, we'll have to wait and see!" She paused to draw her breath as she pondered on the best way to relate the other piece of information that she had for them. "Now, I'm afraid that poor Dawn has not been so lucky. As far as we know, Dawn fell into the river and has been swept away by the strong currents."

"But Tommie, you said that she was in hospital with Mam." Kevin looked accusingly at his uncle.

"I know I did Kevin and I'm sorry that I lied to you. I just couldn't bring myself to tell you the truth last night."

"Is Dawn dead then?" It was a question asked out of innocence but its tone rang harsh around the room.

"Yes, Kevin, I'm afraid your big sister has gone to God. But she will become a little angel and you can pray to her. Her granny and granddad are up there and they will look after her and love her. She'll be okay."

"Yeah, but I loved her too. I'm going to miss her, she was the only sister that I had!" Sarah started to cry and suddenly everyone was off.

"I want Dad, I want Dad!" It all became too much for Kevin and he started to wail uncontrollably. "Make him come home to us, Tommie, make him come home."

The heartache was still evident when Kitty tucked them into bed that night and, although they were fretful, they were worn out and fell asleep in no time.

Tommie was still sitting at the fireside, staring into the angry flames when Kitty reentered the kitchen. His eyes were swollen and his sorrow great. He had lost two relatives in a matter of days and his sister's life still hung in the balance.

"The kids have fallen asleep at last." Kitty sat beside him and gazed into his sad eyes. "God help them, they are shattered."

"It's not going to be easy on them, is it? Remember how we felt when Sylvie disappeared?"

"Yeah! Oh Tommie, it only seems like yesterday and I can still smell the fear that hung in the air that night. This is not going to be easy on any of us at all! Rosie will be heart broken when she wakes up. I still can't believe that this is happening! It's like something that you see in a sad movie or read about in a book. But what I can't understand about it all is why Rosie and Dawn were down at the river in the first place. I mean, it was snowing quite heavily so why did they decide to go for a walk?"

"Kitty." Tommie knew that the moment of truth had arrived, the moment he had been dreading. "There is something that I have been meaning to say to you since all this happened but, between one thing and another, I haven't had the opportunity."

"Go on, this sounds serious!" Her heart skipped a beat as she waited for her brother to continue.

"You know that we all attended the reading of the will." He eyed her and wondered if she was strong enough to accept the awful truth that he was about to unfold.

"Yes, and Harrison left the estate to you."

"Aye, but that's not all, he left the Manor house to Dawn."

"He what? Why on earth did he do that?" She raised her eyebrows and wondered if he was only having her on.

"Dawn was his daughter." There was nothing for it but to give her the blatant facts.

"Ah, come on now! How was that possible?" Kitty thought that she was hearing things but after all that had taken place lately nothing would surprise her now.

"It seems that after mother died Harrison turned his attention to Rosie. He told me himself that he had found a new love but that she was lost to him. I think that they were having an affair all along. Anyway, he owns Dawn and left the Manor house to her in his will. Rosie tried to pawn her off as Robbie's and we all believed her!"

"That's what caused this upset?" Kitty sank back on the chair in a bid to settle herself and honestly did not know whether to be sad or furious.

"Yes, Dawn left the room as soon as she heard the contents of the will and ran out into the snow. It was the only way she knew of coping with the truth, God help her, and must have made for the river. Rosie followed her, she had left before I had realised it, and Lord knows what happened next! Dawn probably lost her footing in the snow and got carried away by the currents. The river is fairly high and dangerous at the moment."

"Oh my God, my God! How horrible! The poor, poor child falling to her death like that! And knowing what she knew about her father! It doesn't bear thinking about. But what in the name of God was Rosie playing at all? She can't seriously have been keeping Harrison's bed warm for him. Sure he was years older than her. What would she have seen in him at all? But you know, now that I think about it, I remember seeing him at the doorstep once blowing kisses to her. It was the night of his birthday, you know the night we had that big party! I tackled her about it the next day but she denied it. Said it was my imagination! Being the fool that I am I believed her and thought no more about it since. But how could she do it? In the name of God what possessed her? Sure he was a doddery old man, well past his prime. Jesus, I wonder is that why Robbie left. Did he find out about the affair?"

"Probably! You know we may ring him and let him know what has happened. The kids will need him at a time like this."

"I don't have a phone number for him." Kitty was trying to think straight but was finding it hard.

"Well then, we may send him a telegram. He's in Meath isn't he? Brook farm, wasn't that the name of the place he bought?"

"Yeah, that's it! I'll go down to the post office first thing in the morning and send one. He has a right to know alright! After all he is still her husband and technically Dawn's father. Maybe with a bit of luck he will come back home for good."

"Maybe he will!" Tommie agreed with his sister but did not hold out much hope.

Robbie, however, arrived at Dalesport as soon as he received the telegram. Tommie met him at the cottage and brewed him a cup of tea.

"Sit down old chap" he indicated the chair at the fireside. "Terrible weather, isn't it?" He felt that the small talk was necessary to break the ice.

"Yeah, the snow is really coming down alright. They say that we're to have it for a couple of weeks yet."

"God, I hope not. The house never seems to be heated when there's snow on the ground and it's hard work keeping all the animals fed. They get so hungry in the cold!"

"Yeah" Robbie was silent for a moment and his face was grave. Suddenly he looked at his brother in law and he was sad. "Tommie, tell me, how has it all come down to this? What have we done to deserve it at all?"

"I don't know, I don't know!" He shook his head and could think of nothing else to say.

"How is Rosie doing?" There was definitely an element of concern in his voice.

"It's hard to say! Kitty was at the hospital this morning and it seems that she hasn't awoken yet. The doctors think that she is in some sort of shock and will only awaken when her mind stops torturing her."

"God, what an awful tragedy. And there is still no sign of Dawn's body?"

"No. I'm afraid not!"

"Maybe she is not in the river at all! Maybe she will turn up one of these moments out of the blue and ask us all what we are worrying about!" Robbie knew that he was clutching at straws but he needed to be hopeful.

"I hate to say this, old chap" Tommie felt that he had to be brutally honest here. There was no point in allowing Robbie to hope for the impossible. "But I think that it is safe to assume that the poor girl is dead at this stage. She'd never stay away this long, she's too young. It's hard to come to terms with but there you are! Such a tragic waste of a beautiful innocent life!"

"I still can't believe that all this has happened. One minute we were all so happy and looking forward to starting a new life at Brook Farm and the next this! Oh my poor Dawn, my poor Dawn, why had it all to end like this for you?" He cried bitter tears for the loss of his child and Tommie began to feel uncomfortable. He was no good in situations like this and he wished with all his heart that Kitty were here. She would know what to do!

"Robbie." Tommie looked at the older man as soon as he had dried his tears. "I know this is not the best of times to ask you this but why did you leave Dalesport in such a hurry?"

Robbie was silent for a moment as he played with the wet tissue and then he shrugged his shoulders. "It doesn't matter now, let's just say that I had my reasons."

"Please Robbie." Tommie was almost begging him. "I really need to know."

Robbie placed his head in his hands for a moment and released a heavy sigh. Could he explain to his brother- in- law the real reason for his departure? He supposed that he'd find out sooner or later so there was no point in holding back. Too much truth had been hidden already and look at the mess that had erupted. Sighing heavily he looked into Tommie's handsome face.

"You won't believe this, I still can't believe it myself, but I found Rosie and Harrison together!" It was said with so much heartache that Tommie felt sorry for putting him in the position.

"When? When did you find them together?" He was being cruel now but he longed to confirm his suspicions.

"Does it matter?" He would prefer not to have to talk about it at all.

"I need to know!" Tommie wished the conversation was over but he had to discover the truth.

"On Christmas day, the day that Harrison died." The sadness in his voice was suddenly replaced by bitterness and he could visualise the pair of them in his mind's eye. "Rosie said she had a headache and was going for a walk to try and clear it. When she didn't return I began to get worried and decided to go in search of her. And where did I find her? In the study with Harrison and the two of them at it for all they were worth. It must have been too much for the old git, though, didn't he die shortly afterwards! Listen Tommie, to be honest with you I don't want to talk about it, it's too painful and I still feel so bitter, so very, very bitter. Anyway you did well out of him, didn't he leave his entire estate to you."

"Robbie." Tommie failed to hide the emotion in his voice and wondered how Robbie would react when he divulged his next piece of information. "Harrison left me his estate because he was my father. It seems that Rosie was only the second Bordoni woman that he had bedded."

"Your fuckin father? Jesus Christ above, I don't believe you!" Robbie's face went as white as a sheet as he stared hard at Tommie.

"Yes, it's true, he told me on Christmas Eve, the day before he died. And there is something else that you will discover too so I might as well tell you now. Prepare yourself for a shock Robbie because there is no easy way of saying this! I'm afraid that he was also Dawn's father."

"Now I know that you are lying." Robbie's reply was loud and angry. "How can you even say such a thing? Sure it's impossible! Dawn is my child, my flesh and blood! Do you hear me? Wasn't I there the night that Rosie told me we had created her?"

"Harrison left the Manor house to Dawn. He stated in his will that he was her father. That was why she left the room in a hurry and headed towards the river. She was shocked to the core and, you know, Rosie wanted to go after her but I stopped her. I thought that the girl would be better off on her own. If only I had let Rosie go, things might have been different! I'm so sorry to be the one to have to tell you all this but you'll find out in time anyway. It seems that my sister has conned you

17

into believing that the child was yours. Rosie has been conning people all her life and as soon as she is well again I mean to have it out with her."

Rosie, however, never did receive the sharp edge of Tommie's tongue. She remained in her demented state for weeks on end and was eventually transferred to a nursing home to recover. Tommie visited her once or twice but after that he stayed away. When Dawn's body was finally washed up at the old mill the family grieved once more and it took a long time for all of them to come to terms with their loss.

CHAPTER THREE

By the time Tommie had reached the age of twenty-five he was indeed a very wealthy young man. His farm had prospered beyond his wildest beliefs but it hadn't happened overnight. Driven by sheer will and determination he had spent every waking moment on his farm. His employees found him to be a hard yet fair task- master but he needed to feel confident that Harrison was proud of him. He needed to make the farm profitable for his father's sake. Now, on this the night of his birthday, he had decided to take the evening off and let his hair down for a change. He had arranged to meet his pal, Bill Foley, at the village hall and drive to a dance in Ballyhale. He had no real interest in women but tonight he was going to find one for himself. He didn't want anything serious, just a fling, a one night stand and, as he readied himself at the cottage, he sang a tune that he had heard that morning on the radio.

Life had turned out better than Tommie could ever have anticipated. Rosie had never managed to come out of her demented state but was getting the best care at the Ashtrees nursing home. It was hoped that some day she would surprise everyone and return to the real world. In the meantime Kitty was looking after the children at the Manor and had just wed Mike Dunne, one of the farm hands, and was extremely happy.

It had been Tommie who had suggested the move to the Manor. After all it had been willed to Dawn and if Rosie was around he had no doubts but she would be living there. There was far too much room in the house for him anyway. He had no intention of ever marrying and having children so how did it make sense to live in the big house? He was more than content in his cosy little cottage.

Tommie's unwillingness to trust women stemmed from deep within his past. He knew enough about them to know that they were not to be trusted. He had adored his mother and had discovered that she had been having an affair with Harrison. And then there was Rosie, his guardian angel. Who would have thought that she would betray her husband and fall into Harrison's clutches also? No, women were alright for a bit of fun but that was that! What was the point in adding pressure and hardship to your life? He had the farm to contend with and he was happy on his own. What more could a man want?

As he searched for his razor, to shave his week old whiskers, his mind suddenly drifted towards Robbie, his brother in law. Now there was a man to be pitied! The poor sucker had given himself completely to a woman and look how his life had turned out. Oh, he had his farm in County Meath and by all accounts it was successful but how many years had it taken him to get over his wife's betrayal? Robbie had entered a state of depression that had lasted well over two years and his farm had suffered as a result. It was only now that his life was beginning to knit back together for him. No, Tommie was going to have a good time and enjoy life but that was all. No commitments, good bad or indifferent!

Bill Foley was already sitting on a high stool when he entered the pub and was neatly dressed in a black pair of trousers and a light blue shirt. He was so handsome that all the women in Dalesport lost sleep over him and he had charm to beat the band! Bill wasn't going steady with anyone at the moment but had his eye on Sadie Murphy. Sadie was a quiet girl and although she secretly fancied Bill she kept her distance from him. Bill, however, was feeling lucky that evening and was hopeful.

"How are you Tommie?" he greeted his pal as soon as he arrived. "What are you having to drink?"

"A pint of ale would go down nicely." Tommie nodded his appreciation at Bill. "Not many in here tonight."

"No, but don't fret, sure it's early enough yet. Happy Birthday by the way."

"Thanks." He smiled in contentment.

"Here's the drink coming. Now let's toast to the night we have in store and may we be blessed with the best of the birds."

"Here, here!" Tommie couldn't help but smile at his friend. Bill was a good sort but he was mad for a woman. He had had the privilege of dating several but somehow he couldn't manage to get the one that he really wanted. Tommie was sure that if he were willing to wait long enough Sadie would eventually be his. He had seen the way she had looked at him on several occasions and knew that she fancied him. She was going to be at the dance tonight so who knows what would happen.

"Did ya sell any cattle lately?" Bill was a block layer by trade and did not know too much about the farming profession. He knew that Tommie, however, lived solely for his farm so he feigned interest.

"Sold two the other day to Tom Ryan, from the crosswords. Two nice heifers they were too! The main thing is I managed to get a good price for them."

"That's good, that's good! Nothing like the colour of money to make it all worthwhile. Now let's get another pint here and then we'll head towards the dance. Don't want the finest women to be gone before we get there, do we?"

It was almost half past eleven when they eventually reached the dance hall as they both had been somewhat reluctant to leave their comfortable bar stools but the crowd was still gathering. They paid at the door and walked across the wide hall to the bar. Ordering yet another drink they scanned the hall with their roving eyes and Bill became excited when he spied Sadie. She was sitting at a table, looking more beautiful than ever, with her sister and Dympna O' Reilly. He roughly nudged Tommie in the ribs.

"She's here alright, do ya see her over there? Bet ya five bob that tonight I'll get to taste those beautiful rosy lips. Are you on?"

"You're a devil, do you know that?" Tommie laughed at his friend's eagerness. "But go on, I'll have the bet with you for peace sake!"

The music was loud and the dance floor black with people but Bill decided to have another couple of pints to settle his nerves before he made his move. Wishing him luck Tommie watched as he walked across to where Sadie was seated. Bill's confident air was less evident than usual and Tommie unconsciously found himself mutter a silent prayer for his pal. He'd be devastated if Sadie were to refuse him. He turned for a moment to lift his pint and on looking back across the dance floor he noticed that Bill had indeed succeeded in getting Sadie onto the dance floor. There would be no stopping him now! He'd use his charm on her all right and Tommie could say goodnight to his five bob.

He continued to drink alone for a while and became so lost in his own thoughts that he failed to notice the dark, good looking girl who had approached and was standing beside him. It wasn't until she leaned across the bar to hand in money for her drink that he spotted her. Immediately he was impressed by her appearance but simply nodded his head. She responded by smiling back at him and as he gazed at her he could safely admit that she was the first woman ever who had managed to tug at his heart- strings.

"Hello" he heard himself greet her. Why was he suddenly feeling so shy and awkward?

"Hi, there, you're Tommie Bordoni, aren't you?" She gave him her best smile and he noticed her white even teeth.

"Yes, yes I am, but tell me, how did you know that?" He was certainly surprised that she had recognised him.

"Oh, I've seen you around." Unknown to Tommie this girl had been watching him for some time and had been awaiting her opportunity to speak with him. Standing beside him now, at the bar, had been no coincidence!

"And you are?" He had never seen her before, he was certain of that.

"Eve, Eve Kelly." She held out her hand to him.

"Pleased to meet you Eve." Tommie caught the hand and shook it gently. "Do you come here often?" As soon as he had it said he realised how cliched it sounded but he didn't seem to be in control of his emotions anymore.

"Actually, I come here quite a lot. I've seen you here before too, you know."

"Have you now!" He felt that she was definitely honest.

"Yeah, you're usually with that good looking fella, Bill. Is he here tonight?"

"He is indeed! He's out there dancing." He nodded towards the dance floor.

"Oh, I see him now! He's with Sadie. You know she has fancied him for ages."

"That's funny because he has fancied her too. They'll get together tonight for sure so."

"Do you fancy anyone?" She pulled her eyes away from the dance floor and was staring at him again.

Tommie was a little startled by her direct, personal question. For fuck sake, he hardly even knew her. Glancing in her direction he could feel the tug at his heart so he decided to answer her and answer her truthfully.

"No, I can't say that I do. What about yourself?"

"Yeah, I've fancied someone for a long, long time but I don't think he fancies me." She was thoughtful for a moment and he could not help but be amused at her facial expression.

"God above, I find that hard to believe! A good-looking lass like you? Anyway, how do you know?"

"How do I know what?"

"How do you know that he doesn't fancy you?"

"Well, he has never as much as looked in my direction before. It's a pity really because I have a feeling that we would be good together."

"Is he here tonight?" He looked around the dance hall to see if he could spot anyone whom she might be interested in.

"Yeah, as a matter of fact he is!" She was staring hard at him now but he was beginning to feel less uncomfortable.

"Then why don't you go on over and talk to him. Let him see what he is missing."

"I did!"

"And?" He couldn't understand why she was telling him all this but she was certainly amusing him.

"And nothing! He still didn't realise that I fancied him."

"I can't believe that! Is he blind or what? Are you sure?"

"You tell me!" Her eyes lit up as she gazed longingly into his.

"What do you mean?" She had lost him completely now.

"Oh, for God's sake Tommie, have you any brain at all in that good looking head of yours? It's you! You're the one that I fancy."

"I don't believe you!" How could a good-looking girl like that have any interest in a man like him?

"It's true, Tommie, I have my eye on you for ages. I have noticed, though, that you rarely ask anyone to dance with you. Why is that?"

"I have my reasons!" He hung his head for a moment and she looked surprised.

"Jesus, you're not a homo are you?" Her lower lip dropped, leaving her mouth open in a gape.

Tommie was appalled by her question and wanted to walk away there and then but he found that he couldn't. Instead he looked this direct speaking girl in the eye and began to laugh at her serious expression.

"May God forgive you for suggesting such a thing! Of course I am not a homo. I just haven't managed to find the right girl yet."

"Would you dance with me?" She certainly was not in the least bit shy.

"Is that a question or an invitation?"

"Both." She fluttered her eyelids and he was finding it hard to resist her.

"I suppose there would be no harm in it at all! Let's hit the dance floor."

As soon as Tommie placed his arms around Eve's waist he knew that she was different from anyone he had ever known before. She was so direct yet easy to talk to and the smell of her perfume made his head spin. He was, however, only here for the bit of fun and reminded himself to cop on. The last thing he wanted in his life was the complications of a female partner and, although Eve was definitely tugging at his affections, he held himself back.

At two o'clock the last song had been played and the crowd was beginning to leave the hall. Bill raced over to Tommie, his face alight with those pleasures that only a female can create, and told him to go on home without him. He was walking Sadie home and would call around the following day to collect his winnings. Turning to Eve he gave her a wink and he was gone.

"Would you like a lift home?" Tommie surprised himself at the question but he had to admit that he really had enjoyed her company.

"Are you going to drive after all that drink?" She wanted to be sure that he was still capable.

"Yeah, sure I'm not drunk and anyway there'll be no cops about at this hour of the morning."

"Okay, so, if its not too much bother but you have to promise me that there will be no speeding." Secretly she was delighted at the invitation.

"It's no bother at all and you can let me know when you think that I am travelling too fast. Is that a deal?"

"Yes, it's a deal!" She was so happy at that moment that she thought she would explode. How long had she awaited this encounter? How many times had she secretly stared at Tommie Bordoni and wondered if she would ever manage to talk to him? And now, here she was standing beside him, waiting for him to drive her home in his car! Yes, life suddenly looked as if it was going to improve.

"Right!" Tommie was oblivious to the sheer elation that she was experiencing. "Let's make our way to the car." He caught her by the hand and as she entwined her fingers through his he relished the warmth that immediately filtered through his body.

Eve lived about two miles outside Dalesport in a remote little thatched cottage. Her father was a small farmer and, because he would rather lie down beside the work than actually do it, struggled to make a living. She worked in a grocery shop in Dalesport herself and had to hand up the best part of her wages every week to her mother. Times were hard and money scarce, mostly due to her father's ill management of the farm.

"You have your own farm, haven't you?" She looked across at him through the darkness as he drove along the narrow country road and reveled in his closeness.

"Yes, yes I have." Sure wasn't it his pride and joy, the very essence of his existence!

"And is it true that Ken Harrison was your father?" She most certainly knew how to ask questions!

"Where did you hear that?" Jesus, everyone must know his business!

"Oh, you'd be surprised by what you'd hear when you're working behind a counter. Bored little housewives come in daily for their chat and some of the things they say would make the hair stand at the back of your neck."

"I see!" he wondered how much more she had heard about him. "Well, he was my father but I'd rather not talk about it if you don't mind."

"I'm very sorry, I wasn't trying to pry. I just think that it would be nice to get to know one another, that's all."

"I've never spoken to anyone about my private matters before and it will take a bit of time before I feel that I am ready to. I need to trust someone before I get that far with them, can you understand that?"

"Of course, and I'm sorry but Tommie, I can tell you here and now, you can trust me."

"That's what they all say." Tommie was bitter as he thought aloud.

"Whose 'them all'?" She could not let him away with his assumption.

"Oh all ye women!" He looked at her in surprise, as if the answer had already been a fore gone conclusion.

"You've been badly hurt by some woman haven't you?" Eve was astute in her realisation.

"Let's leave it, hey? No point in rocking the boat! We're out to enjoy ourselves tonight so let's do just that. Now, tell me, which of these crooked roads will lead me to your door?"

Eve asked Tommie to stop the car before they reached the lane at the edge of the cottage, as she did not want to awaken her father. Turning to him she thanked him for the night and waited anxiously for him to kiss her. He knew exactly what she was at and so, moistening his lips quickly with his tongue, he bent forward and took her in his arms. He was naive enough when it came to women but Eve was not disappointed with the kiss. She responded with passion and remained cradled in his embrace for well over half an hour.

When she finally left him that night she had managed to secure a second date with him. As she crawled into her narrow bed she was almost too happy to sleep and thanked the Lord for sending Tommie Bordoni her way. She knew that she had a long way to go with him as he had troubles in his past that he had not yet succeeded in overcoming but she promised herself that she would do everything possible in her power to become his wife. She had loved him from a distance for so long and now that she had the chance she certainly wasn't going to let him slip through her fingers!

CHAPTER FOUR

"Is that one not up out of the bed yet?" Dick Kelly's loud voice seemed to bellow through the still morning air as he questioned his wife on the kitchen hearth. "Jesus Christ, it's gone eight o'clock, time for any normal person to be up and about. Hey, Eve get out of the bed this minute, I want a hand to change cattle to the far field."

"Leave her be!" Maud Kelly was quiet by comparison. "She was out late at the dance last night and she has work tomorrow. This is the only morning she will be able to rest."

"That's exactly what's wrong here" he looked crossly at his wife, his eyebrows almost crossed over in a V. "You're way too soft on her! Let her away with murder if you had to. It's just as well that I am here to put a bit of manners on the pair of you! Eve" his roar echoed all over the small cottage. "Get up this minute or I'll go in there after you."

Eve turned slowly in the bed and sighed. God, he was rattling off again! Was there no peace to be got in this life at all! Her father was a hard man and sometimes she hated him. She couldn't understand how her mother had put up with him for so long. He never shut up and was always ordering her around. She'd gone years ago if that had been her. As it was she couldn't wait to get out of the place herself. At the moment, though, there was no hope of it. Her wages were small and the bit she had left for herself every week was spent on the dances at the weekend. Remembering how good she had felt last night when Tommie had kissed she warmed instantly and decided to ignore her father's black mood. He wasn't going to spoil her day!

"I'll be there in a minute" she called as she wearily made her way from the bed. Pulling on her black skirt and woolen jumper she sighed as she thought of the task ahead. She was tired and the last thing she felt like doing was trudging through the wet fields after cattle. She daren't refuse though or there would be hell to pay!

Her father was pacing impatiently up and down the kitchen when she entered.

"Took your bloody time, didn't you?" he growled bitterly at her as her mother handed her a steaming cup of hot tea. "If you can't get out of bed in the mornings then you shouldn't be going out at night to these dances at all! That's the way I see it!"

She didn't even bother to answer, as she knew that there was no point. He'd only retaliate again with another complaint and she had heard more than enough from him already. Instead, she glanced across at her mother and not for the first time was saddened by the terror in her blue eyes. Again she swore that when she married it would be for love. Her parents had been a made match. Dick Kelly had been thirty-five when he had approached Pat Dalton, the village matchmaker. He had been looking for a wife who could help him on the land and give him plenty of sons. Maud had been the matchmaker's obvious choice for him as she had been young and chaste and strong. She had, however, produced only one son and he had been born delicate. He had had breathing problems as a baby and, despite doctor's best efforts, had died before reaching his eighteenth month. Eve often felt that her father blamed Maud for the death of the baby.

"Hurry on and drink up that tea, I haven't got all day." He was pacing the floor again, his patience completely evaporated.

"Just finished now." Eve hurriedly swallowed the last mouthful of the sweet beverage and cursed silently as she burned the roof of her mouth. Placing the cup on the long table she sighed as she passed her mother and unwillingly followed her father out across the yard.

The muck and dirt that greeted her was appalling and, as she tried to avoid yet another puddle of mud, she wondered if everyone allowed their farm to disintegrate into such a poor state. She didn't think so. In fact she was more than confident that Tommie's farm would be spotless. Rumor had it that he spent almost every waking hour working and that the farm was his first love. Some people even went as far as to say that it was his only love but she had plans to change that! Anyway, no matter what it was like it would definitely have to be cleaner than this place!

Eve was well versed in the affairs of Tommie Bordoni; she had made it her business to find out all that there was to be known about him. She knew that his mother had worked as a housekeeper for Harrison and that she had had an affair with him. She knew that Harrison had turned out to be his real father and that he had willed his two hundred-acre estate to him. She also knew that his sister Rosie had been keeping Harrison's bed warm and that her first born, Dawn, had also been his. That would make her Tommie's half sister instead of his niece. Dawn had died tragically according to sources and Rosie had lost her mind. She was living in a nursing home and did not respond to the world. Her sister Kitty was raising her children and they lived at the Manor house. Eve felt that Tommie had had a very sad life and she longed to be the one to bring a little sunshine into it.

She would certainly try if she got the chance!

"Hurry on and stop loitering" her father's orders broke through her thoughts, causing her to slip on some mud. "Run along there and start rounding up those animals. There's a shower on the way and we don't want to get soaked. Go on, put a stir on yourself!"

Later that evening Dick made his way to the pub as was usual and Mrs. Kelly sat at the fireside with her daughter. It seemed that the only time the woman was completely at ease was when he was out drinking. She knew that it would be twelve or more before he came home so she was able to relax and let the worries of the day drift over her. He'd come in then, full of beer, and noisily stagger his way to the bed. If she were awake he'd usually start an argument over nothing so she always pretended to be asleep. Looking across at her daughter now she wondered how that brute of a man could have produced such a beauty. And Eve was indeed a beauty! Her hair was dark, she kept it short, and her blue eyes were as deep as cornflowers and her skin sallow and clear.

"How did you get on at the dance last night?" She spoke gently and with interest.

"Not too bad I suppose! There was a good crowd there."

"Meet anyone nice?" She bit her lip as she awaited the reply.

"Oh Mum! You ask me that question every week." Eve couldn't help but smile.

"I know I do but I worry about you. You are twenty next month and as far as I can make out you don't fancy any of the fellas at all."

"As a matter of fact that's not entirely true!" Thoughts of Tommie filled her mind and she longed to see him again.

"You fancy someone so?" She sat up on the chair and willed her daughter to answer.

"Yes, yes I do!" Eve's reply was dreamy and caused her mother a little concern.

"You do? Is he nice? Who is he? Would I know him?" Her mother was really interested and almost sounded excited now. She longed for the day when her daughter would eventually find a life of her own and leave the hardships of the farm behind her.

"Promise you won't tell Dad." She didn't want him knowing.

"I promise, I promise. Oh, Eve, give me a bit of credit here, will you! The less he knows about these things the better as far as I am concerned."

"Well, it's Tommie Bordoni." She felt that his name had a nice ring to it.

"Tommie Bordoni?" Mrs. Kelly lost herself in thought for a moment and then looked at her daughter with wide eyes. "Is he the one whom that Ken Harrison fathered over in that estate in Dalesport?"

"Yes, that's him." She had a feeling that a lecture was about to evolve but she would ignore it. No matter what anyone said she would continue to see Tommie.

"Oh God, Eve, be careful there! There's a lot of history attached to that chap, you know. And people say Harrison was a bit of a lady's man. Tommie could very well turn out to be the same!"

"Don't worry mother." Eve stared into the golden flames and told herself that there was no need to heed her mother's warnings. "I know all the history, as you call it, that there is to be known about the Manor and anyway I'm a big girl now. I can look after myself. I really like Tommie and I just want to give it a go with him. If it doesn't work out, well so be it! Can you understand that?"

"Your father will hit the roof when he hears this!" His shortcomings were always foremost on her mind.

"You promised that you wouldn't tell him."

"And I won't but this is a small village and news travels fast. Just be prepared, that's all I'm saying."

Eve looked at her mother for a moment and was almost overwhelmed by a sense of pity. She had aged a lot in the last few years and constantly had black circles around her eyes, bred from all the worries thrown at her by Dick Kelly.

"Why do you stay with him?"

Startled Maud didn't answer for a moment. Then with her sad, tired eyes she sighed heavily and gazed at Eve. "Sure, what choice do I have? Where would I go?"

"Did you ever love him?" Eve had opened a can of worms now and wasn't about to close it until she had the last one out.

"Why do you want to know that?"

"Just tell me, did you ever love him?"

"No, I never loved him, it was a made match, you know that. I didn't want to marry at all but my father left me with no choice. I respected him, I suppose, when we first we. He was the boss and never wasted an opportunity to let me know. In my own stupid way I looked up to him, placed him on a pedestal that he didn't deserve and I believed all the lies that he told me. But now? Now I feel nothing but resentment towards him."

"I wish he'd leave." Eve could no longer hide the bitterness that she felt for Dick, the bitterness that had mutated into hatred over the last few weeks.

"Please Eve, don't say that, if he ever hears you he'll kill you. Anyway, he is your father after all and as such requires your respect. Now wet some tea like a good girl and bring that sponge cake in from the larder. I've been looking forward to a slice of it all day."

As she poured the steaming water into the metal teapot Eve told herself that Dick Kelly was no father to her and deserved nothing more than her disdain. She constantly prayed for the day when he would go off with himself and leave them in peace but she knew that would never happen. In order to rid him from her life she would have to wait until he died. All the more reason for wanting to get out and get married. If she had a place of her own she wouldn't allow him to visit and she need never see him again. He was no fit father anyway! The tinkers had a better father! How many times had he beaten her black and blue when she was a child? And now that she was older he used mental abuse to get to her instead of the stick. Yes, the world without Dick Kelly would be a better place and she must do all that she could to get away from him. It was too late for her mother but she had her whole life ahead of her. If things worked out according to plan she would spend it as Mrs. Bordoni. Yes, that sounded nice, Eve Bordoni! It had a certain ring to it and she couldn't wait until she met Tommie again!

CHAPTER FIVE

Tommie sang on Sunday morning as he happily went about his jobs. The day was wet and windy and a bitter breeze blew angrily across the farmyard but he didn't care. He had enjoyed himself last night and, without being aware of it, he was looking forward to seeing Eve again. He had been really enchanted with her company and she had made him laugh. He had never thought that that was possible. Still, he' d better not get carried away with it all. He'd see her for another few nights and then that would be that. He didn't want to put himself in the position of falling in love. God no, women weren't to be trusted and the less one had to do with them the better!

He had just finished feeding the last of the Friesian calves in the far shed when he heard Bill's familiar whistle in the yard. He, too, had had an enjoyable night and was in high spirits.

"Hello there, me old boy" he greeted Tommie as he made his way across the farmyard, treading carefully to avoid the puddles. "How about that for a night?"

"Not a bad one at all! And I suppose that you came up the way for your winnings."

"Good God no! What ever gave you that idea? As a matter of a fact I'm calling a halt to that bet. The whole thing is off, have you got that? Meself and Sadie got on like a house on fire and I'm meeting her again but be Jaysus if she ever heard about the bet- well that would be that! You know yourself what women are like! So let's not mention a word about it again. It never happened, okay?"

"Fine by me but it seems that you are going soft in your old age." Tommie couldn't help but grin.

"God no! Soft me hat! Old Bill is no softie, let me tell you! But I really do like the girl and I've waited a long time for her. She's a great little ride too!"

"You didn't!" Tommie couldn't believe how fast Bill moved.

"Of course I did, what do you take me for? Sure you must have got one yourself last night."

"No, I didn't!" The idea had never even entered his head.

"Jesus, I don't believe you! You're definitely lacking Tommie but maybe it's just as well."

"What do you mean?" He looked directly at his friend and wondered exactly what was on his mind.

"You do know who she is, don't you, the one that you were with?"

"Yeah, of course I do, she is Eve Kelly!"

"Aye, Eve Kelly who is Dick Kelly's daughter!"

"Dick Kelly? Now why does that name sound so familiar?" He tried to rack his brain but for the life of him he couldn't remember.

"Sure you know him, everyone does! He's your man, the big thick, who stands right up in the front at the marts and roars abuse at anyone who tries to outbid him."

"Fuck! Is that who her father is?" Tommie could see the cross, angry face before him and an involuntary shiver raced down his spine.

"Yeah and by all accounts he's not a simple man. They say he gives the wife a hard time and he constantly plays away from home. I know for a fact that he was dating Maura Creegan! You know the widow who lives in Kate McNeill's cottage! He beat her up there a couple of weeks ago because she refused to give him what he wanted."

"Get out of here, you're making it all up!" Tommie began to wonder what exactly he had gotten himself into and prayed that Bill was joking.

"As God is me witness I'm fuckin' telling you the truth. So you'd better watch your step, me friend. Take it easy with the daughter, if you get me drift! The last thing you want is to have that fella breathing fire down your back."

"You're right there, Bill, but it won't come to that. I have no intention of getting serious with Eve. Another few nights and that will be that."

"Hold onto her till you get your ride and then let her off! You have it all worked out, haven't you?" Bill winked as he smiled at the surprised man in front of him.

"Christ, you have a one track mind, Bill. Are you not capable of thinking of anything else? Anyway, enough about last night, do you fancy going fishing later on?"

"Sorry mate but I've arranged to meet Sadie. I might take her to the river alright but it won't be to see the fishes, if you get my meaning." He winked again and his face twisted into a leer.

"You're an awful fella, Bill Foley, do you know that? No woman on this earth will be safe while you are roaming about. You'd better be careful yourself or you'll end up gettting the girl into trouble."

"Devil the bit of fear. Now I'll be on my way again and I'll catch you later in the week."

"Right Bill, I'll be seeing you so and mind you don't catch cold on the wet banks."

Tommie found himself wandering over to the Manor after lunch for the bit of company. He knew that Robbie was coming down from Meath and was spending the afternoon with his children. Tommie always liked talking to Robbie and it amazed him how he was able to bounce back after the heartache he had endured. If truth were known Robbie's heart would never recover but he made a good job of hiding it.

Saturday evening came round again and Tommie and Bill made their way to Ballyhale as was usual. They entered the local pub and bought a round of drinks. Sadie was along a few minutes after their arrival and came straight over to Bill. He was like a love struck puppy as he threw his arm around her and pulled her close. Tommie found it hard to believe that Bill was actually falling in love as he was such a tough man. But if the look on his face was anything to go by, well then, he most certainly was smitten.

Eve was waiting for him at the door of the dance hall and again his heart leapt at the very sight of her. He seemed to shake uncontrollably whenever she was around and it unnerved him.

His eyes quickly scouted around to make sure that her father was nowhere to be seen. He didn't want to bump into that lad in a hurry!

"Hi there." His greeting was friendly. "I must say that you are looking very fetching tonight."

Eve smiled and thanked the Lord that she had taken so much time to get ready. She had tried on several outfits before she had settled on a red dress and cream cardigan. The deep scarlet set off her dark colouring and gave her a beautiful glow.

"Have you had a good week?" she asked him as they settled at a table with their drinks.

"Not bad all round. And yourself?"

"I suppose it was alright. I was really looking forward to tonight though. Saturday nights are always my favourite. I can get out of the house and let my hair down and there is no one to stop me."

"Have you any brothers or sisters?"

"No, I'm the only one. It's a bit of a disappointment to my father though, he has always wanted a son."

"Dick Kelly, is he your father?" He wanted to be sure.

"Yeah, do you know him?" She prayed that he didn't.

"I've seen him around. He goes to the marts, doesn't he? Not a simple man I'd say!"

"You'd be right there! He's a mean, horrible cranky individual and I hate him." She didn't care who knew!

"Jesus, Eve don't say that." Tommie was clearly shocked for a moment. He had wanted to get to know his own father better but fate had intervened.

"But it's true. He gives us such a hard time. I don't know why my mother doesn't leave him."

"She probably loves him!"

"She does in her tail. Sure how could anyone love that mean old git? Anyway enough about him. I don't want to ruin my night. You never knew your father did you?"

"That depends on the way you look at it! I grew up thinking that Jack Bordoni was my father and he died when I was only a baby. And as you know, it turned out that Harrison was my real Dad and sure, I had worked for him for years."

"What was he like?" She found that he was talking more freely tonight.

"I always got on okay with him but I discovered that not only had he an affair with my mother but he also had a fling with my sister." Tommie bent his head as the pain from his past dampened his spirits for a moment.

"He obviously liked women." She couldn't think of anything else to say.

"Yeah, I suppose you could say that."

"Are you like him?" Her mother's warning was ringing clear in her ears.

"Not at all. To tell you the truth I don't trust women very much."

"Do you trust me?" She needed to know.

"I don't know yet but it's early days. Time will tell, I suppose! Now lets go have a dance before the night is gone on us."

Tommie was more at ease with Eve that evening and by the time he had dropped her home he felt that he had known her forever. She was such an amusing little creature and completely down to earth. Her mouth was warm and fulfilling and she was beginning to stir the first longings in his loins. He kept himself well under control though, too terrified of the consequences, and was the perfect gentleman. However, as he drove back alone to his estate in the early hours of the morning he found that he had begun to question his hatred of women for the first time in his adult life.

CHAPTER SIX

Tommie continued to see Eve every Saturday night for the next four months and found that he thoroughly enjoyed every moment in her company. However, he was beginning to get somewhat nervous of the effect that she was having on him so he decided that the time had come to review his situation. He knew that Eve had already fallen head over heels in love with him and visualised spending the rest of her life on Dalesport Estate.

Every Saturday night for the last month he had promised himself that he would end their relationship but he been a coward and somehow never managed to find the right words. He had to admit that he liked her a lot and he enjoyed their time together but he certainly didn't want a serious relationship. To avoid further heartache later on he swore that tonight he would tell her that it was over.

He was in a somewhat somber mood when he met Bill at the pub. Bill was quite the opposite, being full of the joys of young love and couldn't understand his friend at all.

"What's up Tom?" he asked him as he handed him yet another pint. "Not meeting the sexy Eve tonight?"

"Oh, I'm meeting her alright, that's the problem!"

"What ever do you mean?" Bill was totally lost.

"I'm afraid it's for the last time." There was regret in his voice as he spoke.

"And why is that?" Bill sipped his pint as he looked at his friend.

"She's getting a little too serious on me. Starting to talk about saving money and such things."

"Ah, I wouldn't mind that, all women get serious Tommie! It's up to us fellas to try and ignore them and keep them in their place. Anyway, you could do worse than Eve. Make a pretty little wife she would and I bet she'd be a great help around the farm"

"That's just it, Bill, I don't want to get married."

"That's what you say now but you're still young. In a year or so you'll change you mind."

"No Bill, I won't ever change my mind. I've seen what women are capable of doing to a man's soul and I don't intend to let one of them bring me down."

"Whatever you say, mate, what ever you say. Anyway, was she good in bed?"

"I don't know." It was almost a whisper.

"Jesus, you must have an opinion one way or the other!" Bill drank a mouthful of his beer and wished that Tommie would loosen up a little.

"I didn't have sex with her!" He bent his head as he spoke, too embarrassed to witness his friend's reaction.

"What? Did I hear you correctly? Did you just say that you never had sex with her?"

"Yes!"

"I don't believe you, Tommie."

"I don't care whether you believe me or not, Bill, but as God is my judge I never had sex with her."

Bill shifted about as she stared at his friend in complete disbelief. "What's the matter with you at all, lad? I can't make head or tail out of you! You are happy enough to stand there and tell me that you have been courting her for four months now and you haven't done the business with her? Jesus Christ, I really don't believe you!"

"It's the truth!"

"You're a strange one alright, Tommie, there's no doubt about that." Bill shook his head as he spoke, completely mystified by his friend's confession.

Tommie was in no mood to argue so he let Bill have his say. He was going over in his mind what he had to say to Eve and he wished that he had it all behind him. He was dreading the evening ahead as Eve was a lovely girl and the last thing that he wanted was to hurt her. And she would be hurt, he knew that! How many times had she told him that she looked forward to their Saturday night dates? Wasn't it all that kept her going in her otherwise sad life? God, this was going to be a lot harder than he had first imagined.

When he walked into the dance hall and watched her beautiful face light up he almost chickened out again but he knew that tonight he had no choice. It was now or never! The longer that he let it go on the harder it would become! He sat her down in front of him and nervously looked her straight in the eye. Eve's smile faded quickly as she watched his somber face. She knew that something was amiss and began to feel anxious.

"You're looking very serious tonight, Tommie." It was almost a whisper. "Is something wrong?"

"Oh, Eve! This is the hardest thing that I have ever had to say to anyone but it has to be voiced. I want to, I mean I need to finish our relationship." There he had got that off his chest and now she knew where she stood with him. He watched as her bottom lip dropped and her eyes automatically filled with tears.

"Finish? Why Tommie? Why do you want to finish? I thought we were getting on so well together. Is it something I have done?"

"Oh Eve, no!" he caught her hands and held them gently. He had no desire to cause her any more pain than was necessary. "Don't you see, it's nothing to do with you at all! It's me! I don't want a serious relationship. I have no intention of marrying and I feel that is the way you would like to see us heading."

"Why did you not tell me this four months ago? Why, Tommie? Of course I was getting serious! Why the hell wouldn't I be getting serious? You're the first decent fella that I have ever been out with and I was falling in love with you. Of course I was serious and now, as well as that, it seems that I was such a fuckin' igit."

The tears began to fall and Tommie shifted uncomfortably on the chair. He knew that she would take it badly but he hadn't bargained for this. Trying to avoid the temptation of putting his arms around her he rubbed her forearm and mustered a smile.

"Hey, Eve, look at it this way, maybe you had yourself a lucky escape. Can you imagine what it would be like to be burdened with me for the rest of you life!"

Rubbing her eyes Eve stared hard at him for a moment and knew that she loved him. He had certainly hurt her and her heart was in tatters but he didn't need to know that! She must try and be strong here and hold onto what was left of her pride at all costs!

"Maybe, you're right Tommie, maybe you're right! I thought you were a decent fella but it seems that I was mistaken. You're no better than any other I have known! The only difference is that you did not expect me to jump into your bed after the first date and I appreciated that. Now, if you don't mind, I'll go and leave you to get on with your life, there's nothing more to be said here! It was nice knowing you!"

And with that she awkwardly leapt from the chair and ran across the dance hall to the toilets. Tommie watched for a few moments and resisted the temptation to follow. She was clearly distraught and he was the cause of it. Oh, it was never meant to work out like this! He had never intentionally meant to hurt her. He did have strong feelings for her and perhaps he would regret his decision but it had to be done. She'd be okay again tomorrow, wouldn't she?

Finishing his pint with what little spirit he had left he stood up and, taking one glance around the hall, decided to head for home. Eve still hadn't emerged from the toilets and he knew that she wouldn't want to see him when she did appear. He had lost all interest in the dance now and, as he made for the door, he swore that he would keep away from Ballyhale for the next few weeks. It just wasn't worth the hassle!

Eve's mother noticed that her daughter was feeling poorly the next morning. Her eyes were red and swollen and she refused breakfast, saying that she had no appetite at all. She waited until Dick had gone to the village and then decided to question her.

"Eve, sit down here for a minute." She gently tapped the low stool beside the range. "Come over and talk to me and tell me what's bothering you."

"I'm alright Mam, honest." She sat down anyway.

"You don't look alright. Are you sick?" The worry in her voice was evident.

"No." She was heartbroken, not sick and there was nothing anyone could do to help her.

"You're sure you're not sick, it's not like you to refuse breakfast."

"Oh, stop mitering, Mam, I've told you I'm not sick!"

"You're not pregnant then, are you? Oh Jesus he'll hit the roof if he finds—."

"Mum, for Christ's sake, will you stop! I'm not pregnant. Can't you give me a bit of credit here? I'm not that much of an idiot! Tommie finished with me, that's all."

"Finished with you, did he? And I thought that you two were getting on so well."

"Yeah, so did I! That's the problem! It has come as a big shock to me." Again the tears began to fall and Eve was so sad that she felt she would never recover from the blow she had received. In a short period of time Tommie had become the most important part of her life and she was going to miss him so much. She knew that deep down she was in love with him but a fat lot of good that was to her now! "He doesn't want to get serious. What do you think of that?"

"He's young, Eve and like most fellas his age he is probably afraid of commitment. Look at the age your father was before he married."

"That's because no one would have him." How dare she compare Tommie to Dick Kelly!

"Eve, enough of that, do you hear me? You will have to learn to respect your father. Anyway, give Tommie a bit of space. Happen he'll realise what he has given up and he will come bounding back."

Eve wiped her eyes and for a second she was hopeful. "Do you really think so, Mam? Do you really think that he will come back?"

"Like a dog with his tail between his legs! Mark my words girl, Tommie Bordoni will be back! Sure, where else is he going to find a girl like you?"

"Oh Mother, thank you, you have made me feel so much better. Maybe if I just hang in there he will come looking for me again. I'll have to have a little bit of patience, that's all! If I wait long enough Tommie will come back and believe me I am prepared to wait! Now, I think that I will go for a walk to clear my head. I won't be too long!"

"Make sure you are back before your father gets home."

"Where is he gone?" She didn't really care, one way or the other, but she was anxious to know how much time she had.

"Didn't say. He'll be back in time for dinner though. Can't see him missing that!"

The sun was attempting to shine as Eve walked down the lane and the birds were busily singing in the tall hazel trees. Spring was definitely on it's way again and the thought of the long evenings filled her heart with joy. Then she pondered on her loss and was saddened again.

The funny thing was that she hadn't been going out with Tommie all that long at all but she had fancied him forever. She felt as if she had lost her best friend and the empty hollow that she experienced in the pit of her stomach caused her to heave. She had tried not to fall in love with him but that had proved impossible. Tommie was one in a million and she prayed that her mother's assumptions were correct and he would come back to her.

Following the lane to the right Eve approached her neighbouring farm. Jake Hodgins farmed fifty acres of land here and his son Podge helped him run it. Podge was five years older than Eve and, although he wasn't altogether bad looking, she cringed every time she met him. He was forever making passes at her and kept pestering her for a date. Podge, in fact, was one of those people who had the knack of making your blood boil.

When she had been younger he had roughly pulled her behind one of his father's haystacks and started kissing her. The only way that she had managed to escape was to crawl out of her cardigan and leave it in his hands. Her father had beaten her when he discovered that she had lost her cardigan but she hadn't cared. Anything was better than having Podge's slime dribbled all over her.

Now, as she passed the way, she shuddered just thinking of it. She kept her head low and prayed that she would see no sign of the older boy.

As she turned at the hay sheds she was surprised to hear muffled mumblings coming from within. Stopping on the road for a moment she listened and distinctly heard the heavy moans and groans. Giggling to herself she assumed that Podge was having his evil way with some poor unfortunate creature and was curious as to whom the unlucky individual could be. She decided to tiptoe forward and take a peek. It was probably Helen O'Neill or Tilly Bergin. Those two would let anyone up on them and she had seen them loitering around the farm quite a few times.

Tiptoeing to the hay barn door she held her breath as she tried to look through the open crack. Her vision was restricted as the barn was gloomy but she could see enough at the same time. And, my God, what a surprise she got!

Podge was nowhere to be seen in the barn. It was in fact an older woman and man who were at it hot and heavy. She looked closer and had no difficulty making out the woman's identity. It was Podge's mother, Kitty! But who was the man? From the shape of the frame in front of her she knew that it wasn't Jake Hodgins. He was a tall, thin man but this fella was short and stocky. No, it wasn't Hodgins. Well, then who? Leaning further in the doorway Eve pressed her head to the pillar on the left-hand side and watched as the man turned to face her. Good Jesus, it was her father! Mother of God, Dick Kelly was fucking Mrs. Hodgins in the barn! It couldn't be true!

But as she peeped a second time she was under no illusion at all. The dirty old man was having his fun while her mother slaved at home alone, making his dinner, completely ignorant of his goings on.

Sickened to the core she placed her hand over her mouth and ran from the spot as fast as she could. She didn't want her father to see her or she'd be slaughtered! The dirty old swine! How could he do that to her mother? Jesus, maybe Tommie was right! People were not to be trusted and it didn't seem to matter what age they were. But how could Kitty do that with him? You'd think that she would have more sense! She mustn't be the full shilling either! Leaning over the ditch at the crossroads she pulled her hand away from her mouth and got sick all over the fresh, green grass.

When she had composed herself Eve was certain that she did not want to go home. How was she to face her mother after what she had just witnessed and she knew that she didn't ever want to see her father again. She decided to keep on walking, it would help to sort out her confusion. The late March winds were cold and stung her face but she didn't even notice. She had thought she had problems when Tommie had given her the shove but this was far worse. Her poor, poor mother! How would she feel when she discovered what her brute of a husband was up to?

Before she knew it she had reached Dalesport and was walking in the direction of Dalesport Manor.

Even though it was a Sunday Tommie was in the top field ploughing the furrows. A pale yellow sun was now shining and circles of white seagulls were hovering overhead in the hope of catching an upturned worm. He immediately saw her, strolling somberly down the lane and he slowed down the tractor and came to a halt at the gateway. He was alarmed at the state she was in and immediately jumped from the tractor, full of concern.

"Eve, whatever is the matter?" He stood facing her now, her beauty causing his heart to beat faster.

"Oh, Tommie! I'm so sorry to have to come to you like this but I didn't know where else to go." She emitted a loud sob, instantly startling him.

"Has something happened to you. Has someone hurt you?"

"It's my father. I've just seen him this minute in the shed. He was with Mrs. Hodgins."

"With Mrs. Hodgins? What do you mean?" he failed to see the seriousness of the situation.

"They were doing it, you know! At it like two dogs in heat, they were. It was disgusting."

"My God! Is this Mrs. Hodgins married?"

"Yeah, and she has a son."

"I don't believe you. What is the woman playing at, at all?"

"I don't know, I really don't know. What would she want with the likes of him?"

"See I told you, no woman can be trusted."

"How am I going to face Mother now that I know this?"

"Jesus, I don't know! Maybe it would be best to say nothing to her for the time being. Although you know that she will find out eventually. All these things have a habit of rearing their ugly head when you least expect them." Tommie hung his head for a moment and remembered the hurt of his own past.

Eve noticed that he had suddenly gone quiet and began to feel guilty.

"I'm sorry." She broke the uneasy silence. "I didn't mean to upset you with this but I had to talk to someone. Maybe I should go?"

"No, it's okay." He looked at her lovely face for a moment and was angered that anyone should hurt her. He did not realise that he had caused her much more sorrow the night before. "Listen, why don't you come back to the cottage for a while and we'll have a cup of tea. It will help to calm your nerves and things might look a little better once you've gotten over the shock."

"A cup of tea would be nice, that's if you don't mind." Anything to be near him again.

"Of course not, come on." He held out his hand and as they strolled across the fields they resembled two young lovers, lost in each other's dreams.

Eve was very impressed at how neat Tommie kept his home. The black stove shone like a glowing coal on the hearth and the fire that he had lit earlier had burned low in the grate. The long wooden table in the centre of the room was spotless and the crockery on the pine dresser reflected the shadows around the room. The kettle boiled and Tommie arose to make the tea.

"You have a lovely home here." Eve was already beginning to feel better. After last night she had imagined that she would never see the inside of Tommie's house and now here she was awaiting a mug of strong black tea. No one could tell what tomorrow was going to bring!

"Yeah, it's not too bad, I suppose!" He poured the steaming beverage into the two cups. "It does me anyway!"

"Why did you stay here? Did you ever consider moving into the Manor house?"

"No, to tell you the truth it's too big for me. Where on earth would I get the time to clean up all those rooms? Anyway, Kitty needed the space for the kids." He didn't tell her that the Manor had not in fact being willed to him. There was no need for her to know everything!

"And what will happen when you get married. Will you stay here?"

Looking serious for a moment Tommie handed her the mug. "I wasn't joking last night, Eve, when I told that I have no intention of ever getting married."

Eve might as well have been hit by a ton of bricks. He was deadly serious! Tommie had no intention of ever marrying. Did that mean that he would never want her back? Her mother had only told her that to cheer her up and she had believed her! Oh, what was the point of loving him the way that she did? She was wasting her time but she couldn't control her emotions. The more she saw of him the more she loved him and as she glanced across at his handsome face a warm glow enveloped her.

"You can't say that you will never marry. Someday some woman will come along and sweep you off your feet. Then you won't have any say in the matter." She had to hold out some hope; that was all that was left to her!

"Oh, Eve, you are an innocent little creature, aren't you! You do say the funniest of things! Do you not realise that if any woman were to sweep me off my feet, it would be you! But you see, I won't allow myself to be swept away."

"Why?" How could he control it?

"From what I have seen so far in life I believe that a woman is definitely the ruination of man. Once a fella allows himself to be entangled with one he might as well go ahead and sign his own death warrant. His happiness is shattered and his trust depleted. Take Jack Bordoni for instance. He totally adored my mother and how did she repay him? She went along and slept with Harrison. And then there was Rosie, my sister. Dear Rosie- the girl I'd always looked up to in my youth. She had a great man in Robbie. He was solid and dependable and he loved her more than life itself. And what does she do? Goes off with Harrison as well. And now there's your father and that Mrs. Hodgins. They are also betraying the people who love them. Can you blame me Eve for my lack of faith in human relationships?"

Her heart bled for him at that moment and she realised that he would need a lot of persuasion to overcome his fears. She knew that she wanted to help him but did she have the strength? She found that she was tired lately, tired of all the hardships and heartache and her father's behaviour had really put the tin hat on the lot of it. Still, she thought that it would be worth the try. She didn't want to lose Tommie because of everyone else's horrible mistakes.

"Not everyone behaves like that you know. There are a lot of people who are happily married for years and are content with each other."

"Maybe, maybe but it is a chance to take all the same."

"I would never betray the man I loved by cheating on him." She was surprised when he started laughing.

"What do you find so funny?" She found it hard to hide the hurt from her voice.

"My little Eve, you are a lovely, amusing creature and, you know, I do believe what you are saying. You are too nice to cause pain to anyone and if I were to marry I would be a fool to pass you by. But you have to understand that I am too eaten up with the betrayals of those that I have already loved and it would not be fair to take on a woman under these circumstances."

"Don't you get lonely here?"

"Of course I do!" He thought about all those long, weary nights that he spent by the fireside. There were times when he almost conceded to talking to himself! "Rosie's children often come by and visit but they don't stay long. I keep busy during the day so I don't have much time to think of company. The winter nights are the worst."

"Would you mind if I called over to see you an odd time? I get lonely too and it would be nice to have someone to talk to. We can still be friends even if we're not going to be lovers, can't we?" She had to keep in touch with him some way or another.

"Yeah, I suppose we can." He didn't see the harm in it and he certainly did enjoy her.

"Good! Well, I suppose that I have wasted enough of your time. You have work to be doing and I am keeping you idle. I'd better be getting home anyway and face what's in front of me. No point in putting it off any longer."

"Will you say anything to your Ma?"

"Not for the moment. But I'll be watching that old swine like a hawk and if he keeps on playing away from home I'll spill the beans on him alright."

"That's a wise decision." Tommie didn't tell her that Bill had already mentioned that Kelly had a steady bit on the side. The girl had enough to contend with for one day.

"Will you be at the dance next Saturday?" She was hoping to see him there. Who knows what happen when he had a few drinks down?

"I doubt it but we'll see. Do you want a lift home? It's a bit of a distance."

"Thanks, Tommie, you are indeed a gentleman but I'll be okay. The fresh air will clear my head" and she planted a friendly kiss on the side of his cheek. He tried to ignore the burning sensation in his flesh as she turned towards the door.

Tommie and Eve spent a lot of time together over the next few weeks. He stayed away from the dances but she called to see him on Sunday afternoons and they walked the estate together. The more he saw of her the more he found that he needed her but he was careful to control his urges. Not once since the night that he had finished with her had he made any attempt to kiss her and he intended to keep it that way.

CHAPTER SEVEN

Dick banged the mug nosily on the table and wiped his mouth slowly with the dirty sleeve of his aran jumper. "That was a grand bit, I must say, a grand tasty bit altogether! Pity the rashers were a little burnt though, but there you are."

Eve looked across the table at the man that she had truly grown to hate over the last number of weeks and her stomach turned at the very state of him. There he was, grinning like a Cheshire cat, looking so smug and self- righteous. What was more he never failed to waste an opportunity to have a go at her mother. She was sick to the teeth of him and didn't know how the woman put up with his complaining at all. What was wrong with her anyway? Was she not capable of standing up for herself?

"The rashers weren't burnt." She knew that he would roar at her for back answering but she didn't care anymore. Her mother needed some support here.

"What did you say?" He looked accusingly at her, the grin faded and his voice harsh.

"I said that the rashers were not burnt." She kept eye contact with him and dared him to answer.

"And what makes you such an expert? You of all people! You're nothing but a lazy slut, that's all you are! You wouldn't know one end of a back rasher from another. You'd prefer to be out walking the roads rather than helping around here. Don't think I haven't noticed! Where do you be going anyway?"

"No where in particular." She did not want him to know that she had been spending more and more time up at Dalesport farm in the hope that Tommie would ask her back. He'd surely call her a slut then!

"On the lookout for a man, is that it?" He swallowed the last mouthful in his cup and looked at her, a milk moustache pasted over his lips.

"No." She did her best not to blush but was finding it hard.

"Well then, why do you spend so much time roaming around the place? Answer me!"

"It's none of your business." Could he not just go out and leave them both in peace?

"What did you say?" He looked at her strangely, stung by her insolence. That one was getting more brazen by the day and he had no intention of putting up with it. He'd bring her back down to size if it were the last thing he'd do.

Eve was standing now, her temper taking control and she knew that there was no turning back. As the blood boiled within her veins she looked at him with disdain and disgust and answered him bravely. "I said it's none of your business. I'm sick of listening to you poking your nose in where it's not wanted all the time and I'm equally sick of the way you are always having a go at Mam. Can't you leave her alone? We never dream of asking you where you are going and, God knows, you're never here."

"You brazen hussy, just who the hell do you think that you are talking to?" He picked up the empty mug again and slammed it on the table in an attempt to quieten her.

"You are so self righteous all the time, you make me sick. Anyone listening to you would imagine that you are perfect. But we both know that you aren't, don't we?" She had built up such a rage inside her now that she was unable to stop. She thought about nothing but getting her own back on this man who had deceived her mother.

"Explain yourself, you ungrateful bitch." His spits fell across the wooden table and his eyes burnt in their sockets.

"Do you really want me to spell it out for you? Here in front of Mam?" She was challenging him and he didn't like it.

"Your mother and I have no secrets from each other." Dick looked guiltily at his wife but noticed that she was keeping her head down. She reminded him of an ostrich and wished, yet again, that she would show a little back bone.

"Huh!" The grunt had slipped out before she realised it but she knew now that she had where she wanted him. Knew that she had him worried.

"You'd better watch your tongue, my young girl. You're overstepping the mark here and it's well you know it. What does your poor mother think of her precious daughter now, brawling at her father like a common fishmonger? You must surely be a sad disappointment to her. I know you are to a big disappointment to me anyway!"

"Me a disappointment? That's a joke, isn't it? I dare say that you must be a far bigger disappointment to her than I could ever prove to be! I bet she rues the day she married you. Look at you! You treat her like a servant and there's never any peace in the house when you're around. Always roaring and shouting. And if that wasn't bad enough you have to go and play the field behind her back."

"Play the field? What the fuck are you talking about now?" She definitely had his attention and knew that he was anxious.

"I saw you, you know! You and Mrs. Hodgins, in the barn! At it hot and heavy, you were! You are no better than a ram in the spring. You disgust me!"

"You stupid, interfering bitch, you don't know what you are talking about." Dick arose quickly, knocking his chair over in his fury and was at her side in an instant. He hit her full force across the face with his right fist and sent her tumbling to the floor. As Eve collapsed onto the cold tiles she noticed her mother's sad face and knew in an instant that she had definitely gone too far.

"Eve, Eve can you hear me?" It was three hours later and darkness had begun to spin her web around the farmhouse. Mrs. Kelly had been sitting at the side of the bed, wiping her daughter's brow with a cold sponge since Dick had left and she was distressed and worried. How had it come down to this at all? Would Eve ever awaken and dispel her worst fears? Looking at the still child she knew that the fist had left a dirty black mark around the jaw and it was becoming larger by the second. She couldn't help but wonder what the neighbours would say when they heard. Neighbours is right! Mrs Hodgins was a neighbour and look what she had done. Past caring she turned her attention back to her daughter and was delighted to see that Eve had begun to open her eyes.

"Eve, Eve, how are you feeling? You gave me a terrible fright. I thought that you were never going to wake up and I was afraid to ring for the doctor."

Eve sat upright in the bed, her head paining, and touched her swollen jaw. It was tender and sore and she knew that it was bruised. In a matter of seconds the memory of the evenings events returned to her and she felt her head begin to spin. She couldn't stay here any longer, couldn't bear to face the man after what he had done to her. If she got the chance she'd kill him and then what would happen? She'd end up in jail and Tommie certainly wouldn't want anything to do with her then. No, she had to go! But where? As the tears began to spill down her face she realised that she was fed up living.

"Ah Eve, please don't cry." Her mother held her daughter to her and tried to comfort her.

Looking into the sad, anxious face Eve knew that her mother was in a far worse predicament than she was. At least she had her whole life in front of her but what had Mrs. Kelly?

"Mother." Her voice was gentle. "You know that I cannot stay here any longer."

"Eve, don't be silly, of course you can stay here. This will all blow over and in a couple of days it will be forgotten about altogether. You know what he is like."

"No, mother, it will not be forgotten about this time. I will never, ever be able to forgive that man for what he has done. He has definitely gone too far this time. Do you know that I actually hate him."

Mrs. Kelly gasped as the realisation of what her daughter had just said hit and saddened her. Things had definitely gone from bad to worse around here and there was absolutely no hope of improvement.

"Oh Eve, how can you say that? He is your father and you can't possibly hate him. You are not meant to hate him! You are hurt and angry at the moment and you are confusing your feelings with hatred. Tomorrow everything will look better."

"No, Ma, things will not look any better in the morning. For so long now I've been afraid of him and I found him hard to tolerate but the day that I saw him in the barn I suddenly knew that I hated him and always have. What I can't understand is why you don't hate him after all the misery that he has caused you in your life and now this. He cheated on you with another woman. How does that make you feel?"

"To be honest, Eve, I don't really care. Mrs. Hodgins is just that-another woman! Granted I had credited her with more sense but there you are. He has been going out with women since shortly after you were born."

"And if you knew why did you stay with him?" She couldn't believe that her mother was so calm.

"It was the easiest thing to do. You were small and needed your father. And anyhow where would I go? Who would want me after being with him? As far as I was concerned the more women he was with then the fewer times he came bothering me in my bed. That was the way I wanted it."

"And what about now? Would you leave him now? Come with me and we'll rent a little house together. We can live on my wages and we won't need him anymore."

"Oh Eve, darling, if only it were as simple as that. Dick may not be the best husband in the world but in his own way he needs me."

"Yeah, to do his cooking and cleaning!"

"How can I explain it to you? Your father and I have been through a lot together and I have my marriage vows to consider. You go your way, my little one, but I will stay here. I am bound to your father for better or worse."

"It's your call mother but I have to tell you that I definitely intend to go. In fact I will be gone before he gets home. I don't want to face him ever again!"

Rising she made her way to the wardrobe and opened the heavy pine door. Scrambling about inside she eventually found her black rucksack and roughly began to throw her clothes into it.

"Where will you go? It's late, wait until tomorrow at least."

"No, I'll go tonight! I don't want to be here when he comes back full of his beer. I have no idea where I am heading but as soon as I'm settled I will write to you. And, if you ever change your mind about leaving, you will know where I am."

"I wish you wouldn't go, Eve, I'm really going to miss you! Take care of yourself, won't you and keep in touch." Mrs. Kelly tried to curtail the flow of tears from her eyes. Her daughter, the only friend she had in the entire world, was leaving and she didn't deem it fair to stop her. Maybe it was for the best! Maybe it was what she herself should have done years ago but it was too late now. She was far too old and weak. Anyway Dick would search the earth for her and bring her home and then he'd probably beat her senseless. She couldn't take that chance.

"I will mother." Eve hugged her tight and then, taking one last glance around the bedroom where she had spent so many unhappy childhood days, she grabbed her bag, walked towards the door and was gone.

Tommie turned down the volume of the radio and settled himself in the fireside sofa. He had had a hard day and was dog-tired. His limbs were aching and his back felt as if it were about to break at any minute. He was looking forward to relaxing for the night and he glanced at the fire to make sure that there was enough wood to keep it burning before he closed his eyes for a catnap.

It was windy outside and when the first timid rap came to the door he ignored it. The second rap was more demanding and it was only then that he realised it wasn't the wind playing tricks. Cursing quietly he moved towards the door. The last thing he wanted now was one of Rosie's children making noise about the place. He was far too exhausted to deal with their goings on!

Opening wide the door he got the surprise of his life when he saw Eve standing there. He was even more alarmed when he noticed the horrific bruise that literally pulsed from her jaw.

"My God, Eve, what has brought you all the way out here at this hour? And what on earth has happened to you?"

"Tommie." It was a mere whisper. "I'm so sorry to bother you but you see I didn't know who else to turn to! Can I come inside?"

"Yeah, sure." He led the way to the kitchen and pointed to the chair near the fire. As soon as she had settled he looked at her again and frowned. "Are you alright, Eve? What in the name of God has happened? Have you been attacked?"

Even in her distress Eve could hear the concern in his voice and it comforted her.

"It was my father. He did this to me." She swallowed hard as she shamefully admitted her distress.

"Your father? Suffering Jesus, why?" He examined the bruise to see if any permanent damage had been done but as far as he could ascertain no bones had been broken.

"I vexed him. I told him a few home truths and he didn't want to hear them. He preferred to lash out instead." She rubbed her jaw slowly. "I hate him. I've left home and I'm never going back."

"You could go to the guards with this, you know."

"What would be the point? He'd talk so sweetly to them and they'd end up believing him.

I'd come out the villain as usual. You don't know what he is like, Tommie." She knew that his suggestion was hopeless.

"But you can't just let him away with it." Tommie was angry that someone could intentionally harm another like this and not have to pay the price.

"He has got away with it already as far as I am concerned but let me tell you I have no intention of seeing him ever again. I will never go home as long as he is there."

"And where are you going to go?"

"I don't know yet. I was wondering if I might be able to stay here for a couple of days until I get a house of my own organised." She was pleading with him now, trying to reach the inner depths of that soft heart that she had already experienced. "Do you think that would be possible?"

Tommie looked serious for a moment and found that he was unable to answer. The last thing he wanted in his life were the complications that were facing him right now but he felt that he was indirectly involved in the situation. He supposed a couple of days would do no harm.

"It will only be for a couple of days mind. I can't have everyone around wondering what the hell you are doing here. And if your father happens to darken the door then I'm afraid you will have to go. I want no trouble, do you understand that?"

"Of course, Tommie, and thank you very much. I'll be gone by the end of the week, I promise. And my father won't appear. He doesn't even know that we are acquainted."

"Well then, we'd better get you settled in a room. The bedroom to the right there is a grand one but hasn't been used in an age. We'll make up the bed and air it out and it should be alright."

"Oh Tommie, I don't want you to go to any trouble for me. I feel bad enough as it is. I'd be happy enough to sleep here on the sofa."

"Don't be silly! We'll have the bed aired in no time and it'll be far more comfortable for you. Now do you fancy a cup of tea?"

When Tommie awoke the next morning he had to admit to himself that he was a little excited at the prospect of seeing Eve. He definitely enjoyed her company but denied the fact that he harbored any feelings for her. "We're just good friends" he told himself as he buttoned his shirt. "Sure I'm only helping her out! That's what friends do!"

Eve was already up and had breakfast waiting for him on the table.

"Sit down" her smile melted his heart. "And eat some of these sausages and eggs. I've been waiting ages for you to arise."

"There was no need to go to all this trouble. What time did you get up at anyway?"

"About half six! I couldn't sleep. And it is no bother, no bother at all. Sure isn't it the least I can do after you helping me out. I'm taking a few days off work, don't want to go in with this black eye. News would be all around the village in no time and I couldn't handle that!"

"You're dead right" Tommie cut one of the sausages and popped it into his mouth. "Take as long as you can. You could do with the break anyway."

"I was wondering if you needed any help around the farm today. It will stop me from thinking of my troubles and I'm a dab hand at it. Had plenty of practice!"

"I'm sure that I can find something for you" he was suddenly looking forward to working with her. "I won't leave you idle anyway!"

The day seemed to fly as together they laughed their way through the various farmyard chores. Eve seemed to be more content and was delighted that Dick Kelly did not come looking for her. He would never guess anyway, that she was at Dalesport farm, would he?

And so one day lead into another and before either of them had time to stop and think she had been at the farm for more than a week.

It was Monday evening and the pair sat around the fire chatting and relaxing after yet another hard day's toil. Eve had just bathed and had dressed herself in a long white cotton frock. Her skin gleamed from the delicate fragrant soap she had used and her face practically glowed from the heat of the stove. As Tommie watched her he could feel his loins quiver at her sheer beauty and he began to get fidgety and nervous.

"What are you staring at?" She caught his stare and suddenly smiled sweetly at him, causing his heart to skip a beat.

"I'm not staring!" He had to deny it just as he had been trying to deny his feelings of late.

"Tommie, you may not realise it but you have been staring at me for the last five minutes. I've seen you!"

"You're fibbing Eve, imagining things! Anyway, even if I was what crime is there in it?"

"Oh, there's no crime involved at all but don't you know that a girl will get her hopes up when she sees a fella staring at her like that?" She was holding his gaze now, her eyes full of love and desire.

"And did you?" He looked at her again and knew in that moment that he still fancied her.

"Did I what?" She decided to tease him.

"Did you get your hopes up?"

"Oh, Tommie I always have my hopes up about you, you should know that!" The love she held within her never ceased to hope that someday he would fall in love with her too.

"Eve, oh Eve, if it were only that simple!" He didn't really want to get into any of this but he seemed to be drawn to it by a force.

"Do you find me attractive?" She needed to know how he was feeling at that particular moment in time.

"What sort of a question is that?"

"Well, do you?" she had him now, exactly where she wanted him, and she wasn't going to give up.

"Yes, of course I find you attractive. Sure what man wouldn't?" There was no point in denying it.

"Tommie." It was a slight whisper. "Will you kiss me?"

"Do you think that that is a good idea?" He knew that if he touched her at all, if he felt her soft skin mingle with his, there would be no turning back.

"Yes." She certainly couldn't think of a better one.

Eve leaned over in her chair until her head rested near his. Staring into his large brown eyes she recognised the want that was lying there and so brazenly she caught his face between her palms and found his lips. Tommie was surprised but responded with passion. He hungrily sought her mouth again and again and released some of the built up longings that had mounted inside of him.

Without warning he was unbuttoning her dress and allowed his hands to caress her breasts. Their warmth excited him further and he moaned as he felt an unfamiliar longing deep within.

Eve was aware that he was totally lost to his passions but she was fearful that he might suddenly awaken and come to his senses. She didn't want him to stop; this was the moment that she had spent so long dreaming about and now it was a reality. He couldn't stop now, he just couldn't!

Tommie, however, had no intention of stopping. He felt that he had died and gone to heaven and all practically had been obliterated from his mind.

He was on top of her at this stage and she knew that he was fumbling with her underwear. He was going to enter her! She couldn't believe it. As he undid the zip of his trousers he suddenly began to feel a little nervous but she knew that there was no turning back. Tommie would be hers after tonight. He would realise that he loved her and she'd spend the rest of her life here, with him, on Dalesport farm. She need never see Dick Kelly again!

As she felt his erect penis probing between her legs she closed her eyes and was lost to the moment. The initial sudden thrust pained her and she cried out but after a few minutes her body became accustomed to the pressure and she found that she was actually enjoying the experience. Tommie was gentle and as he came within her she did not feel any disappointment towards her lack of orgasm. Tommie Bordoni had made love to her and that alone warmed her heart.

The remainder of the night was spent making love and it seemed that now Tommie had started, he just couldn't get enough. When Eve finally closed her eyes she smiled to herself as she contemplated what had just happened. Dick Kelly would be furious if he could see her now but in fact, without realising it, he had actually done her a favour by hitting her. Hadn't he led her straight into Tommie Bordini's bed! What would he say if he ever discovered the truth?

CHAPTER EIGHT

Eve was still asleep when Tommie wearily aroused himself the next morning and crept quietly out to the kitchen. He felt that he had a lot to sort out in his mind before he spoke to her and he needed time alone to think. He didn't stop to boil the kettle for a cup of tea, he was fearful that the cheerful humming might awaken her. Instead he carefully opened the cottage door and stole out into the cold early morning.

The dew was still glistening on the lush grass and a fox stole stealthily near the hedge along the stile. Morning had broken but the countryside was still quiet and Tommie felt like an intruder as the noise of his footsteps echoed towards the woods.

Jake was waiting in the diary and had already four of the cows in for milking. He was far too chirpy this morning for Tommie's liking and he was finding it hard to respond to him. Eventually he sent him off to feed the calves and finished the milking alone, absorbed in his worried thoughts.

What had possessed him to do what he had done last night? He had made love to a woman for the first time ever and he had thoroughly enjoyed it but, God above, he had broken one of the rules that he had always sworn to abide by! Broken one of his few commandments!

If truth were told Eve had come to mean more to him than he had ever imagined anyone would. He denied the fact that he was in love with her but yet he experienced a warm, tender feeling in his heart every time he thought of her. If he wasn't careful he would wrangle himself into the situation where he was unable to live without her. That could not be allowed to happen at any cost! What they had done last night could never be repeated, under any circumstances. The experience had been special but could never recur. No, he would never make love again to Eve Kelly as long as he lived no matter how much his body tempted him to.

Tommie was under no illusions; he knew that in order to stick to his decision he would have to ask her to leave his cottage. Oh God! How on earth was he going to get around that one? Eve would be full of the joys of last night's experience- hadn't she every reason to be- and he supposed that he should be too. She would be devastated when he told her but it had to be done. And the sooner the better! He raced through the last of the milking and nervously made his way back to the cottage.

Eve was making a pot of tea when he entered and, as she turned to smile at him, his heart suddenly began to melt. She looked so beautiful as the early morning sun smiled on her pretty face and he did have deep feelings for her. He couldn't deny those facts! Could he go through with it at all? It was going to break her in two and God alone knew what it would do to him! But what other way was there around it?

"Hello there, lover" she greeted him with a kiss. "I didn't hear you get up. And how are you this wonderful morning?"

"Not bad. And you?" He turned to face the window, the guilt gnawing away at his body.

"I feel fantastic. I've never been so happy in all my life. Oh Tommie! I still can't believe that we made love last night."

"Neither can I!" he sighed heavily as he turned to look at her. "Neither can I! Eve, will you sit down for a moment, I need to talk to you."

She looked at his anxious face and was immediately put on her guard. As the butterflies began to chase one another around her stomach she had an idea of what was to come. She knew that she didn't want to hear it but had no choice.

"What's the matter Tommie?" He was regretting his actions already. Had she not satisfied him?

"Oh, Eve! I don't know how to tell you this but last night should never have happened."

"What do you mean 'should never have happened'? Did you not enjoy it?"

"Of course I enjoyed it. Can't you see that that is exactly the problem! I have already told you that I am never going to get married so why the hell did we do it?"

"Why did we do it?" She raised her voice and was almost shouting at him, her anger now suppressing her anxiety. "How can you even ask such a question? We did it because we both wanted to and because we both love each other. You do love me Tommie, don't you?"

"Jesus, I don't know. I don't even know what love is supposed to be like. All I know is that I don't want to fall in love and this can never ever happen again."

"How can you say that? Of course it must happen again. Wasn't it wonderful? Didn't you enjoy it? I love you Tommie and I want to make love to you forever. I want to give my whole life to you."

"No, Eve, no! You must not say such things. It is not possible. We've been through all this before. I'm a bachelor at heart and that is how I intend to stay. I am not looking for a wife, you know that, and we should never have made love. It only deepens your hurt and pain and I don't want to be the cause of any of that. I should have had more sense! You are far too dear and sweet."

"So what happens now?" She fought the tears that stung her eyes. The last thing she wanted was for him to see her cry. "What do you suggest, eh? We go about the cottage ignoring each other? Ignoring these feelings that we have for each other? Is that what you want Tommie, is it?"

"No, Eve, that is not what I want at all. Even I am not stupid enough to realise that that could be possible. The only conclusion I can come to is that you will have to leave."

"Leave? You want me to leave after having sex with me? Is that it? You only used me Tommie, do you realise that? I should have known better but I loved you and trusted you and I was hoping that you felt the same way. Oh, I've been such a fool."

"No, Eve, please don't say that! I didn't use you! I will always treasure what we had last night. It will stay in my heart forever but you have to try and understand where I am coming from."

"No, I can't, I can't understand at all! In fact I could safely say that as long as I live I will never be able to understand where you are coming from and do you know, all of a sudden, I don't even want to! It seems that I have to pay for the sins of all the women who betrayed you in the past and it's not fair. Do you hear me, Tommie, it's just not fair! You will have to grow up and learn to live beyond your pain. We had something special going here but you have ruined it. But no matter! It is your loss and I know that in time you will realise that. The only sad thing is that I won't be there for you when you come running back. Now, I'll pack my things and I'll be gone before lunchtime."

"Where will you go?" He was genuinely concerned.

"I haven't decided yet but don't you worry about it. It needn't bother you."

"Ah, Eve don't be like that. Surely we can still be friends." He reached out to touch her arm but she backed away from him.

"Don't you dare touch me Tommie Bordoni. You can't have it every way you know. Now, I'll thank you for your hospitality and I'll won't be bothering you again."

Tommie, knowing that he alone had created this mess, decided to leave her in peace to make a start on her packing. The sooner she was gone then the sooner he could get on with the rest of his life. That was what he wanted after all, wasn't it?

However, as he walked through the door, he turned to look back at her and for a split second wondered if he really was doing the right thing. He had grown accustomed to having Eve around the place and he knew that he would sorely miss her. Still, it was as she had said, he had made his bed and now he must lie on it! He'd get used to the long evenings alone again and soon she would become nothing more than a haunting memory. He didn't need a woman to make his life complete. He had his farm!

It didn't take Eve long to pack her belongings and when she had finished she sat on the bed and wept. Smoothing the blankets with her right hand she found it hard to believe that only hours earlier she had made love here with Tommie. She had no regrets. She would take the memories of that wonderful night with her to her grave.

In the meantime she had to learn to nurse her broken heart and decide where she was going to go. Faced with no alternative she knew that she had to swallow her pride and head for home.

What other choice was available to her? She would return to the farm for a few weeks but she'd never give up the quest of looking for a place of her own.

Mrs. Kelly was half- heartily washing the breakfast dishes at the sink and turned her head sadly to look through the window. Life had always been hard for her but it had definitely worsened since Eve had left! Dick was in a foul mood all the time and slammed every door that he walked through. He was spending more and more time in the village and she knew that he was consorting with women. She didn't care! She just wished that one of those women would take him away altogether. Things might be a little more bearable then. Before, at least, she had Eve but since her daughter's hurried departure she was feeling pretty lonely all the time. She didn't blame her for leaving. She would have done the same under the circumstances but, oh, how she missed her so!

Squinting her eyes she suddenly noticed a figure coming towards the cottage and she tried to make out who it was. It took her a few minutes to focus as her eyesight had deteriorated over the last two years but as the figure began to draw nearer she imagined that it was that of her daughter. But it couldn't be! Eve had sworn that she would never return while he was there.

However, there was no mistaking the identity of the person now, as she was only a matter of feet away from the window. It was Eve all right and she was looking so sad and forlorn. Wiping her hands quickly in her apron Mrs. Kelly raced across the kitchen and flung open the door. Tears of joy mingled with worry as she pulled the girl to her and hugged her.

It was only after they had settled inside with a cup of strong, black coffee that Eve related her grief to her mother. Mrs. Kelly listened and felt that her heart would break. Eve was such a kind, gentle person yet she had been given a hard path in life. Where was the justice in the lot of it? Oh, if she could get her hands on that Tommie Bordoni she'd wring his scrawny neck for him. Imagine the cheek of him to take advantage of her daughter and then throw her out of his house! He was a bad sort all right. A chip off the old block you could say! Sure didn't Harrison make a pastime out of bedding women and he never committed himself to one either. However, her main priority at the moment was her daughter. Tommie Bordoni would come later on.

"Eve." Her voice was soft as she looked at her heartbroken daughter. "I know that right now you might feel that you're life has ended but you will get over this. Tommie Bordoni is not worth your tears. You are far too good for the likes of that fella and the quicker you realise that the better. He couldn't be any other way anyway when you consider who sired him. You will meet someone in time and you will fall in love and all thoughts of Tommie will leave your mind. The only worry I would have about it all is that you have slept with him. I pray that he did not leave you with child. If he did, well then, that will be a different matter altogether."

"Jesus, I never thought of that." Eve found herself almost wishing that she were pregnant. At least then she would have some hold over him. Tommie would stand by his child -she knew that.

"Well, we'll cross that bridge when and if we come to it. For the moment we must get you settled and back to normal."

"What'll he say when he finds out that I'm back? Do you think that he will kick me out?"

"Don't be silly! He's never here long enough to notice anything. Always out riding women! He'll get a disease one of these days if he's not careful."

"I hope he does and it falls off him. He deserves no better, the dirty animal. I'm still going to find a flat you know. I'm not staying here for long."

"We'll see, we'll see." Mrs. Kelly rubbed her daughter's arm and prayed silently that she would never leave again.

It was eight o' clock that evening when Dick Kelly returned home from his ramblings. He was full of beer, as usual, and was in a foul mood as Peggy Treacy, from the lower bog road, had refused his advances. He had had to make do with Molly Rodgers and she was a dried up old prune. Still beggars can't afford to be choosers and he had got his release. He'd be waiting till the cows came home if he were depending on that wife of his to satisfy him. She never had much in her anyway and all she seemed to be doing was moping around since Eve had left.

Her face was enough to turn milk sour and he didn't relish the thought of looking at it at this hour of the night. He'd have his supper and he'd go straight to bed.

On entering the kitchen he thought at first that his eyes were playing tricks on him. But no! He was seeing clearly. There was his brazen daughter sitting in his kitchen as if she had never left it. God above, what next? Striding across the room he stood in front of her and opened his mouth. The stale smell of whiskey penetrated the air and Eve could feel her stomach weaken.

"And where may I ask did you spring from?" He had no idea that Eve had been living at Dalesport Farm for the past few weeks.

Before Eve could open her mouth to reply Mrs. Kelly stood abreast of her husband and glared at him.

"It doesn't matter to you or me where she was! All that need concern us now is that she is home again and she is going to stay for a while."

"Oh, she is, is she?" He tried to get past his wife but staggered from the alcohol.

"Yes, and that is the final word on the matter. There's some cold stew in the pot there if you want it. Heat it up yourself."

Dick made his way to the stove and started shuffling around the saucepan. Secretly he was glad that his daughter had returned. He hadn't been managing the farm work very well on his own and he needed to change around some of the stock tomorrow. And what about the way his wife had stood up to him? Jesus there was a first time for everything!

"Oh, let her stay then." He muttered away to himself as he placed the plate of stew into the hot oven. "She's more use to me here anyway and she might help to take that sour look off her mother's face."

And so nothing further was said on the matter. Within a couple of days Eve felt that her stolen days with Tommie had been only an illusion, a figment of her imagination, a dream that she had created to lessen her sorrows in life. Why then did she anxiously await the due date of her periods?

CHAPTER NINE

The wet April days yielded to a warm, sunny May and Tommie's workload around the farm tripled. He took on Kevin, Rosie's thirteen-year-old son, to help him out at the weekends and during the long bright evenings and paid him well. Kevin was delighted with the money and worked like a little Trojan.

Tommie was content enough during the days but at night-time, when he made his way back to his lonely cottage, his heart felt heavy. It was then that he missed Eve most and he found that she was constantly on his mind. He had not seen her since the day he had dismissed her from his home and he wondered how she was faring out. Bill had mentioned that she hadn't attended the dance in Ballyhale for a while and he assumed that she had left Dalesport altogether. Maybe it was just as well! She would be out of Dick Kelly's way and he wouldn't be able to harm her.

There were evenings, however, when he just had to hold himself back from going over to her father's farm to see if she was there. He would shake himself then and warn himself to cop on. He didn't need Eve in his life so why, oh why, did his heart ache so much?

It was a warm Thursday evening in the middle of May when Bill drove into the farmyard in a state of excitement. It had well over a week since he had seen his pal and he was looking forward to the chat. Tommie had become a bit of a loner lately and Bill couldn't understand it at all. He knew that things

69

hadn't worked out for him and that Eve one that he was hanging around with but sure wasn't there plenty more fish in the sea. The only trouble was that Tommie would never find one hanging around the farm. He needed to go back to the dances again. Maybe he could manage to persuade him to!

Turning off the ignition he alighted from the car and made his way towards the barn where Tommie was shoveling dung.

"Hi, there me old pal. Long time no see! What are you up to at all?"

"Oh, hello Bill. I'm just cleaning out the shed here. I let the calves out last week and the ole place needs to be done badly. It's a mess after the winter."

"Well, stop shoveling that shit for a minute and sit down here and talk to me. I haven't seen you for ages. Gave up on the dances did you?"

"Haven't the time for them to tell you the truth."

"You should make the time you know. All this work will get you down and life is short."

"I know, I know!" Tommie placed the shovel to one side and sat beside Bill.

"You won't find a woman in the hay sheds there. You may just get out and about and get some action."

"I don't want a woman, Bill. I'm happier on my own!"

"Can't understand that at all! Meself, I'd never live without one."

"That's your call, Bill. Anyway, anything strange with you?"

"Be God there is but you won't believe it Tom! I'm going to go and get meself hitched!"

"For fuck sake Bill, you're having me on!"

"Deed and I'm not, 'tis true alright. Come the fourth of August I'll be an old married man."

"Get away with you. Am I right in assuming that it is Sadie that you are marrying?"

"Aye, sure who else would it be."

"But you haven't been going out with her that long."

"That's true enough I suppose but I've been with her long enough to know that I love her. What's the point in wasting any more time?"

"You'd want to be certain sure before you do anything. Marriage is for life you know."

"I know that Tommie but I really do love Sadie and she loves me. Sure you know yourself how long I have worshipped her from afar. And I haven't told you the best bit yet. Sadie is having a baby. My baby! Can you imagine that! I'm going to be a Dad. Me, mad Bill Foley, is about to become a father!"

So that was it! Bill had knocked the girl up and now he was doing the right thing and standing by her. Fair play to him. Well, if that was what he wanted in life so be it. He hoped that the two of them would be happy.

Jesus, a terrible thought suddenly crossed his mind. What if Eve had become pregnant after their one night of passion? Would he stand by her and marry her? He knew that he would have to or else Dick Kelly would murder him. But there was only a slight possibility of Eve becoming pregnant wasn't there? It would never happen after the first time.

"You've gone awfully quiet all of a sudden." Bill looked at his friend and knew that he wasn't happy. "What's the matter with you?"

"Nothing, nothing at all! I'm really glad for you Bill and I hope it all works out okay."

"Thanks, Tommie. You'll come to the wedding won't you?"

"I wouldn't miss it for the world."

"Great, that's that settled then. Well, I'd best be on my way. I'm meeting Sadie in an hour and I want to change my clothes. See you later Tom. Hey, why don't you come along to the dance on Saturday? Let you're hair down so as to speak."

"We'll see, we'll see." But he knew that he had no intention of going.

When Bill had left Tommie returned to his shoveling but his mind was not on his work. He couldn't take it in, Bill Foley was to get married and become a Dad. Bill who loved to play the fool and date scores of women was ready to settle down with Sadie, a girl he had only being going out with for a few months. Tommie couldn't understand how he was able to commit himself to take the chance. What if it didn't work out? What if he decided in another while that he didn't really love Sadie at all? Still it was Bill's life and he could do with it whatever he liked.

In one way he had to admire his friend's courage. He himself would never be able to enter into the promise of marriage. Yet, when he thought of Eve, his heart skipped a tiny beat and he felt a sorrow creep over his body. He prayed that he had not left her with child. What in the name of God would happen then?

Tommie had just finished clearing the dung when he noticed a red ford come into the yard. He knew straight away that it was Robbie. He had heard Kitty say that he was coming down to take the children to Meath for a couple of days. God, there was a man who had come out on the wrong side of marriage. As far as he knew Robbie had never touched another woman since his break up with Rosie. Oh, he was still married to her but who could blame him if he had fallen for another? Rosie was living in the land of no return and at this stage they had all given up hope of her ever coming back to reality.

Noticing how thin Robbie had become Tommie tried to keep the sympathy from his tone as he greeted him.

"Hello, there and how are you?"

"Not bad at all Tommie. Kept busy but that's the best way I suppose. What do you think?"

"I don't know. Sometimes all this work would get to you. Down for the kids?"

"Yeah. They're looking forward to coming up for a few days. You should come up yourself sometime. You'd enjoy it."

"Maybe I'll surprise you one of these days." He laughed at the very thought.

"Bring the girlfriend up with you." Robbie had a grin on his face as he waited for Tommie's reaction.

"Girlfriend? What girlfriend? I haven't got one." Surely Robbie hadn't heard anything?

"Ah go on outta that! Kitty told me that you had a woman in your life. It seems that she was living in the cottage with you for a little while. Am I right?"

"I helped a friend out that was all. Anyway Kitty has no right to go mouthing to you or anyone else about my private affairs." So they had all been wondering what had been going on and it looked like they had jumped to their own conclusions.

"Hey Tommie, keep your hair on! She wasn't mouthing as you call it. She was just delighted that you had some company for a change. She worries about you, you know."

Well, she needn't bother, I'm fine." He was in a defensive mood now and wished that he had not come over. "And you can tell her that when you see her!"

"She's looking forward to the day when you finally settle yourself down with a woman and start a family."

"She wouldn't want to hold her breath on that score! She'll be sorely disappointed."

"What do you mean?" Robbie wondered what he had said to annoy him so much.

"I'm never going to get married Robbie."

"Deed and you will. Sure didn't we all say that."

"Yeah and you'd have been better off if you had stuck with your initial decision. Sure what has marriage ever done for you only caused you heartache? And how many more are there out there like you?"

"Don't base your opinion of marriage on mine, Tommie. There are a lot of good marriages you know." His voice quivered as he spoke, his sorrow engulfing him completely.

"Do you ever get lonely, Robbie? Have you ever thought of taking another woman?"

"Yeah, I do get lonely but to be honest with you I have never even looked at another woman. I still think about what I had with Rosie and imagine that it was real. I loved her more than I could ever hope to describe and sometimes I dream that I will experience that love again. A fool's hope, I suppose, but there you are. It keeps me going."

"Have you really not looked at another woman?"

"No, why would I bother? Rosie was the only woman in the world for me and I will live with her loss. It's hard sometimes but I can cope with it."

"Fair play to you" Tommie figured that the man was a saint, awaiting a fitting for his halo. "Anyway I'd best be making tracks, I have a lot of work planned for the day."

"I'll see you so, Tommie but before I go let me give you a word of advice. Don't be too hasty with your decisions. Remember, if you happen to meet a nice girl hold onto her and don't be too quick to let her go. You might just find that you will spend the rest of you life regretting it."

Tommie absently nodded as he left the yard but deep inside he wondered if he would indeed regret giving Eve the push.

She was as nice a girl as you would find anywhere and he had let her go. No, he convinced himself that he had done the right thing and from now on he was going to forget about women altogether. He had tasted the fruits of passion and their memories would help sustain him for the rest of his life.

CHAPTER TEN

It was a beautiful Friday evening at the end of May and Eve was on her way home from work. The deep yellow sun slanted cheerfully in the pale azure sky and the trees had skillfully arrayed themselves with fresh green leaves. A cuckoo tried to sing in the distance and the last of the spring primroses smiled shyly from underneath the thick hedgerows. Eve walked slowly, practically exhausted as the day had been particularly busy and she hadn't slept well the previous night. Her mind, as always, had been full of Tommie Bordoni and no matter how she tried to forget about him she found that she couldn't. He was certainly coming between her and her reason.

Oh, she knew that he didn't want to have anything more to do with her, he had made that perfectly clear but that didn't stop the longings that she felt in her heart. Every time she recalled the touch of his hands on her body and the smell of his naked flesh as he made love to her she weakened. Tommie had come to mean everything to her in a short space of time and she was finding it hard to live without him. He had left an empty void in her life and she was unable to fill it anymore.

Her mother had advised her to go out and look for another fella. "Plenty more fish in the sea" she had said. "Don't waste your time waiting around for the one that you can't catch. One of these days you will wake up and find that you are old and then it will be too late."

Eve knew that her mother was right but at the moment she didn't have the energy to start looking. She had even given up going to the dances at Ballyhale as she had lost complete interest in them. What was more she had also abandoned the idea of moving away from home. Her father spent so little time in the house these days that she rarely saw him. That suited her and she kept out of his way as much as possible. Her periods had arrived approximately three weeks after her return home so any hopes that she might have had of bearing Tommie's baby had vanished.

Turning the corner at Hodgin's farm she cringed when she noticed Podge sitting sullenly on the stone wall, his skinny legs swinging frantically in front of him. She planned to keep her head down and pass him as quickly as she could but he was down from the wall in a flash and was keeping step with her.

"Hello there, Eve." His smile conveyed a missing tooth in the front of his mouth. "How are you this fine evening?"

"I'm fine, and you?" She tried to be pleasant, as she knew that there was no point in taking her troubles out on him.

"Oh, okay. Looking for a bit of excitement but, you know yourself, nothing like that ever happens around here." He was delighted to have the opportunity to talk to her as he had fancied her practically all his life. He had sat beside her on several occasions in Primary school and had always conveniently forgotten his books so that he could share hers.

"You're right there!"

"What do you do yourself for excitement?"

"What do you mean?" She wished that he would just go away and leave her alone. This was the last thing that she needed right now.

"At the weekends. Where do you go?"

"Nowhere really." She sighed as she was beginning to find the conversation a bore.

"Would you like to come out with me this weekend?" Podge knew that he was chancing his arm and he hoped that it would be worth it.

"No thanks." Not in a million years!

"Ah why not?" He sounded surprised and disappointed.

Looking into his unshaven face Eve felt that he must already know the answer to that but she was too gentle a person to remind him.

"I don't have the time." It seemed to be the kindest answer and it would have to do him.

"Some other time then?" He wasn't about to give up hope.

"We'll see."

Podge seemed to be happy enough with that reply and he nodded his farewell and made his way back to the wall, a silly smile plastered on his country face. As Eve walked the remainder of the way she found herself pondering on the cruelty and irony of life. There was Podge and he would do anything to go out with her but she really had no interest in him. And then there was Tommie and she'd do anything to have him but he didn't want her. Where was the justice in the lot of it? She tried to imagine what a date with Podge would be like as she walked the last few remaining steps and quickly dismissed the idea from her head. It really didn't bear thinking about!

Her mother had her dinner ready when she entered the kitchen and she ate ravenously. She noticed that her father was absent from the table.

"Where is he?" She didn't really care but she wanted to know if he would walk in at any minute.

"He's gone out. Won't be back till dark."

"Where is he gone at this hour of the evening." He rarely missed his dinner.

"To the pub, I suppose! I don't know! He didn't say." She didn't care one way or the other!

"Gone off to meet a woman I'd say." She felt bitter as she cleared the dishes from the table. "Keep him nothing to eat, it might teach him a lesson. You know, of course, that he is still cajoling with almost every woman in the village and he is the talk of the town at this stage?"

"To be honest Eve I don't care anymore. He can do what he likes as far as I am concerned as long as he leaves us alone."

"Yeah, I suppose you're right there! By the way you'll never guess who asked me out just now."

"Who?" Mrs. Kelly was all ears and was delighted that her daughter trusted her enough to confide in her.

"Podge Hodgins." She stifled a giggle.

"Podge from next door? I don't believe you! And what did you say?"

"What do you think I said? I told him that I hadn't time to go out."

"Do you think that was wise? Podge is a grand fella you know and he will own all that land one of these days. You could do worse than marry Podge, Eve."

"Oh mother, will you just listen to yourself. If you think that I would go out with Podge for his bit of land then you are mad. I'd rather stay single all my life. Anyway it's Podge I'd have to take to bed with me and not his bit of land!"

"Well at least don't dismiss him completely until you have thought the whole thing through." Mrs. Kelly wished that Eve would abandon her idea of reconciliation with that Tommie fella. He wasn't for the likes of them at all!

"Yes mother." Eve found herself agreeing for the sake of peace and then changed the subject. She was sorry that she had mentioned Podge at all. He would, of course, be her mother's idea of a good catch. He was a hard worker, keen and reliable. Not to mention the big farm that would become his any day now. Oh, Podge would indeed be a suitable catch for someone, some day but Eve knew that he was not for her.

Meanwhile down at the Sparrow's Inn Dick Kelly was filling his gullet with pint after pint of bitter ale. He was feeling a little down and he thought that the drink might help to cheer him up. Mrs. Hodgins had begun to cool down of late and didn't seem to require his manly love as much as she once had done. Jesus, there was a time, not too long ago either, when she had been gagging for it! She couldn't even wait until he had his trousers fully down. Now the bitch was turning sour on him and he didn't like it. It wasn't that he loved her, oh good God no! Women were ten a penny and he had no difficulty in getting one to lie with him. He just felt that she had an awful nerve to reject his advances. Well, he'd show the stuck up cow! He'd have his evil way with her one last time and then she could go to hell. He looked at his watch and noticed that it was just gone seven o' clock. She'd be out feeding the hens in fifteen minutes and if he hurried along the road he might be in time to encounter her. Raising the half-full glass to his lips he finished the cold ale in one mouthful and then slowly climbed off the bar stool.

His steps were staggered as he made his way towards the door but he managed to open it without making too much noise. The hot and heavy May evening hit him as soon as he went outside and he blinked his eyes in the bright sunlight. Pulling his trousers up around his hips he set for the road home and, despite his drunken state, managed to make it to Hodgins farm in good time.

There she was, throwing grain to the hens, just as he had predicted. She did not appear to be at all happy about his sudden appearance but Kelly didn't care. The bitch was asking for all that was coming to her!

"Hello, Kitty!" he greeted her in a friendly tone. "Isn't it shocking warm for this time of the day?"

"To hell with the weather, what the fuck brings you up here?" She threw the last of the grain to the plump hens and stared him right in the face. "Jake is just up the fields and will be back any moment and Podge is inside in the house. Do you want them to find out what we have been up to?"

"No, no of course not. Let's go into the barn for a moment, I want to talk to you."

"Listen Dick, you know that there is no point in talking anymore. I said all I wanted to say to you the last time and as far as I am concerned that is that. There is nothing more that we need say to each other and we both have to get on with our own lives from here."

Dick was not going to be put off as easy as that. He took one look at the fine looking woman in front of him and he could feel his member harden inside his trousers.

"Get into the barn when I tell you" he roared at her and she was frightened for a moment.

"You've been drinking haven't you?"

"And what business of yours is it if I have? Now get along to the barn before I have to force you to go."

Kitty was silent for a moment and then considered that she had better do what he had requested in case her husband came along and wondered why, in the name of God, the two of them were yelling at one another across the hen yard.

Closing the makeshift gate behind her she followed him like a meek lamb and told herself that she was going to give him five minutes to say what he had to say and that was all. Oh, she rued the day that she had ever let him lay a finger on her. What had she seen in him anyway? Looking at him now in this sorry state, with his trousers hoisted up around his waist, she knew that it certainly hadn't been his looks. She had been lonely, that was all. She had craved the warmth of another body beside hers and had longed for the passion and excitement that resulted from sex. Her husband had given up the act years ago. Impotent, that's what the doctors had said and it looked like he would never be able to make love again. Dick Kelly, on the other hand, while he was no prince charming, knew how to get a woman excited. He was like a sex machine and she had enjoyed their tumbles for a while. Now she had had enough and the very sight of him turned her stomach. She found it hard to believe that she had actually allowed him to crawl into her. The very thought caused her to shudder.

When they reached the barn Dick pushed her roughly inside and he bolted the door behind him. Turning to face her he knew that she was afraid of him and the knowledge excited him further.

Grinning to himself he made his way towards her and caught her by the arm.

"I know that you have said that we're finished but I thought that we could do it one last time. Just for old time's sake. What do you think, hey?"

"You have got to be joking, haven't you. I meant what I said and there is no going back! You and I are definitely finished. No more hanky panky for us! Is that clear?"

"Oh, it's clear alright but the problem is that I don't agree with you. I think that we should indulge in some good old passion and we're not going to be finished until I say so! Have you got that into your stupid little mind? I am going to have sex with you, with or without your consent."

Before she could reply Dick caught her roughly by her long thick hair and pulled her to him. Staring at her terrified face he bent forward and kissed her full on the mouth. The kiss was wet and sloppy and she retched, as she smelt the stale ale on his breath. She found that she was unable to break free and her heart pounded in her chest as she fought with him. Dick dragged her to the bed of hay in the corner of the barn and tore the blouse from her body. As she struggled to cover herself he began to suckle her large breasts and handle them roughly. He played with them until he was fully aroused and then he lifted her skirt and peeled away her underwear. Pulling down his trousers he shoved his member into her and continued to shove until he reached satisfaction. Grinning he got off her for a moment and then, without warning he was on top of her again. He ignored her sobs, as he thrust himself time and time again into her unwilling body. It took him a lot longer to climax the second time and when he did he took such a fit of coughing that he thought he was going to die. Pulling himself up off the hay he redid his zip and stood over her grinning.

"Not so high and mighty now, are you bitch?" He spat at her as she tried to pull herself together. Kitty remained silent and that seemed to aggravate him.

"Say something, you stupid slut." He kicked her across the legs to get a reaction but still she remained quiet, too tired and bruised to answer.

"You're a fuckin snob, do you know that?" Pulling her up he looked her straight in the eye. She was still naked but showed no recognition of the fact. "A high and mighty bitch. Too good for old Kelly, are you? It's not so long ago that you were begging me for it you know! What would your husband say if he knew that you were rolling in the hay with Dick Kelly, I wonder? Shall we go out and call him in? I'm sure he'd love to see you in this state." He caught her left breast and pinched her so hard that she squealed.

"You're a bastard, Dick Kelly, a right bastard. What I ever saw in you the first day, I'll never know. I can't understand what in God's holy name ever possessed me to allow you to lay a finger on me! And if you mention a word of this to my husband it will be you that will come out the sorry one and not me. He'd pull you apart limb from limb and leave your bones for the crows to pluck. I would deny any consent. I'd tell him that you raped me, just like you have done now. You're a horrible, mean disgusting man and I never want to lay eyes on you again as long as I live."

"You fuckin ungrateful slut." Dick was clearly agitated but was somewhat afraid of Hodgins. The man was big and was known for his fiery temper. Rumour had it that he was as strong as an ox. He could lift two bags of cement and throw them over his shoulders without effort. If Hodgins were to get his hands on Dick Kelly he'd make mince meat out of him for sure! He had to do something, had to quieten this woman somehow! She'd tell her husband that she had been raped and then it would be lights out!

Looking around the barn with darting, mad eyes he vowed that he would make her afraid of him, make her too terrified to go running to her husband with silly stories. He'd make her afraid of him and then she'd be quiet!

Spying a tractor spanner near the old rusted potato sprayer he quickly made his way towards it. Without warning he grabbed the spanner and rushed at Kitty with it. The heavy blow that she received to the temple sent her spinning and within seconds she had fallen to the floor. The blood spurted from the side of her mouth and dropped onto the golden hay in a heavy red flow. Dick gasped as he realised that he had caused the woman more harm than was his original intent and he bent down beside her and gently called her name. When he received no response he checked her neck for a pulse. He couldn't find one!

"Mother of Jesus I've killed her." He broke out in a sweat as he looked at the spanner, which he still held in his hand. "She's as dead as a fuckin maggot, holy hand of God what have I done at all?" He scanned the shed automatically to see if there was anywhere he could possibly hide the instrument but on failing to locate any suitable place he decided to bring it with him.

Stopping at the barn door he glanced around the yard for movement. The last thing he wanted now was for some one to see him emerge but luckily all was still! Quickly he made his exit and scaled the wall like a man half his age. He didn't stop running until he had reached his farm. Making his way towards the shed he grabbed a spade and walked out across the haggard. He dug for five minutes and then buried the spanner in the rich brown soil. His wife watched, mystified, through the little window in the back kitchen.

CHAPTER ELEVEN

When he had completed his gruesome task Dick slowly made his way to the house and scrubbed himself in the bathroom for at least ten minutes. He wanted to ensure that all traces of blood had been washed from his hands before anyone saw him and he cringed as he watched the red stains twirl round the white sink and race down the plug hole.

When he eventually entered the kitchen he ordered his wife to make a cup of tea and sat at the table with his head in his hands. His body was all a tremble and he knew that he was really for the high jump now! He had not meant to kill the bitch, that was the God's honest truth! He had wanted to hurt her alright, make her afraid of him and so stop her from blabbing to her husband about her ordeal but that was all. He had to make sure that no one would suspect him of the murder. No one must ever know that he was hanging around with Mrs. Hodgins. Looking up he noticed his wife staring strangely at him.

"What the fuck are you looking at?" He was in no humour to deal with her right now. Hadn't he enough on his mind?

"I want to know what you were burying this minute in the haggard." She looked critically at him and did not like the terror that she witnessed in his wild eyes.

"What the fuck are you talking about?" Surely she did not know what was going on? How could she?

"I was watching you while you were busy burying something out there and I want to know what it was."

"It's none of your fuckin business, that's what it was, and I want you to forget that you ever saw anything. And if anyone happens to come by and ask if I was at home this evening I want you to say that I never left the house all night. Have you got that?" He looked at her crossly, his eyes buckled into a squint.

"I'm sure you were seen in the pub." He was up to something and he wanted her help to cover up his tracks! What had he done? Had he stolen from someone in the village?

Dick silently cursed. She was right of course! The bitch had more sense than he would have given her credit for.

"Well, say that I was here after seven. Say that I went out early for a quiet drink and that I was home by seven. Have you got that?"

"What have you done?" He was looking as guilty as hell and his face was ashen.

"What do you mean what have I done?" How could she suspect anything?

"Why do you want me to lie for you?" She'd get to the bottom of it if it killed her.

"Listen here woman." Dick was red in the face at this stage and his terror had been replaced by anger. "I have done nothing so get that through to your thick, stupid skull. You just do as I have told you to and everything will be fine. Okay?"

"Yeah." She didn't want to argue with him but as she started to do her ironing she wondered again what trouble he had managed to get himself into now. And he was in trouble, she knew from his strange behaviour and frightened eyes!

He never left the hearth for the remainder of the night but sat slumped on the chair, with his head in his hands. For once in his life Dick Kelly did not as much as open his mouth and you needn't be Sherlock Homes to figure out that he had committed some sort of a crime.

Podge Hodgins shuffled around on his chair and suddenly began to wonder why the house was so disturbingly quiet. Glancing at the clock he noticed that it was ten to eight and his mother had not yet called him for the tea. That was unusual! They usually ate at half past seven, just after she had seen to the hens.

Arousing himself he eventually decided to go through to the kitchen to see what the delay was. He was so hungry now that he could almost eat a horse.

Upon entering the kitchen he noticed that the room was empty and his mother was no where in sight. Worse still there was no tea started! Where the blazes was she? It wasn't like her to be late with the meals. His father would be in at any moment now and there would be hell to pay if he had to wait for the tea. She knew that as well as he did!

Strolling out to the hen house he was surprised to find that there was no sign of her there either. The hens had been fed alright! He could see the remains of the grains of barley on the dusty ground so she couldn't be too far away! Closing the gate behind him he made his way across the yard and noticed his father walking close to the cattle shed. Perhaps he knew where the woman was.

"Have you seen mother?" he called when he was close enough to be heard. "She's not inside and there's no tea ready."

"Did you check the chicken coop?"

"Yeah, the hens have been fed but she's not there."

"Maybe she popped down to the village to get a loaf or something."

"I hardly think so, not at this time anyway. Sure most of the shops are shut at this stage. I'm starving with the hunger. I wish she'd come back."

"She'll be back, don't you worry, sure she never goes too far. I'll tell you what to do. You go on in and make a start on the tea and you'll find she'll be back before you have it ready."

"You must be joking, sure cooking is women's work!" Podge wasn't going to be landed with that one.

"Do you want to eat or not?" Jake was clearly annoyed at the disturbance and yelled back at his son.

"Yes, of course I do but-" He was a little afraid of his father but still he did not fancy the job of cooking.

"But nothing! Go on in and start cooking and I'll be along in five minutes."

Knowing that it was useless to argue anymore Podge reluctantly returned to the house, pulled the heavy frying pan out from under the cooker and began to fry some eggs and sausages. The meal was cooked within fifteen minutes and still Mrs. Hodgins had not returned.

"So much for the ole lad's predictions" Podge muttered as he placed the eggs on the heated plates. His father came in and joined him at the table and still there was no sign of the woman. In fact the table had been cleared and the delph washed up and she had not appeared. Mr. Hodgins suddenly became anxious and was forced to admit that the whole thing was very strange.

"Where the devil can she be?" He straightened his hat on his head and scratched his forehead. "She never told me that she was going anywhere. Did she say anything to you?"

"No." Podge looked through the kitchen window into the stillness of the late evening. "She went out to feed the hens and she never came back. Most peculiar."

"And you checked the hen house? She didn't fall and bang her head out there did she?"

"No, she's not there." He was certain of that.

"Emh, I think that I'll go have a look around the farm just to satisfy my mind. There's a simple explanation for her absence but I can't figure out what it is. Are you coming?"

"Yeah, I suppose so." He didn't feel like moving but he was curious as to where his mother could be.

Podge followed his father out into the warm evening and together they searched the fields and sheds. On their way back to the house they passed the barn and Jake Hodgins noticed that the door was a little ajar. That door seemed to be open a lot lately even though he was always so sure that he closed it behind him. He'd bet a pound to a penny that his wife was inside. Throwing wide open the door he allowed the evening light to cascade into the barn, brightening even the darkest corners. He gave his eyes a moment to adjust to the change and when he looked the sight that he witnessed before him sickened him completely.

There, on the floor of the barn, imbedded in a mound of hay lay the body of his missing wife. She was practically naked and what little clothes she wore were in complete tatters. To make matters worse there seemed to be thick red blood everywhere. He knew straightaway that she was dead, her body was still and her eyes staring ahead. He tried to stop his son from entering the barn but Podge was in before he had recovered his senses. He screamed when he saw the dead woman and rushed to her body and began to weep like a child. After a few minutes he looked at his father through red stained eyes and spoke.

"She's dead Da, she's dead!"

"I can see that, son but what I would like to know is what the fuck has happened here?"

"Looks like someone attacked her." Podge was stating the obvious but his mind was not working correctly. "What are we going to do?"

"Jesus, I don't know! This is awful! My poor, poor Kitty, who has done this to her at all? I think that we had better call the guards. Run to the house and phone them straight away! Whoever has done this to my wife will pay dearly."

Podge took one last look at the lifeless body in front of him and, without uttering another word, staggered across the yard to phone the guards.

Sergeant Molloy was out in fifteen minutes accompanied by his assistant. He made his way slowly into the barn where Jake Hodgins was bent over the body of his dead wife. Podge sat in the corner of the barn, near the potato sprayer and was silently crying. Molloy thought he had never witnessed such a pitiful sight in all his life.

"Jake, I'm terrible sorry for your troubles." He extended his hand to the grieving man. "This is a desperate business altogether. You'd never think that the likes of this would happen in a place as small as Dalesport."

Jake looked at the sergeant and there was anger in his eyes. "You have to catch the man who has done this. I want to see for myself what sort of a monster he is! She was a good woman was Kitty, she didn't deserve this at all!"

"No, no one deserves a death like this and I promise you that we will certainly do our best to find this criminal." He took a look at the still body in front of him and began to examine it for clues. "Have you any idea who would want to harm your wife?"

"No, none what so ever! Like I said she was a good, quiet woman. Never did a days harm to anyone."

"Where were you when this awful tragedy occurred?"

"I was in the fields attending to the animals."

"And your son?" He glanced towards Podge who was now rocking his knees and staring like a madman at the corpse.

"Podge, where were you." Jake was reluctant to release his hold on the lifeless body.

"In the house. I was in the sitting room." Still he stared ahead.

"And neither of you heard anything?"

"No, not a whisper." Jake stroked the dark hair and cleaned some blood from the face.

"The clothes have been removed from her body. Looks like there was an act of sexual intercourse here. Your wife wasn't having an affair with anyone was she?"

Hodgins growled deeply and looked at the sergeant with wild eyes. "Of course she wasn't having an affair. What sort of woman do you think she was? She was attacked. Do you not think that that is clear enough from what you can see in front of you here?"

"Yes, yes it is clear but I have to ask these questions. Whoever attacked your wife wanted to make sure that she didn't tell any one afterwards. It might just be possible that she knew the attacker. Now, did either of you see anyone lurking around the farmyard this evening?"

Both of them nodded their heads in unison.

"We'll get to the bottom of this, don't you worry. In the meantime we will have to get your wife's body to the hospital for an autopsy. Looks like a severe blow to the head but with the right help we may be able to discover exactly what sort of an instrument dealt the blow. Tom" he turned to the assistant. "Go inside and ring for an ambulance. It is okay to use your phone I take it."

"Use it away." Jake was clearly in a state of shock.

"I don't see any old instrument lying around here. Whoever has done this horrific deed obviously has taken it with him. But it will turn up, these things usually do. We'll get to the bottom of this alright, don't you worry Jake. We'll have this criminal behind bars before the end of the week! We'll catch this creep alright, have no worries." He was trying to convince himself as much as convince Jake.

"The sooner the better," he stroked his wife's head again and gave way to the tears that had been welling up inside of him.

Sergeant Molloy rang at twelve o'clock that night and apologised for the late hour.

"We've just had the autopsy completed" he told Jake. "I was right in my theory. Mrs. Hodgins was struck quite viscously on the side of the head by a heavy steel weapon. She suffered severe damage to the brain and her skull was fractured in several places. She had been raped, more than once I might add, by the attacker. His semen was all over her body! By the way, I'm sorry to say that the baby had no chance of survival at all."

"Baby, what baby are you talking about?" Jake was tired and worn out and wondered if he had heard correctly.

"You must have known that your wife was pregnant."

"What?" Jake was in total disbelief. She couldn't be pregnant. Sure he hadn't touched her in years, he wasn't able to!

"Just a couple of months, that's all. Maybe she mightn't have been aware of it herself. Anyway it only deepens the sorrow of this awful tragedy. We will be starting a full-scale investigation first thing in the morning so I would advise you to get good nights sleep, if that is possible. We will need all the help we can get on this case and if there is anything at all you or your son can remember please don't hesitate to call me."

Hodgins slowly put down the phone and stared at the hall table for an age. So his wife was having an affair after all! Who was the man she had become involved with? Was he the one who had killed her? He couldn't answer these questions but the more he thought about it the more he realised that this man had in fact actually done him a favour. If he had found out about the affair, which was bound to have happened in time, he would definitely have killed the woman himself with his own bare hands. Better for a stranger to be put on trial for the murder than he himself!

CHAPTER TWELVE

"I'm coming, I'm coming." Maud Kelly ran her fingers through her greying hair as she curiously made her way towards the door. It was not yet eight o' clock and she couldn't for the life of her think who would be calling at such an hour. She wasn't up long herself and felt that she hadn't properly awoken yet.

She was surprised but not shocked when Sergeant Molloy and his assistant confronted her. Hadn't she been expecting something to happen or someone to appear since she had witnessed Dick in the haggard yesterday evening?

"Good morning." The Sergeant tipped his hat and tried a smile. "Forgive me for bothering you at such an early hour but I am investigating a murder in this area and need all the help I can get."

"A murder?" Maud could feel her stomach retch and she could hardly swallow. Whatever she had imagined Dick doing it hadn't been that. Was he capable of murder? Pulling herself together she looked the handsome man straight in the eye.

"I'm afraid that I can be of no help to you, guard. I know nothing of any murder."

"Oh, I never said that you did but I would like to ask you a few questions if I might."

"Okay, come on in." Anything was better than standing at the door.

She led the way to the tidy kitchen and offered them a seat. Eve and Dick were still in their beds so the house was quiet.

"Would you like a cup of tea?" She was dying for one herself and would have taken something stronger if she had had it in the house.

Both men nodded and while she brewed she was very conscious of the two staring around and taking all in. As she laid the cups on the table she noticed the assistant pulling out his notebook and pen. This was as serious as you could get!

"Now if I can begin." Molloy looked at the woman in front of him and sensed that she was a little nervous. "Last night a terrible murder was committed right next door to your farm. Mrs. Hodgins was attacked and raped and struck down in cold blood with a heavy instrument. We have not as yet discovered the instrument but I can tell you that we will find it."

"Oh my God, not Kitty!" She placed her hand over her mouth as the horror of the situation registered in her brain. This was far worse than she could ever have possibly imagined. But surely Dick did not have anything to do with it? He certainly was a lot of things, a coward, a bully, a cantankerous old git but a killer? Surely not!

"Yes, I'm afraid Mrs. Hodgins met her death last night and whoever is responsible for it is still out there at large. I want to get to the bottom of this as quickly as I can and put this brute behind bars. While he is still roaming around there is a chance that he may strike again."

"Oh my God!" It was all she could manage to say. She felt that she was dreaming. Surely Dick was not responsible for this. It was just a coincidence that he had been digging in the haggard yesterday evening. Fiddling with her fingers she looked across at the assistant. She could tell that he was writing at top speed in his notebook and she wondered just exactly what he was putting in there.

"What time did the murder occur?" It was a strange sort of question to ask but she needed to know.

"We're not sure of the exact time but we reckon that it was between seven and eight. Podge saw her go out to feed the hens at seven and went looking for her a little after eight."

Jesus, it had been around ten to eight when Dick buried whatever it was he was burying out in the haggard. This was not looking good at all!

"Did you see anyone peculiar or hear any strange noises around this time?"

"No, I heard nothing. I can't believe that that woman was been slain to death a couple of fields away and I heard nothing."

"What were you doing at that time?" Molloy sipped at the tea as he watched her fidget. If he didn't know any better he'd say that she was hiding something but she was such a small, frail looking woman and Kitty Hodgins had been big. She'd never have managed the murder on her own!

"I was clearing up after the tea."

"Does anyone else live here with you?"

"Yes, my daughter Eve and my husband."

"And were they both here last night?"

"Yes." She tried not to sound guilty for her lie.

"All night?" Molloy was biting the top of his pen, his mind working overtime. This woman was hiding something, he was sure of it!

"Well, Dick went down to the local early on in the evening for a few pints but he was back by seven." Why was she covering for him? She didn't know. Perhaps she wanted a chance to confront him herself first and see what he had to say for himself.

"And where are they now?"

"Both are in bed." At least she was telling the truth now.

"You may call them for me. I want to question them too. You never know, maybe one of them might have heard something."

Maud slowly walked towards the bedroom door and called her daughter.

"Be there in a moment Mum." Eve was her usual good-natured self.

She didn't take a chance on calling Dick. Instead she entered the darkened bedroom, pulled back the heavy cream drapes and shook him in the bed. He wasn't in the least amused.

"For God's sake woman, will you let me be. What has a man to do to get some sleep around here?" He growled and pulled the blankets back over his balding head.

"You may get up, ya big ape" she was angry with him. "The Sergeant and his man are sitting in the kitchen. They want to ask you a few questions."

He shot up straight away and she noticed the terror that had washed over his face.

"Question me? About what? You should have told them I wasn't here. You're a daft woman. Do you hear me? A daft igit of a woman!"

"I may not be as daft as you think, you know!" Maud felt a bitter resentment towards this man she had married. He was a low down coward and any pity she had felt for him in the past had died. "Anyway, they know you are here now and are waiting for you in the kitchen."

"What do they want to question me for?" Terror gripped him and he could feel the sweat begin to form on his brow.

"As if you didn't know." She muttered these words to herself, afraid to utter them aloud.

"It appears that Mrs. Hodgins was murdered last night and they are looking for the killer. They want to see if you heard anything strange going on around the place."

"I hope you told them I was here all night."

"Yes." She said it in a matter of disgust and threw his trousers at him before leaving the room.

Eve was already in the kitchen when she returned and she was answering all the questions that were being thrown at her. No, she had heard or seen nothing. She had been in her room all evening listening to records and hadn't been outside at all. Yes, her father and mother had been in the house also and hadn't left to the best of her knowledge. Yes, she had known Mrs. Hodgins and she had been a lovely woman. No, Podge was not strange and he had been devoted to his mother. It felt a little peculiar to be defending Podge but for all his shortcomings she was confident that he was not the killer. She made a mental note to call around later on to see how he was coping.

All heads turned at that moment to the doorway where Dick Kelly had suddenly appeared. He was badly in need of a shave and his hair (the bit that he had left) was uncombed. His shirt was buttoned wrong and his trousers hoisted up about his waist. He was anything but a welcome sight and Maud noticed the exchange of glances between the two guards.

"You must be Dick Kelly." Sergeant Molloy stated the obvious. "I am Sergeant Molloy and this here is Tom, my assistant. Your wife has probably explained to you the reason that we are here."

"Yes, indeed! Awful business! How may I help you?" He was trying to look cool.

"We were wondering if you saw anyone peculiar hanging about last night."

"No, I saw no one." His reply was far too hurried and definite.

"And you were in the pub early on?"

"Yes, I just went down for a little while. I left early enough though, anyone can tell you that. I don't like to leave the wife on her own too long, you see she tends to get a bit nervous so I go out early and come home early. Just as well too with the way things went round here last night!"

Maud cringed as she listened to him talk. How could he sit there so calmly and tell lie after lie when he knew that he had committed the worst sin of all? And he had committed the murder, she had no doubt about that at all now!

"And what time were you home at?"

"I don't know exactly. A little before seven, wasn't it love?"

It had been a long time since he had called her that and Maud nodded in surprise.

"You would have to pass Hodgins farm on the way home. Am I correct?"

"Yes." He couldn't deny it.

"And that would have been around seven. You heard nothing going on there? A scream or an argument? You see the murder happened between seven and eight."

"No, I heard nothing, nothing at all."

"It's most peculiar." Sergeant Molloy looked him up and down. "A dreadful murder has taken place and no one has heard anything. Mr. Hodgins was in his field and heard nothing. Podge was in the house and heard nothing and you were passing by the house and heard nothing. Most strange, most strange indeed."

Dick began to shift uneasily and his movements didn't go unnoticed. Sergeant Molloy arose and thanked them for their time. He said he would return to the scene of the crime and hunt for more clues. It was his only hope! He bade farewell and walked out into the early morning with Tom.

"What do you make of that fella?" he turned to his assistant as soon as they were out of ear shot of the farmhouse.

"Seems a little odd to me. What did you think yourself?" It was an understatement and he knew it.

"Yeah, he's odd alright! Seemed to be a bit jumpy too. We'll have to keep a close eye on him."

"I don't fancy that at all." Tom grinned as he got into the garda car. "Anyway, let's go back up to Hodgins and see if we can find anything there."

Dick Kelly wolfed down his breakfast and hurriedly left the kitchen before his wife had a chance to start pestering him with her silly questions. He was going to take himself up to the hill and cut the thistles there. He needed a peaceful environment if he was going to think and there wasn't anywhere more peaceful than the hill. The only sounds that were to be heard up there were the singing of the brown thrushes and the gentle lowing of the maiden heifers.

Maud was glad to see him leave. She had no intention of saying anything to him until she had managed to clear a few things in her head and one of them included digging up the haggard.

"Eve." She spoke softly to her daughter, who was still eating breakfast. "Do you have to go to work today?"

"Why?" It was a funny sort of question for her mother to be asking and took her by surprise.

"I wanted you to stick around for a while. Things might turn nasty here."

"I suppose I could always take the day off if you really need me to but what ever do you mean? What's going to turn nasty?"

"I don't want to say too much until I'm sure and certain but I think that your father was involved in Kitty's murder."

"Involved? How do you mean involved?" She couldn't be serious, could she?

"I think that it was he who killed her." It sounded worse when she said it aloud but it was all that was going through her mind and she wanted to discover the truth as soon as possible.

Eve put her cup down on the table and stared at the woman in front of her. She must be gone mad! Her father a murderer?

That was a joke! Oh, she knew that he was a wicked man and she had no love what so ever for him but he was too much of a coward to kill anyone.

"Why do you say that? Sure wasn't he supposed to be in love with her? Didn't I see the two of them myself with my own eyes? At it like two animals they were!"

"You don't have to be in love with someone to do that you know! God, Eve you really are innocent to a lot of things. You have a lot to learn about life, haven't you? Anyway the reason that I think he did it is that he was acting strange when he got home last night."

"He's always acting strange" Eve interrupted. "There's nothing new there!"

"Yeah, I know but this was different. He told me that if anyone asked I was to say that he was here all night. Why did he think anyone would be bothered asking about him? And he sat on the chair when he came in and never opened his mouth or moved all night. But I could tell by him he was agitated."

"But that doesn't proof that he killed the woman."

"Oh, I know that but you see I haven't told you the best bit yet. I might be able to come up with the proof."

"How mother?" Eve was all ears now.

"Well, last night I saw him out in the haggard. It was just after he came home from the pub. He had a spade and was burying something in the ground."

"What? What was he burying?"

"I don't ⊾now but I intend to find out. My guess is that it was the weapon he used to kill her. The sergeant did say that he couldn't find it."

"Oh Jesus, Mary and Joseph, do you really think so?" Eve was utterly shocked by the revelation.

"There is only one way to find out, isn't there? I'll do the digging and you can keep an eye on the fields to see if he is returning." Maud was determined to discover the truth, no matter what the cost.

"Do you think it is safe?" Eve was not anxious to be caught.

"Is it safe not to? If he had already killed one woman who's to say he won't do it again. And it could be one of us next time." She was being a bit dramatic now but she couldn't do this without her daughter's assistance. Her ploy worked.

"Come on so, the sooner we find out the better." She wanted to get the ordeal over and done with.

They left the house through the back door, took the spade from the side of the shed and made their way across the yard to the haggard. The morning was beautiful and the air so sweet that it was hard to imagine a murder had been committed in the area the previous evening.

Eve stood at the gate of the haggard and watched the fields with one eye and her mother with the other. She felt ill at ease because, although she hated her father for all the misery that he had caused her, she didn't like to think of him as a murderer. It was far too frightening.

Maud did not have any difficulty in finding the exact spot where her husband had dug the previous evening. In his frantic state Dick had failed to cover his tracks very well. Sods of clay lay scattered in untidy heaps and the ground he had messed with looked fresh in comparison to the rest of the land. She began digging and three minutes later she felt the shovel hit something hard in the ground below. Casting her tool aside she beckoned at Eve to come and help her and the pair dug with their hands until they had uncovered the spanner.

Lifting it slowly from the ground both of them gasped as any seeds of doubt that they had harbored in their minds vanished in that instant. The weapon was covered with patches of red blood. Dick had killed Kitty and had used the spanner in his crime.

"Sweet suffering Jesus, the dirty bastard did kill her!" Eve began to feel nauseated as her body temperature rose and she threw up all over the haggard. Maud was also feeling weak and had turned as white as a ghost.

"What do we do now?" She looked at her daughter blankly, the spanner still in her hand.

"What do you think we do? We go to that sergeant and tell him our suspicions. If he did kill Kitty, and there appears to be no doubt about that now, then he will have to pay for his crime. He needs to be locked up behind bars. I, for one, do not fancy sharing my house with a murderer. Do you?"

"And who is a murderer?" The voice of Dick Kelly thundered behind them and froze them to the very spot. Eve could feel her heart leap within her chest and Mrs. Kelly's blood pressure immediately soared. Terrified, they both slowly spun around to face him.

"Well, whose a murderer, you stupid bitch?" His face was as red as a beetroot with rage and liaisons of froth had started to form at the side of his mouth.

"You are Dick." It was Maud who answered. "You killed Mrs. Hodgins."

"Says who? Who says I killed her? You? Have you lost your reason altogether? What proof do you have?"

"I have this." She produced the spanner from behind her back and waved it at him.

"Where the fuck did you get that?" He was totally surprised by her find.

"Where do you think I got it? It was in the clay where you buried it last night."

"What are you talking about? I buried no spanner. You're more daft than I had imagined."

"You're lying and it's well you know it! I saw you! I told you last night that I saw you dig the ground and bury something. I was in the back kitchen and I saw you. And even if I hadn't come out here and found this, it would only have been a matter of time before the guards located it. You didn't manage to bury it very well, did you? There was a lot of loose clay around the area. Sure, my God, you don't think that the guards are as stupid as you do you? You killed Mrs. Hodgins and now you are going to have to pay the price!" She was screaming directly at his crazed face, all fear forgotten, and loathed the man that she had wasted so many years of her life on.

Dick shuffled around on the clay, the sight of the stale blood on the spanner unnerving him. Looking at his wife he wondered if there was any point in denying her allegations. She had already guessed the truth and had all the proof that she needed, clutched in her right hand.

"And so what if I did? Are you going to tell the guards? Are you going to rat on your own husband?" He spat the words at her and she cringed.

"Why? Tell me why you killed her." She didn't fear him at all now; in fact all she felt at that particular moment was severe hatred.

"I'll tell you why, shall I?" His eyes were blazing and his face twisted in anger. "The bitch had it coming to her. She was too high and mighty and thought she was a bit above the rest of us. I only meant to hurt her but I brought her down to size alright, I can tell you. She won't make any more complaints now."

Maud looked at her husband and noticed the mad, glazed look that was springing from his eyes. That was it! He had completely lost his marbles! Why had she not noticed it before?

"You'll have to tell the guards. They will find out anyway."

"I won't be telling the guards and you better not either, if you know what's good for you. Do you hear me?" He was roaring now and Eve, who was watching silently at the side, began to fear for her mother's safety. What if she annoyed him so much that he snapped again? She couldn't bear it if anything bad were to happen to her. Already his face had taken on a crazed look and his eyes were starting to roll around in his head.

Glancing around she knew that there was no one in sight. It was just be herself and her mother against this maniac. She had better do what she could to stop the conversation before it went out of control altogether.

"You two should have more sense." She was glaring at the man whom she had called father and the hatred that she felt for him was eating her up. "Just look at the pair of you shouting at the top of your voices for all the world to hear and, Mother, you are waving that murder weapon around as if it were a toy. What if the guards were to come back now? It would be easy enough for them to solve their case after what you have just said. If you want to argue I suggest that you go inside and continue this conversation. And bring that thing with you." She nodded at the spanner.

Dick looked at his daughter and for the first time in his life he noticed how beautiful she really was. Her hair was as black as coal and her cornflower blue eyes were wild. Her breasts were ample and her waist well formed. She had lost that skinny look that had haunted her for so long and had matured into a lovely young woman. She was any man's fancy now but as far as he knew she had no man friend. He couldn't help but wonder why.

"You're right of course, as usual." His tone was sarcastic but his mouth was twisted in a leery grin. "We'll all go in and have a cup of tea and see if we can come to some arrangement on what to tell those bleeding guards. We're all in this together now mind so it is up to you to help me out as much as possible."

"To hell we are." Eve muttered as she followed her parents across the haggard. What a sad life they had etched for themselves and it was definitely going to get worse before it got any better.

Putting the kettle on to boil she ignored both of them for the moment. She knew that they were each lost in their own thoughts and she felt that it was better to give them space to work things out. How was she to know that her father's thoughts were now fixed on her and not on the cruel deed that he had completed. He had already forgotten about Mrs. Hodgins, she was history, and he was wondering what this young girl would be like between the sheets. He felt that she would be fiery and he could get a great deal of pleasure from her. He had passed the line of no return and no deed seemed too wicked for him anymore.

"Well!" Maud finally broke the silence as she stared into her mug of steaming tea. "What is it to be? Do you tell the guards or do I?"

"You fuckin bitch!" His roar was so terrifying that Eve spilled her tea all over the tablecloth. "You tell the guards? Is that what you want to do? Tell them away then but it'll be the last thing you will do I can assure you. I'd have you dead before they'd arrive. There will be no guards, do you hear me? Let them come to their own conclusions on this. We can tell them that we suddenly remembered seeing an old tramp hanging around yesterday afternoon and they can concentrate on looking for him."

"They're not that stupid you know. Sooner or later they will put two and two together and will come looking for you. There's that spanner for instance. No matter where you hide it they will find it." Eve regarded her father closely as she spoke. "The best thing that you can do is give yourself up and save a lot of heartache later on."

Dick jumped up from his chair and made his way towards his daughter. The venom in his eyes frightened her and she tried to back away from him.

"And who died and made you God?" He spat the words at her, shaking her to the very core. "Let me tell you something for nothing, you're no better than that Hodgins woman when all is said and done and deserve the same treatment that she got! Think you're above your own father now, do you? Well, I'll show you that you are no better than any of the rest of them."

Grabbing her by the arm he shook her violently and she let out a piercing scream. Before she could do anything to stop him he had ripped her blouse from her chest and exposed her breasts. Excited by the round, red nipples he roughly began to feel the soft flesh and lost complete control of his mind. He did not hear his daughter crying for mercy nor his wife roaring at him to leave her alone. He was a man on a mission and this bitch had been begging him for it!

He ignored Maud when she pulled at his arm and kicked him in an effort to stop him. She knew what he was up to and she was going to do everything in her power to prevent this horrendous act. He could do what he liked to other women but, by God, he was not going to harm her daughter! Digging her teeth deep into his right arm she bite down hard until she drew blood but unfortunately only managed to stop him momentarily. The pain that raced through him lasted merely a moment and as he turned around he pushed her and threw her against the wall.

"You're next ya stupid slut." His words had a viscous ring. "Kept away from me for years and wouldn't give me what was rightfully mine. That's why I had to resort to other women and look at the fuckin mess that that has bred. Well I'm going to have a go at you in a minute whether you like it or not! This is as much your fault as it is mine."

The hatred she felt for him was suddenly turning to fear. She knew that she should run for help but she was unwilling to leave her daughter here, alone with this mad man. What could she do?

She watched in horror as her husband lifted his daughter's skirt and felt the warmth of her inner legs. When he began to caress the top of her thighs Maud suddenly felt ill. What sort of a monster was he to want to do this to his own daughter? To want to do this to anyone? He was nothing more than an animal and needed immediate help. He had definitely lost his mind- there was no question about that. This was how poor Mrs. Hodgins had died. The poor woman had suffered at his hands and now here he was attempting to inflict the same pain on his own flesh and blood. Well, it just wasn't on- he would not rape Eve. By God he wouldn't! Not while she still had a breath in her body! She'd see him dead first!

Fumbling to get up from the floor she rubbed her head and noticed a little blood trickle from a cut at the side of her face. Ignoring the pain she looked across at her daughter and gasped as she saw Dick undo his trousers. Jesus, he really and truly intended to go through with it and if she didn't react soon it would be too late. What was she to do?

As Eve fought to free herself Maud staggered her way across the kitchen and spotted the bread knife gleaming on the wooden table. "That would do nicely," she thought as she picked it up and examined it's sharp edge.

Without giving the matter as much as a second thought she hurriedly ran towards Dick and, full of loathing and disgust, she drove the weapon straight into his back.

As the knife stabbed his right lung Dick stumbled and let out a roar of sheer agony. He began to gasp for air and, falling in a heap on the cold floor, he cursed his wife before breathing his last.

Eve was clearly still in shock as she pulled her clothes around her and got off the sofa. She ran into her mother's outstretched arms and as the relief began to filter through her body she started to cry. She found that once she had begun she couldn't stop but she was delighted to free her body of the tension that had seized it. After five minutes she pulled her head up and looked at the sorry sight in front of her. She felt no remorse for the loss of the man that had borne her.

"He'll never hurt anyone again, that's for sure, the dirty bastard! Oh Mam! What would I have done if he had raped me? Thank you for stopping him. I'd have killed myself if he had managed to enter me."

"Sssh, don't talk like that my dear. It's all over now and Dick Kelly has left this world and will never harm another soul again. Not a minute before time either, I can tell you. The funny thing now is that I will be the one facing a murder trial and not him."

"There will be no murder trial facing you, mother. What you did you did out of self-defense and love for me. The police will understand that, sure they will have to! We will have to tell them everything we know and then apologise to the Hodgins for all the pain that he caused them. What spurned him to do it do you think?"

"Oh, I don't know. I imagine from what he has said that Kitty had given him his marching orders. Said her good-byes and he wasn't able to accept it. She paid the ultimate price that anyone should ever had to pay for an affair. God help the woman!" She blessed herself hurriedly and looked away from Dick.

"I wonder if the guards are still down in Hodgins. Shall I ring them and tell them to come up?"

"You do that my child. The sooner we get this mess cleared up the sooner we can get on with our lives. I don't want that body on my kitchen floor any longer than it has to be. And don't change your clothes before they come. Get a cardigan or a gown and cover yourself up. We'll need all the evidence we can get for our defense."

It was Podge who answered the phone and he sounded so sad and demure that Eve immediately felt sorry for him.

"How are you doing, Podge?" she asked him. "This is Eve here. I'm very sorry to hear about your mother. She was a lovely woman and didn't deserve such a fatal end. I'll call down and have a chat with you in a day or two when things are cleared up. In the meantime is Sergeant Molloy still up there?"

"Yes, he's still here. Do you want him?"

"Please."

Sergeant Molloy was puzzled when he heard who was looking for him but he was hopeful that the young girl had remembered something that would open up this case. So far all he had was dead ends and he was becoming flustered.

"Hello, this is Molloy."

"Eve Kelly here. I was wondering if you could come up here for a few minutes."

"Up to your farm? Why?" This was a puzzler, there was no doubt about that!

"I'll tell you when you get here. But please hurry. It's an emergency."

The garda car was parked outside within four minutes and Molloy brazenly made his way in through the open door. He gasped when he saw Dick on the floor, the knife still protruding from his back.

"What in Christ's name has happened here?" He could scarcely credit the sight in front of him. "There's been a second murder. My God, who has stabbed this man?"

"It was me." Maud was quiet but a little frightened. "I stabbed him and before you ask I have no regrets. I would do the same again in a minute if he pushed me to it!"

"You?" He was finding it hard to believe that this timid looking woman could be capable of killing a strong man such as Kelly. "And why, may I ask, have you committed such a criminal act? What possessed you at all?"

"He was trying to rape my daughter- his daughter. Can you believe that? This monster was going to force his only child to have sexual intercourse with him. I couldn't stand around and let it happen. Eve, take off your cardigan and show the sergeant."

Slowly Eve allowed the cardigan to drop to her waist to reveal her torn clothes. Her breasts were red where he had groped her and her neck sore but she didn't care. She was glad to have made such a lucky escape and would be eternally grateful to her mother for saving her.

"My God!" Sergeant Molloy was obviously shocked. "What sort of a man would want to do this?"

"A man that has lost his mind, that's who. Dick Kelly went completely mad before he died. He is the man you are looking for. He is the one who killed Mrs. Hodgins."

"That's a very serious accusation you are making. Are you sure?" Maybe this woman was only trying to clear herself here. He'd have to tread very carefully.

"Yes, as sure as I have ever been about anything in my life. He was having an affair with her and he killed her because she ended it."

"And why did you not tell me about the affair when I was here earlier?"

"I wanted to be sure before I said anything."

"And you definitely sure now?"

"Yes. That was what started this argument here. You see he came home in a state last night and I knew that something was up. He went out to the haggard and started to dig before he came in and he never said a word all night. I went out there this morning to find out what it was he had buried out there and I found this." She took the spanner from the dresser and handed it to the sergeant. "This is the spanner he used to kill poor Kitty. He admitted it to the two of us before he died."

"Good Jesus," Molloy wiped his brow. "Here, let me see that spanner." He took the weapon and noticed the blood on it. Handing it to his comrade he sighed and rubbed his brow.

"Looks like there is no doubt here at all so. I'd better go down and tell Jake. He will be glad to know that the killer has been brought to justice. You should ring the undertaker and get him to sort out this body. And thanks for all your help."

"Sergeant." Maud called him as he turned to go.

"Yes, Mrs. Kelly."

"Will I be charged with the murder of my husband?"

"I wouldn't think so. What you did you did out of love for your daughter. Self defense, that's what I'm calling it! Anyway he was a wanted killer and so it is safe to assume that there will be no charges pressed."

"Thank you." Maud sighed with relief and, after organising the undertaker, went to run a warm bath for her daughter.

CHAPTER THIRTEEN

Kitty Hodgins was laid to rest in the cemetery at the back of the country church the following Wednesday morning and Dick Kelly was buried on the Thursday. On both occasions the church had been filled to capacity, as the villagers did not wish to miss out on either event. News of the murder had spread quite quickly and the little village had not yet recovered from the shock of the horrific tragedy.

Not as much as a tear had been shed at Dick's funeral as most people were delighted to see the back of him. He had never been what you would call a popular man but his latest escapade had sent horror shocks throughout the community. No one felt any sympathy towards him; their thoughts and prayers were with Maud and her daughter and they wondered what on earth had possessed her to stay with him for so long. She had given him the best years of her life and this was how he had repaid her. He got his true deserts now and the Lord would deal with him.

Maud remained calm throughout the ceremony but as soon as she saw the coffin being lowered deeper and deeper into the cold dark earth she knew that she had a strong desire to spit on it. Spit on it and all it signified! Spit and maybe some of the pent up hatred would escape. It was only the presence of Eve, who stood calmly by her right side, which prevented her from disgracing herself.

Eve indeed had made a marvelous recovery from her attack but remained tight-lipped and refused to talk about her experience. Maud worried about her but said nothing. She did not want to put her daughter under any further stress than was necessary and longed for the day when the whole sorry ordeal was well and truly behind them.

Later that afternoon Eve surprised her mother by saying that she was heading over to Hodgin's farm.

"What do you want to go over there for?" Maud was not sure that there would be a welcome there for her when she arrived.

"Oh Mum, you know that it is because of this family that they are forced to suffer all that grief so I thought it would be a good idea to go over and apologise. Explain to them that we are not all tarred with the same brush as he was. Let them see that we care about them."

"Do you not think that may be a bit too soon? Their pain is still very raw. Jake Hodgins might run you off with a pitch fork."

"I'm willing to take that chance. Look I won't be too long."

As she wandered down the dusty road Eve's mind as usual returned to Tommie. It had been so long now since she had seen him and she really missed his handsome face. She had to admit that she was a little disturbed when he had not shown up for the funeral. The least he could have done was made an appearance for her sake. After all she had given him her body and felt now that she was one with him! However, no matter how many times she had scanned the graveyard there had been no sightings of him. He had no feelings for her, that much was obvious, and she vowed for the umpteenth time that she would put him out of her heart once and for all. He just wasn't worth it! Still it would have been nice if he had been there to hold her when she had needed him most. It would have been lovely to feel his muscular arms around her and seek comfort from his strong masculine body.

"Oh, Tommie." She sighed as she stopped for a brief moment. "If only you needed me too!"

Podge was cleaning out the hencoop when she approached the farm and Jake was no where in sight. She thought that he was looking rather fragile and her heart instantly went out to him.

"Hello Podge." Her voice was gentle. "Are things any better with you?"

"Eve, what brings you up the way?" He was a lot quieter than the Podge she knew.

"I came to apologise, on my father's behalf, for the agony that he has bestowed on you. I'm so very, very sorry about your mother."

"Thanks, I know you are. She was a good woman, you know, and didn't deserve the death that she received. It was cruel. I still can't believe it. I can't believe that she won't be coming back."

"How is your father?" She could almost feel his pain.

"Not good at all. He is in a world of his own and stays out late every night. He misses her more than he pretends to. We both do!"

"Oh, Podge I'm so sorry." She didn't know what else to say.

"T'wasn't your fault Eve. You are not to be held responsible for the terrible deeds of your father. What sort of a man was he anyway? How could he do what he did? What was he thinking about?"

"I don't know, I really don't! He was a horrible little man. He made our lives a misery for so long. I know that I shouldn't say this but I'm not sorry that he is dead."

"The guards told me what he tried to do to you. It's just as well that he died or else I would have went up there and killed him myself."

Eve was touched by the remark and, for the first time in her life, she found herself smiling at Podge.

"Thanks, Podge but it wouldn't have been worth it. You would have ended up doing time for him and what good would that have done?"

"If I had ended up in prison would you have come to visit me?" He had noticed the softness that was about her today and he intended to play on it.

"Probably." What else could she say?

"Oh Eve! What are we like? What way are our lives turning out at all? Here we are stuck in this backwater of a place and there seems to be no way out. Since Ma died I feel so trapped. I had been planning all along to move to Dublin as soon as I got the money together, get out of here once and for all, but I'll have to stay here with the old chap now. I can't leave him on his own, not in the state of mind he's in anyway!"

"You were planning to move away?" Why did she feel a little saddened at the prospect? Sure hadn't she spent half her life avoiding him!

"I was thinking about it alright. I don't like it around here anymore. People in this village don't take me serious at all. In fact I think that the half of them look on me as some sort of simpleton."

"Don't be stupid Podge! Of course they don't. And anyway why do you care what the villagers think of you? Haven't you got this nice farm to earn your living from and I'm sure the farmhouse will be yours someday. You won't need the villagers at all. I'd say that you are luckier than most."

"The only catch there is that the farm will not be made over to me until I marry. And at that I will have to marry a girl that my father approves of. No Protestants or townies! That's what he told me. He has strange ideas too."

"That's a tall order alright but I'm sure that you will have no difficulty in complying with his rules though. I'd say that there are a lot of girls out there who would jump at the opportunity of going out with you."

Podge lay the sprong aside and looked at Eve for a moment. She felt that he was studying her face and she was a little uncomfortable.

"I asked you out more than once and you refused."

"I'm different! I've known you forever. We're more like good friends. I was talking about the girls at the dances. Why do you never go to them?"

"I don't feel comfortable there. I've been to one or two but I'm no good to ask a girl up to dance. I hate it when she refuses me."

"You'll get over that in time."

"Do you go to the dances?"

"I used to." Her reply was so sad that he wanted to hold her to him.

"Have you ever been out with a fella?"

"That's a very personal question."

"I'm sorry. I was just curious." Podge hung his head as if in shame and Eve could not help but feel pity for him. He was alright really! Not as bad as she had always imagined but then she had been so besotted by Tommie that she was blinded to everything else.

"I've been out with a few boys."

"Anyone special?" He realised that he definitely needed to know something of her past.

"Yes, there was someone special once but not anymore." The reality of her words pained her as she spoke.

"I'm sorry. What happened?"

"He had no real interest in me. Never even came to the funeral. He's best forgotten about I think." She fiddled with her fingers as thoughts of Tommie swept through her mind.

"He obviously is a twit and doesn't deserve you at all so I wouldn't go wasting my time on him! Any man that would have no interest in you must be soft in the head! Now I've finished here so do you want to come inside and have a cup of tea?"

"No, thanks. I'd better be getting home. I just came to apologise and see how you were. Say hello to your father for me and tell him I'll see him again."

"I will Eve and thanks for coming. It means a lot." His smile was so soft and his face so happy that her heart melted slightly.

"Goodbye, Podge." She returned his smile and waved her hand.

Turning she made for the road and was surprised when she heard him calling her. The evening sun caught the tints in her hair as she spun around and the rays on her face heightened her beauty. Podge's heart stood still as he gazed at her.

"Will you call to see me again?" His voice was full of pleading.

"Yes, yes I will and soon." And she meant it. They could comfort one another in their grief, if nothing else.

As she walked the road home Eve wondered why on earth she had always ignored the humane side of Podge. He really was a nice fella and she knew in her heart that he was every bit as lonely as she was. He needed company right now so what was the harm in an odd visit every now and again?

Bill handed the pint to Tommie and wished him good health.

"Slainte, yourself." Tommie grinned at his pal. "Won't be long now."

"Three more days. Can you believe it Tom? Three more days and I'll be a married man! No more stopping off for pints whenever I feel like it. No more dancing at Ballyhale on the Saturday nights! I'll be under the thumb, that's for sure but I'm looking forward to it. Sadie means everything to me and I'm going to make her the happiest woman alive."

"She's a lucky girl and I hope that she realises it. I wish you both the very best and may you have many happy years together." He lifted his glass and winked at Bill. He was a little overcome at how happy this fella in front of him was. God Almighty, if he was to marry in a few days time he'd be a nervous wreck. Still there was no fear of that! He was too clever to get himself mixed up with that sort of thing, wasn't he? See how he had handled Eve! She never even called around anymore and he thought about her less and less as the days went by. He had had a lucky escape there. What with that business with her father and all! No, Tommie was happy living the bachelor life and, while he wished Bill all the best, he was not in the least envious of him.

"Look who's just walked in." Bill was nudging him and pointing to the door. Through the smoky haze in front of him Tommie looked and was surprised to see Eve. What a coincidence! He had just been thinking about her and now here she was in the flesh, looking every bit as beautiful as usual. She was not unaccompanied though, Podge Hodgins stood on her right side. Continuing to stare Tommie was well aware of the fact that she was ignoring him and when Podge had ordered at the bar the couple took their drinks and sat into the snug at the back of the pub.

"Well, wonders will never cease!" Bill was laughing. "Who would have put those two together?"

"Who the hell is he?" Tommie was a little miffed and he did not know why.

"He's none other than Podge Hodgins!" Bill had seen him before.

"But aren't those two neighbours?" He had heard Eve talk of him.

"Looks a little more than that to me. Do you see the way he was looking at her? And now that I think of it I remember seeing them together one night in Ballyhale."

"At the dance?"

"Yeah. They looked more than neighbours that night too."

"What do you mean?" Was he getting anxious? Tommie placed his hand on his stomach and tried to deal with the knot that had suddenly grabbed hold of his insides.

"They were holding hands and kissing, that sort of thing. Did I not tell you all this before?"

"No, you certainly did not! I think I would have remembered if you had."

"A most unlikely affair, I must say, after all the troubles and everything! Sure wasn't it her father that killed his mother?"

Again all Tommie could mutter was another 'yes.'

"Did you go to that funeral after?" Bill was a little surprised by his friend's reaction to the newcomers. As far as he was aware Tommie had given the girl the shove a long time ago and that could mean only one thing. He wasn't interested in her! So then why was he behaving like a child that had lost it's favourite pet?

"No, I didn't go near the funeral. I couldn't! It was an awful business wasn't it?"

"Be God it was. And did you hear that the ole Kelly fella went about raping his own daughter? Now tell me what sort of a scum bag was he at all?"

"Jesus, I have no idea! He's no loss I can tell you. You know I kept meaning to call up to see how she was but I never got around to it."

"And now Podge has beaten you to it. You missed out there, me old mate. Still, like I always say, there are plenty more fish in the sea. You may go fishing again, Tom, and see what the next catch will reel in. Go for someone with fewer complications next time. Do ya hear me?"

"Yeah!" Tommie finished the last dregs in his glass and ordered another pint. He was going to get drunk tonight, that much he knew, and fuck Eve Kelly and Podge Hodgins. After all they were none of his business anymore and he hadn't wanted her, had he?

CHAPTER FOURTEEN

The sun shone warmly on Sadie as she proudly made her way
to the church to become Bill's wife and the villagers all agreed
that they had never seen a happier looking bride. Her condition
was not as yet noticeable and her pale ivory dress was in deep
contrast to the baby blue of her bridesmaids. With her hair
tightly secured away from her face she was indeed a picture
to behold and the petite silver tiara on top her head gave her a
regal appearance. Bill took her arm with pride, a warm smile
plastered across his handsome face, and thought he would burst
open before he had a chance to say ' I do'.

As soon as all the photographs had been taken the party
made their way to Carroll's hotel in the centre of the village
where the reception was being held. The meal was mouth
watering and the drink flowed as the dancing began.

Bill, however, remained sober throughout the entire afternoon
and not even Tommie could persuade him to take a pint.

"Sorry, me ole chap" he had smiled at him when he had
offered to buy him a drink. "I promised me wife that I would
stay away from the alcohol today and I mean to stick to it!
God, I'd better get used to saying that- 'me wife'. Sounds nice,
doesn't it?"

"What ever you say!" Tommie failed to see the 'niceness'
in the situation but remained tight-lipped. The last thing he
wanted to do was spoil Bill's day. "Sadie won't notice if you
just have the one, surely be to God."

"I suppose not but I don't want to chance it all the same.
Women are cute creatures, they have a strange way of knowing

these things and I don't want to get into her bad books on the first day. I'll tell you what you'll do, you have a drink for me and then get yourself out and do a spot of dancing. Some of Sadie's friends are a bit of alright, if you know what I am saying."

"Don't let her hear you say that for Christ's sake. You'll have to try and keep your eyes off the other chicks from now on!"

"No worries on that score, mate. Sure look across at Sadie there, isn't she everything that a man could want!"

The happy couple said their good-byes to their guests at around eleven and left for the airport. Bill was taking his bride on her honeymoon for a fortnight to the States and, as it was to be his first time on an airplane, he was really excited about it. He had read a few books about New York and knew that he was going to have a whale of a time there.

Tommie waved them off with a heavy hand and slowly returned to his lonely seat at the counter. Ordering a double whiskey he looked around and noticed that he was one of the few guests who sat alone. Almost everyone at the reception had a partner. Was that what life was all about? Settling down with a woman and raising a family? He had no one, now that Bill had wed. His only drinking partner was gone and Tommie was not looking forward to the idea of propping up the bars alone. But what was his alternative? Should he go off and find himself another woman? He felt that he didn't have the will for that but one would certainly be good for the night.

Glancing around he suddenly spotted a rather timid looking girl seated alone at a table. She was dressed in a blue flowery summer dress and wore her long dark hair around her shoulders. She was no Mona Lisa but suddenly Tommie felt the basic need for company. He was a little down now that Bill had left and the fact that Podge was dating Eve did not help cheer him up.

Finishing off the whiskey in his glass he left his comfortable spot and strolled over to her. Smiling sweetly he faced her nervously and quietly asked if she would like to dance. The girl was rather surprised but flattered none- the -less and accepted his offer.

Leading her onto the dance floor Tommie was delighted to discover that the music had suddenly slowed down. He had never been one for a fast dance as he lacked any sense of rhythm and, as he placed his arms around her, he knew that he had definitely missed the closeness of a female body.

"I'm Tommie, by the way" he introduced himself as he held her in his arms. "I'm a good friend of Bill's."

"And I'm Mary O' Reilly" she looked into his eyes as she spoke, causing his heart to flutter. "I'm a second cousin of Sadie's, on her mother's side."

"You don't live around here, do you?" he detected a strange drawl in her accent but not for the life of him could he figure out where she was from.

"No, I live in Cork, Mallow to be precise. I'm only here for the wedding and I'm heading home early tomorrow."

Tommie was delighted with her imparted information, as it was exactly what he needed to hear. Cork was a long way away so this could only ever be a brief encounter. After the wedding he would never see her again so he might as well enjoy her company while he had it.

The remainder of the night was spent dancing and when the music finally stopped Tommie suggested that he walk Mary back to her lodgings. She was staying with Sadie's mother on the outskirts of the village and made no objections when he held her hand and led her out into the night air. It was two o' clock in the morning but it was still warm.

As soon as the fresh air hit Tommie he began to feel a little woozy and cursed himself for having drunk too much whiskey. Trying to compose himself he glanced at the young girl at his side and was delighted that she had not noticed his wobble.

"It's a lovely night." He stared at her round, innocent face. "Would you fancy a walk down by the river? It's grand at this time of the morning."

"Whatever you like." The reply was so timid that Tommie felt hopeful. Anything that he might suggest would be alright with Mary but could he really find it in himself to take advantage of her? He would have to wait and see!

They walked hand in hand along the road and left the village behind them. The atmosphere was quiet and not another soul was around. On approaching the riverbank Tommie sat on the green damp grass and indicated Mary to follow. She took his lead, all the while listening to the soft, calming gurgle of the water as it made it's way towards the Nore.

After a few moments Tommie turned to face the girl and gently took her in his arms. As he began to kiss her soft, inviting mouth he was more than surprised by the passion that was emphasied in her kiss and was not to know that Mary had been longing for a fella for the last six months. All her school friends had boys and she had ever only been out with the one. He had turned out to be a waster and had left as soon as he had managed to get her into his bed. Tommie might not be able to get away from her as easily as he thought!

They kissed for approximately half an hour and Tommie began to feel that old exciting tingling again. He automatically slid his hand up underneath her dress and, on witnessing no resistance what so ever, brazenly began to fondle her small breasts. Their warmth and softness excited him even further. When Mary allowed a tiny moan to escape from her lips Tommie read it as a sign to continue. As his body began to harden he pulled up her dress and fumbled at her underwear.

Feeling the soft, wet vagina with his fingertips he longed for the moment of entry and he kissed her hard. Mary was definitely excited but stopped him when she noticed that he was undoing his zip.

"We can't do that Tommie." She sounded a little nervous. "Do you hear me, we can't do this."

"Do you not want to?" He prayed that he might persuade her some way or another.

"It's not that."

"What is it then?"

"I might get pregnant." She sighed heavily as she spoke, suddenly feeling rather childish.

"Deed and you won't." He stroked her hair and tried to reassure her. "It's not as easy as that and anyway I'll pull out before I come." He was gone too far now to turn back and his manhood was throbbing inside his trousers.

"Oh, I don't know! To be honest with you I'm a little afraid and it's too risky. What if you don't pull out in time?" Mary was scared to take the chance.

"You want to do it, don't you?" His voice was soft and encouraging.

"I don't know."

"You'll enjoy it, Mary, really you will. Have you ever done it before?"

"Yeah. Once! But I didn't enjoy it. It hurt like hell."

"Well, there you are then! It only hurts the first time. This time you'll enjoy it and I can promise you that I will be gentle. Oh Mary, come on, give it a try."

"You will pull out on time, won't you? Promise me!" She needed to be reassured.

"You have my word."

Content that she could trust him on his word she pulled him roughly to her and began to kiss him. Before long she too was caught in the moment and as he entered her body she sighed with contentment. They writhed on the grass as the gentle waters crept by and neither remembered to stop before the finish. Both of them came together and Tommie's sperm was deposited deep inside her womb.

Lying back on the bank with her head gently nestled in the security of his arm Tommie felt totally fulfilled and very content. Mary on the other hand was rather nervous.

"You never pulled out." She looked at him in accusation. The moment was over and the harsh reality bit her.

"I know and I'm really sorry. I meant to but I was too excited. You're a great little lover, Mary. You made me lose control of myself."

"Am I really?" She forgot her anger for the moment.

"Yeah, the best."

"Oh Tommie!" Delighted by the compliment she was on top of him again and as they consummated their relationship for a second time, all thoughts of unwanted babies completely dispelled.

They sat on the damp banks until the dawn broke through and another day was born. Mary asked him to write to her, she longed to keep in contact with him, and she scribbled her address on a box of matches that she had robbed from the hotel foyer. Tommie promised her that he would write as soon as he could and he kissed her before leaving. Mary looked after him as he strolled down the road and felt that at last she had met her husband. Tommie was not going to get away from her as easily as he thought.

CHAPTER FIFTEEN

Bill returned from his honeymoon full of the joys of marriage and made his way to Dalesport farm. He found Tommie sitting in the kitchen fingering a letter that had just arrived in the post. He was looking very serious and Bill wondered if he had had some bad news.

"What's up pal?" he asked as he pulled a wooden chair up beside him and sat on it backwards.

"Ah, nothing much Bill. Glad to see you home again. Did you have a good time? What was the States like?"

"God, Tom, they were lovely. Totally different from here, I can tell you. Everywhere is so built up and the buildings go all the way up to the sky. We had a great time there and I'd advise anyone who had a chance to go. You should head over yourself sometime. See if you can catch a bird for yourself."

"Jesus, don't talk to me about birds. They'd break your fuckin heart."

"Heard from Eve then?" Bill wondered what he had missed in his absence.

"No. Haven't seen her since that night we went out. I made the unfortunate mistake of getting together with one of Sadie's cousins at the wedding. It was after you had left and I was feeling low. Too much whiskey and that sort of thing."

"Which one of her cousins was it?" Bill's ear perked up.

"Mary, Mary O' Reilly!"

"Be God, fancy that, you and shy little Mary! And did you get your ride?"

"Jaysus, Bill, you're mind is a sewer!"

"Well, did you get it or not?" Bill was dying to hear all the details.

"As it turns out I did." Tommie looked sheepishly at his friend to see how he would react.

"What's the problem then?" He was finding it hard to understand him.

"This here." He waved the letter at Bill and sighed heavily. "She was a sure bet for me as she was from Cork and I thought that I would never have to see her again. It seems, however, that she is coming up the way at the weekend. Going to stay with her aunt and she wants to meet me."

"And you don't want to see her?" The penny was beginning to drop at last.

"Jesus no! It was a one-night stand as far as I was concerned. I wouldn't have gone near her otherwise. I want no women in my life."

"You don't know what you are missing boy! Look at me now! I can have my ride whenever the mood takes me. No more going out and getting oiled up beforehand. Anyway, I still don't really see your problem. Can't you just tell her that you want anything more to do with her?"

"It's not as simple as that!"

"What do you mean?"

"Here, read it." He threw the letter into Bill's lap and as Bill pulled the pink, rosy paper from the envelope he was overcome by the smell of perfume that rose to his nostrils.

"Dear Tommie" he read. "I've been waiting every day for the postman to bring me your letter but am always sorely disappointed. I am assuming that you have either lost my address or that you have not had time to write so I decided that I would take pen to paper myself. I have been thinking about you all the time since the wedding and I long to see you again. Every night I dream of making love to you and I look forward to our next meeting. I am returning to Dalesport this weekend to visit my aunt and I want you to meet me. I will be down at the river on Friday evening at around eight and I will see you there. I have something very important to discuss with you go. Something that might change both our lives forever! Looking forward to seeing you. Love you forever, Mary."

"How many kisses has she put on the end?" Bill couldn't help but snigger. "You made an impression on her alright."

"What does she want to discuss, that's what I'd like to know." Tommie was a little worried but Bill was finding the whole situation amusing.

"She's going to ask you to marry her." He laughed at Tommie and nudged him in the ribs.

"Jayus, be serious for a minute will you!" Bill was doing nothing to help the situation. "You don't think that she's pregnant do you?"

"For fuck sake how would I know?"

"If she is would I have to marry her?" His face was so grave that Bill stopped laughing for the moment.

"She's not pregnant, you silly git. Sure didn't you only do it the once? Anyway, it's not even three weeks ago so she wouldn't know yet."

"I hope you're right because I can tell you one thing, pregnant or not pregnant I have no intention of marrying her."

"As far as I know she's only seventeen. You'd want to be careful Tom or the next thing you know you'll be brought up for cradle snatching. Wait till I tell Sadie!"

"You're no help at all, let me tell you. And if you mention a word of this to Sadie or anyone else for that matter I'll have your head on a platter."

"Okay, okay. I'll keep my mouth shut. But tell me this much! Will you meet her?"

"Dunno! I haven't my mind made up fully yet. I'll let you know on Friday."

"You're a funny bugger alright, Tom. No woman will ever steal your heart, will they?"

"No." It was merely a whisper as memories of Eve's scent wafted through the walls of his mind.

Friday was a cool but dry day. A soft wind breezed over the meadows and unsettled the grazing cattle. The starlings were gathering on the wires, contemplating their inemient departures to warmer shores and the squirrels in the woods were already foraging for winter storage.

Tommie finished his milking a little earlier than usual and ran a warm bath. As he lay soaking in the soft bubbles he wondered whether or not he should go and meet Mary. He presumed that if he reneged on the meeting she would eventually enquire about his whereabouts and turn up at his house. He certainly didn't want that! Kitty would never stop nagging him if she were to see her. Anyway what had he to lose by meeting her? All he had to do was explain his position to her, like he had done with Eve, and that would be that. If it turned out that she was pregnant then that would be harder to face but he still meant to get rid of her. She was only a child after all!

It was five to eight when he approached the village and as he turned at the post office he noticed Eve walking in his direction. What should he do now? Continue on and chose to ignore her or stop and say hello? He didn't know! All he was aware of was her radiant beauty and her pleasant smile as she approached. She spoke first thus dispelling his anxieties.

"Hello there, Tommie, long time no see. How are you doing?"

"Oh hello, Eve. I'm fine and you?" His knees suddenly began to shake and he felt tongue-tied.

"I'm okay now." The sorrow in her voice was clearly evident.

"I'm sorry to hear about your bit of trouble. 'Twas an awful business." He felt that he had to mention it.

"Yes, it was!" She was thoughtful for a moment. "I'm doing my best to put it behind me and get on with my life."

"Can't be easy." He was feeling a bit strange as he watched her. It was hard to credit that he had made love to this girl earlier in the year. It seemed like a lifetime ago now but she was still so beautiful and she had filled out so much!

"No, it's not easy at all!" She bit her lip as she looked at him.

"I would have went to the funeral but I was busy." Why did he feel the need to explain himself to her and why did the very sight of her still cause his body to tremble so much?

"It's okay, I understand. Most of the people who came anyway were only there out of curiosity."

"Did he harm you?" He needed to know for sure. All different sorts of rumours had been circulating and one had been worse than the next.

"No, he tried to but thank God my mother saved the day."

"That's good, that's good! By the way I hear that you are seeing Podge now." He needed to change the subject as he was become increasingly uncomfortable.

"Yes." She wondered how he felt about that.

"How is that going?"

"What do you mean?" Tommie was always one for asking strange questions.

"I mean are you happy? Do you like him? That sort of thing!"

"Yes, yes I do like him. The funny thing is that I spent so long running from him and I never knew what sort of a person he really was."

"I'm delighted for you, I truly am." He didn't really mean it but it had to be said.

She looked at him for a moment and then she smiled.

"Thanks Tommie, that means a lot to me. There was never any real hope for you and me, was there?"

"No, Eve, I'm afraid not! I'm an out and out bachelor and that's the way it will always be."

"It's a pity Tommie. We had a good thing going together and you know it took me a long time to move on. But I'm over you now and am trying to get on with my life. Podge is good to me and I like him. I may not love him yet but that will come in time."

"Good, good, well I best be going. I have an errand to do."

"Right, it was nice to see you again. Take care" and she kissed his cheek before continuing down the road.

Tommie sighed as he made his way towards the river and wondered, in years to come, if Eve would still have such an effect on him.

Mary was pacing impatiently up and down the banks when he approached but on seeing him she ran to him and threw herself into his arms. Smiling, she hugged him and held onto him so hard that he felt his life drain away.

"Oh, I've missed you so much Tommie, I just couldn't wait to see you again." She let him go and gazed into his handsome face. "Have you missed me?"

"To be honest with you, Mary, I haven't had time to miss anyone. How have you been keeping?"

"I'm great. I have some news for you." The excited tone in her voice was evident and unnerved him.

"Yeah, you said as much in your letter." He was a little anxious now and beads of sweat began to form on his brow.

"Guess what it is." She was dying to tell him and was practically leaping up and down on the bank.

"I can't." Why was she delaying the agony? Why not just come out and say what was in her mind and be done with it?

"I may tell you then I suppose!" She smiled as if her bit of news was really going to make his day. "I'm thinking of moving up here to Dalesport."

"You're what?" Jesus, that was all he needed but at least she wasn't pregnant.

"I'm thinking of moving up here. I'm going to get a job and stay with my aunt." She was beaming now and didn't notice the sour expression on his face.

"And what would you want to do that for?"

"Ah come on, Tommie, don't be stupid! I'm moving to be near you of course. We can't manage our relationship when we are both miles apart. You even admitted that you had no time to write to me. If I were living close at hand then you wouldn't need to write. We could see each other every day. What do you think?"

"I don't think that it would be a good idea." He had to knock this one straight on the head, there would be no pussy footing here!

"Why not?" The smile quickly faded from her face and was replaced by a childish scowl.

"Because we do not have a relationship. We spent one night together and that was all. I don't want a girlfriend, Mary, and that's the bottom line."

"But I thought you liked me! We had sex didn't we?" She felt that she was going to cry but no tears came.

"Yes we did, but that's all that it was. Sex! Don't get me wrong, Mary, you are a grand girl and I do like you but we have no future together. I'm sorry if I led you to believe that we had."

"I hate you Tommie Bordoni." She suddenly screamed at him, thereby confirming the fact that she was indeed still a child. "You just used me, that's what you did. My aunt warned me to keep away from you. She said that you would turn out to be like your father and I wouldn't believe her. But you know what, she was right! I hope to God you rot in hell." And with that she spun around and ran from the bank in floods of tears.

Bill later told him that she had departed from Dalesport the following day and had been heartbroken. At least she wouldn't be bothering him anymore and Tommie vowed for the umpteenth time that he would never ever look at a woman again. He couldn't cope with them at all. You gave them an inch and they took a mile. This time he truly meant to stick to his guns.

CHAPTER SIXTEEN

A light fall of snow heralded a cold Christmas Eve. The air was bitter and the skies a dull grey and a promise of heavier downpours lay on the horizon. Eve's fingers and toes were practically numb as she sat in the old ford with Podge. He hadn't wanted to bring her inside as his father was sitting by the fire and he had something important to ask of her. For weeks now he had tried to pluck up his courage and decided to do the deed before Christmas. At least that way he would know where he stood in the New Year.

"Eve." He gently called her name as he caught her frozen hand. "You know that I have grown to love you over the last few months."

"Yes, Podge, I do." At least she could be sure of him.

"And do you love me?"

"Yeah." She did in a funny sort of a way. It was, in fact, more of a need than a love but he did make her happy.

"Well, I was wondering if you would do me the honors of becoming Mrs. Hodgins."

"Are you saying what I think you are saying?" Eve was definitely surprised.

"Yes, Eve, I am asking you to marry me."

"Oh, Podge, I don't know what to say!" She hadn't been expecting this at all.

"Just say yes my darling and make me the happiest man in the world."

As she looked into his eyes Eve could see the deep devotion that had matured there. Podge would treasure her until he died and that was something that she longed for. He would provide her with the reassurance and security that she would never get from Tommie. But was that enough? Did she love him? She honestly didn't know. She had grown very fond of him and she knew that she enjoyed his company. She depended on him and if he were to leave in the morning she knew that she would miss him sorely. Yes, perhaps in her own peculiar way she loved Podge. It was a different love than the one she had held for Tommie. That had been an all-consuming passion but had ended prematurely. Yes, marrying Podge might not be so bad after all.

"Well, what do you say?" Her silence had begun to frighten him and a cold shiver had escaped down to the base of his spine.

"Oh, Podge, I would be delighted to marry you."

"Eve, my darling, that's wonderful. You have made me the happiest man on this side of the Sliabh Blooms and I can promise you, here and now, that you will not regret your decision. I will do all in my power to be the best husband in the thirty-two counties and provide you with everything that you deserve. Now I have a little something here for you."

Reaching into the dark depths of his coat pocket he produced a round red box and handed it to her. "Happy Christmas, my darling" he whispered as he watched her open it slowly. A bright, shiny solitaire stared back at her and as Podge placed it on her finger she was overwhelmed with happiness. Putting her hand out in front of her for inspection she glowed inwardly.

"I'm an engaged woman, imagine that!" She leaned towards him and kissed him full on the lips.

"What about a Spring wedding?" Podge was anxious to set the date. "April is such a lovely month."

"Yes, April has always been one of my favourite months. All the daffodils will be in bloom and the new life of spring abundant in the fields. We will get married in April, Podge."

"Shall we go inside and tell my father the news? It will cheer him up immensely. He really likes you Eve, you know, and he's a little down at the moment. This is the first Christmas he has spent here without mother."

"Yes, let's go inside." She was delighted at the suggestion. "My hands and feet are frozen solid and I'm sure he has a good fire going."

Abandoning the old ford the pair skipped to the back door, rather like a couple of giddy school children, and made their way to the kitchen. The heat of the glowing coal fire hit them instantly and Eve made her way towards the flames. As she held her hands over the embers she nodded at Jake and he smiled.

"Too cold this evening to be out courting in the car, eh?" He grinned and revealed his toothless mouth.

"Yes, it is a bit." Her hands had begun to tingle from the heat and were raw with the pain.

"We're not finished with the snow by a long shot yet, you know. Come morning we might be all snowed in"

"Let's hope it won't be that bad."

Podge shifted restlessly as he listened to their small talk. God he loved that woman so much and was delighted that his father thought so highly of her. It made everything so much easier.

"When you two are done discussing the weather there is something important that I would like to share with you, father."

"What is it son?" Jake's attention was suddenly diverted from this dark beauty at his side.

"I have asked Eve here to become my wife and she has consented. We are to be married next April." He gleamed proudly at his girlfriend as he caught her tingling hand. Jake sat upright in his chair and beamed.

"Well, that's the best news that I have heard in a long time. Congratulations to the pair of you. We'll need a drink to celebrate. There's some whiskey in the bottom shelf of that dresser over there. Pull it out Podge and we'll toast your future."

Mrs. Kelly was equally as happy when she received the news. She was delighted that Eve would still be close at hand and this wedding would mean an end to the old hankering after Tommie Bordoni. He was no good for her daughter and it was a blessing that the Lord had finally listened to her prayers and allowed her Eve to come back to her senses.

Tommie heard the news of Eve's engagement on New Years day. He had been down in the shop purchasing a loaf of bread and had bumped into Bill outside the post office. Bill had broken it gently to him as he was under the illusion that his friend still carried a torch for Ms. Kelly but Tommie assured him that he was delighted with the tidings. Eve deserved to be happy and if she had chosen Podge to spend the rest of her days with, well then, good luck to them! That was all he could manage to say!

However, as he milked his cows that evening he found his mind wandering back, yet again, to that tender, warm night so long ago when he had made love to her. The joy and exhilaration of their union had never abandoned him and he felt that it would be locked inside the chambers of his heart until the end of his days. Eve had definitely been a special woman and he had to admit that he did still harbour deep feelings for her. He supposed he had loved her but he had made the decision to forsake her for the sake of his beliefs and he could not reverse his actions. So be it! He would live with that knowledge of his loss for the rest of his life.

PART
TWO

CHAPTER SEVENTEEN

Eve heaved a sigh of relief as she carefully folded the colourful tea towel, laid it on the kitchen table, and sank wearily into the fireside chair. The house was unusually quiet and as her body ached from the hardships of work she meant to make the most of her time alone. Podge had just left for the market five minutes previous and had taken Joe and Pete with him. She was not expecting them back for at least another two hours. Podge had a crate of vegetables to sell and three baskets of eggs and she knew that he would not settle until the last one had been bought. Money was tight and the produce that they sold on market days was essential to help keep their heads above water.

Reluctantly pulling herself up Eve walked across the warm room, filled the kettle under the kitchen tap and slowly plugged it into the white socket on the wall. She needed a nice cup of tea to settle her mind and to help her relax.

As she waited for the water to boil she gazed out the wide window and wondered why on earth she had been feeling so down lately. She had tried to convince herself, over and over again, that her worries were all money related but, if truth were told, she knew that the problem was a lot more deep-rooted than that. Eve did not love Podge!

Oh, she had desperately tried so hard over the years to love him in the way she was supposed to, the way a wife is supposed to love the man she marries, but it seemed that no matter what she did nothing ever worked. She respected him all right and liked his company but that was as far as it went. For the last fifteen years she had been living a lie and now, at the age of thirty-six, she was fed up to the teeth with it all. She felt that her life was passing her by and she craved excitement but knew that she wasn't going to get it from her husband.

As she poured the boiling water into the flowery teacup Eve reached for a spoon and suddenly found herself looking back over her married life. She had come to this farm with great expectations but they had all too quickly been shattered. Jake Hodgins had turned out to be an extremely hard man to live with and himself and Podge fought constantly. How many mornings had she awoken to the sound of their raised voices in the kitchen? Eve had tried to remain impartial, she had no desire to become involved, but secretly she felt that Jake was a little harsh on his son. He had certainly ruled the roost while he had lived with them and she had shed no tears when he had suffered a fatal stroke three years ago. She thought that his death might help her become closer to her husband but instead of improving things it somehow managed to make matters worse, if that was possible! He willed his farm and house to Podge but there had been so much debt on the place that life had been a struggle since. Even with Dick Kelly's farm things had continued to be tough as most of what was earned was eaten up by bank debts and so the market was the only chance of survival.

Eve had begged Podge to sell the Kelly land. She knew that it would fetch a good price, most of the farmers in the locality would kill each other for it, but Podge had refused. He had clearly stated that he had no intention in letting the entire countryside know that he was in debt and that is exactly what they would be saying as soon as they saw the land up on a poster. In fact Podge had been slightly depressed for a long time after his father's passing and then his depression had turned to anger and bitterness. He felt hard done by, not that she blamed him, but she thought that there was no need for him to take it out on the rest of the family.

Thinking of her two sons brought a rare smile to her otherwise tight lips. They were good boys really and, while they were a little frightened of their father, they did everything in their power to help him out. Joe had been born a year and a half after her marriage and had certainly been a bit of a handful at first. He was a colic baby and cried for nights on end. Eve was constantly exhausted but her mother had been around then and she had helped her out. Only for her she felt that she would never have came through the experience. Sadly Mrs. Kelly had been knocked down by a car and killed when Joe had been only five months. Eve grieved for an age after her mothers passing and wouldn't let Podge come within a mile of her. Slowly though she returned to normality and eventually allowed her husband back into her bed. Nine months later Pete was born. Joe was approaching three at that time and Podge was as proud as could be of his siblings. He took them everywhere with him and introduced them to farm work at a very early age. Eve had also been kept busy with chores around the farm and never had much free time to contemplate her life.

Now with Jake's passing and the boys doing most of the work that had once been hers she seemed to have a lot of idle hours on her hands. Instead of putting them to good use she found herself looking back into her past and did not like the results that were being bred.

How many times, over the last four years in particular, had her thoughts strayed to Dalesport Manor and to Tommie Bordoni? She didn't dare count but she knew that, even at night when she lay beside Podge, it was Tommie who filled her dreams. Tommie with the dark hair and the hazel eyes! Tommie who had grown more handsome with age!

Eve was convinced that he had definitely been her soul mate and she scolded herself for letting him go. She had been so young back then but she should have been more insistent. Tommie might have relented if she had pursued him with vigour but it was too late now. She was stuck with Podge, for better or worse, and there wasn't a lot that she could do about it. She knew that Tommie had never married and, if the rumours were correct, he was indeed a very wealthy man. He wasn't breaking his back like Podge just to keep his bills paid and food on the table. No, Tommie was what could have been described years ago as upper class and Eve would have had a much better life if she had married him.

"Ah well, there's no use sitting here reminiscing" she scolded herself and, throwing the last dregs of tea down the kitchen sink, she wandered out into the garden. The July sun was bright and the day extremely hot. The scent of late Honeysuckle and

133

Sweet Williams filled the air and the sparrows chirped happily as they pecked the cobbles for food.

Eve shuddered as she came to the old barn and could never understand why Podge had not burnt it down. Every time she had to pass by the bitter memories of his mother always filled her with foreboding and reminded her of her evil father. Today she hurried past and didn't stop running until she met the brow of the hill. Sitting on the dry burnt grass she allowed her body to filter in the heat of the sunrays and gazed across at the peaceful countryside. She was up on a height and could see for miles around.

The village was far away on the left and, over the horizon, to the right lay Dalesport Farm. She wondered what Tommie was doing at that particular moment and, closing her eyes, she tried to conjure up his face in her mind. As the afternoon sun beat down heavily on her she lay on the grass, totally immersed in her own thoughts, and before she knew it she had fallen asleep.

It was Joe who aroused her several hours later. He had returned from the market with his father and when Podge realised that she was nowhere in sight and had no tea ready he became angry. He had roared at his son to go in search of her and Joe had been too frightened to protest. He advised his mother to get home as quickly as possible and as he helped her up she realised that she was burnt from the sun. Ignoring her sore arms and legs she followed her son back to the farm and was breathless by the time she entered the kitchen. She could tell straight away that Podge was in a foul mood.

"And where the hell were you, may I ask?" he almost growled at her. "This is a nice how do you do, isn't it? We come home from the market, wall falling with the hunger and not only do we find that you have gone missing but you also have no tea ready."

"I'm sorry! I'll get you something straight away." She always felt that he treated her like a servant.

"You do that and be quick about it. Where were you anyway?"

"I went for a walk and I must have dozed off."

"Who did you walk with?" He was looking accusingly at her and she didn't like it.

"What do you mean?" She knew exactly what he meant, wasn't he always harping on at her whenever she innocently spoke to another man, but she had to pretend innocence.

"I mean who the fuck were you walking with?" His face was twisted with jealousy and he sighed heavily as he awaited her answer.

"Why are you asking me that? I was with no one, I went for a walk by myself." She found his insecurity hard to manage.

"Am I supposed to believe that?" His face was almost touching hers now and she could see the angry in his eyes.

"Of course you are!" Why was he being so unreasonable?

"Well, I hope for your sake that you are telling me the truth. If I find that you are messing about behind my back I'll kill you, have you got that?"

"Oh Podge, for heaven's sake, will you calm down." She turned and cracked an egg onto the pan and watched as it sizzled in the hot fat. "Why would I be stupid enough to go messing about? Isn't one man more than enough for any woman?"

When he didn't answer she looked at him for a moment and could see that already he was beginning to cool off. God, he was so possessive and insecure! No matter how many times she assured him that she was not having an affair he found it hard to believe her. Was it as a result of his mother's unfaithfulness or was he just like Tommie? Maybe all men were the same! A woman would be better off on her own after all!

Eve was aware that Podge was watching her as he ate his supper. She could feel his eyes boring through her sunburn. God, she was going to be sore tonight! How on earth had she managed to fall asleep in that heat? She couldn't understand it at all!

"By the way, I met an old friend of yours at the market." He studied her face, afraid that he would miss her reaction. "Tommie what's his name from that big Manor. He was asking for you."

So that was what his mood was all about! He had bumped into Tommie and had felt insecure in his presence. She had better not show much interest in the meeting if she knew what was good for her.

"Did you?" She tried her best to sound casual but was dying to know what Tommie had been inquiring about. "That was nice for you."

"Huh." It was more of a groan than a comment and Eve was surprised by the response. Placing her hand on the steel teapot she felt it best to change the subject.

"Have another cup of tea. There's plenty on the pot."

"Aren't you even going to ask how he was?" Podge looked at her curiously. He knew deep down that his wife still harboured feelings for Tommie and he never gave her a chance to forget it.

"I can't be bothered and anyway I'm sure he is alright!"

"That's a good one, I must say!" He held out his cup and nodded at her to refill it. "And there was I was under the impression that he was the love of your life."

"Don't be so stupid Podge." She was angry now and she was conscious that Pete was looking at her curiously. "Tommie and I were a long time ago. You came along and changed everything, remember? It was you I married, wasn't it?"

"I suppose!" Podge was quiet for a moment. "It just bothers me to think of how well he has done for himself on his farm while here we are still struggling along. Depending on good prices at the market to get by from week to week while he swans around like the Lord of the Manor without a care in the world."

"I know we're not well off." Eve tried to be gentle with him in an effort to calm. The last thing she wanted was an angry Podge on her hands for the night. "But we are happy, aren't we? We have each other. Who on earth has Tommie got at the end of the day." She was surprised that she could sound so convincing but she certainly didn't want a depressed husband.

"I suppose you are right, as usual! I'm sorry Eve. I shouldn't be taking out my problems on you. It's just that when I think of the two of you together all those years ago I still get jealous. Can you understand that?"

"There's no need for any jealousy" she lied to him. "I have no feelings for Tommie Bordoni. They died a long, long time ago and you're the only one that I want now."

But in bed that night Eve found that it was Tommie who was filling her dreams yet again. She dreamt that she was drowning in a watery abyss and it was Tommie who reached out to save her. He told her that he loved her and wanted her in his life. However, the cold reality of morning dawned and another day of pretence was borne.

CHAPTER EIGHTEEN

Tommie ran his hand through his wet hair and wiped the beads of sweat that had formed along his brow. The late September afternoon was sultry and sticky and he was looking forward to jumping into the bath as soon as he had finished work. He wasn't complaining about the weather mind! No, indeed, wasn't he glad of the bit of sunshine to get the harvest finished. He already had the hay in the barn and the barley cut. He was at the straw at the moment and as soon as he had that finished he'd be nearly squared up for another while. At least until the cows started calving again!

God, there seemed to be no end to this farm work at all and he was feeling worn out at the moment. He spent every day from early morning until the approach of dusk working the land and it left him little or no time for socialising any more. He was so exhausted by the end of the day that he had no energy left to head to the pub.

Rosie's youngster, Kevin was still helping him out on the farm and he was glad of his company. Bill called over an odd night and Robbie came down from Meath every two weeks. Still Tommie felt that there was something missing from his life and he was terrified to admit to himself what that something really was.

He jumped down from the tractor and, as he gazed along the golden field, his mind began to stray towards Hodgin's farm. He hadn't seen Eve for about five years and he wondered how she was getting on with Podge. Was she still as beautiful as ever? Did he ever cross her mind in the same way that she constantly crossed his? God, he was never going to get her out of his system and he wondered if their paths would ever meet again.

As it turned out the encounter was closer than he could ever have cared to imagine. The following Thursday Podge was laid up in bed with a late summer flu and Eve had to go to the market with the vegetables. She took Pete with her and left Joe at home to attend to his father's needs. Podge was as contrary as a bag of cats when he was laid up and needed a full time nurse.

Packing the vegetables into the old Ford Eve admitted to herself that she was more than a little excited at the prospect of her trip. At least she would be away from the farm for the afternoon and have a chance to converse with some of the villagers. She was not the best driver and so she took the roads pretty slowly. Never the less she arrived at the market a few minutes earlier than anticipated.

The square was already thronged with people and the hustle and bustle that filled the air was like music to her ears. She set about putting up her stall immediately. Pete placed the carrots and cabbages together while she looked after the lettuces, cauliflowers and beetroots. Her products were fresh and home grown and were a big hit with the local housewives and so within twenty minutes she had most of her stall sold and she turned to clear some of the empty boxes from her path.

And that was when she saw him! There he was, standing about three feet away, looking every bit like the ' Lord of the Manor', just as Podge had said, staring at her unconsciously. When she smiled shyly at him he walked over to her and stood beside her.

"Hello, there Eve." As she watched his face light up Eve's heart began to sing. Tommie was still as handsome as ever and he was delighted to see her.

"Hello, there yourself. Long time no see!"

"Yes, it has been quite a while. How have you been?"

"Great," she lied. "And you?"

"Ah you know! Busy as usual! Podge not here today?" He knew that he wasn't.

"No, he has a touch of the flu so I came along instead."

"Ah good! It's nothing too serious then! How is married life treating you anyway? Is it everything that you imagined it would be?"

"Yes, yes it's fine. You never took the plunge yourself after?"

"No." Did she detect a certain sadness in his tone? "I never married although sometimes now I'm sorry that I didn't. Life can become boring when you have no one to share your dreams with."

She nodded as she tried to compose herself. She did not need to hear this, not now anyway! Tommie was sorry that he had no wife! Why was it so hard to imagine? It looked as if she hadn't waited long enough! No, she had jumped straight at the chance of marrying Podge because she had felt that there would never be any hope as far as Tommie had been concerned. Well, there was nothing she could do now, she had made her bed and now she must lie on it. She wasn't going to give Tommie the satisfaction of knowing that she too had made a mistake.

"This is Pete here." She decided that it was time to change the subject. "He's giving me a hand today."

"Hi Pete." Tommie smiled at the youngster. "We've met before, haven't we? I've seen you here several times with your Dad."

"That's right. You were talking to my dad the last time he was here."

"There you are Eve, we're already acquainted. And I must say that he is a mighty fine boy. He is a credit to you and Podge."

Eve had to stop the tears from forming on her eyelids. A credit to her and Podge! That's what he had said and indeed he was right. But if only he had been Tommie's son! If only things had been different and she had married Tommie instead of Podge! It was he whom she still loved even after all this time and seeing him here in front of her had made her realise it even more.

"Well I'd better be going." Tommie broke the uncomfortable silence that had developed. "It was nice seeing you again. Give my regards to Podge and tell him that I hope he is feeling better soon." And with that he turned and was gone.

Eve watched as he walked away from her life yet again and wished that she could run after him and plead him to take her with him but she had to stay where she was and no amount of hoping could change that.

"Damn you, Tommie Bordoni" she muttered to herself as she tried to focus on packing up her stall but the joy had disappeared from her afternoon. When she looked up Tommie had disappeared and she felt sad and desolate.

Podge was feeling a lot better when they arrived back at the farm and was actually siting at the table eating his tea. He glanced at her as soon as she entered the kitchen and began to speak through a mouthful of streaky bacon.

"Well, how did you get on today? Did you sell much?" He thought that it would be a poor taking when he had not been there to oversee.

"Yes, we had a great day. Everything went fairly quickly and I would have sold as much more again if I had had them."

"That's good, that's good. We need all the money we can get from that market stand. It's our only hope of survival until things start to pick up again."

"I was giving that some thought on the drive home and you know I came up with a great idea!" She looked across at him to ensure that he was listening.

"Yeah? And what was it, may I ask?"

"I was thinking that I could bake some buns, cakes and brown bread, that sort of thing and go along with you to the market each week and sell them. The women would love them; you know how quickly homemade stuff disappears! They would bring in a few extra pounds. What do you think?" She had come up with the idea when she had been wondering how on earth she could manage to bump into Tommie more often. She knew that she could never have him but still she wanted to see him, to be near him, to talk to him. It was better than nothing! All she needed now was her husband's approval.

Podge was silent for a moment and then he began to laugh. "You know my dear, I always said that you were far more than just a pretty face. That's an excellent idea! I don't know why we didn't come up with it sooner. The extra money will help us to pay the loans off in no time and we'll be back on our feet before we know it."

Not just a pretty face! Eve smiled to herself as she contemplated Podge's words and when he made love to her that night, all his insecurities quieted for another while, she closed her mind and imagined that it was Tommie who lay beside her. Tommie with the handsome face and muscular arms! She could have her fantasies if nothing else and no one could ever take them away from her!

CHAPTER NINETEEN

Tommie sat alone at the counter and twirled the flat ale around in the end of his glass. It was Friday night and he had wandered down to the local inn out of sheer boredom. The evenings had started to draw in and he knew that he was spending far too much time sitting alone in the cottage. The walls were beginning to close in on him at this stage and he simply couldn't wait for the cows to start calving again. At least then he would have something to occupy his mind with.

At the moment he found that his mind constantly seemed to be with Eve Kelly, or Eve Hodgins as she was now! Eve had taken to accompany her husband to the market over the last few weeks and had sold record amounts of home baking. Hadn't he himself bought many a square loaf of brown bread from her and relished their taste knowing that they had been baked with her fair hands.

Tommie knew that Hodgins had gone to the neck in debt, he had heard the rumours circulating around the pub, but still he wondered at him allowing his wife to sell her produce. He was such a proud man! Now if he himself had married her there was no way that she would have had to lower herself to selling bread. No, Eve was above all that and deserved better. Still she wasn't his problem anymore. Why then could he not erase her from his mind? Way did she constantly seem to be haunting him? Why did his heart ache so much and why did he long to hold her in his arms? He was too terrified to answer these questions and was delighted when a familiar voice broke through his thoughts. He turned to see Bill standing beside him.

"Jesus, you were the last person I expected to see in here tonight. How's it going me ole pal."

"Not so well at all. I came down here to drown my sorrows." Bill looked a little forlorn and as he ordered a pint Tommie wondered what on earth was the matter with him.

"Everything alright at home?" Tommie had a worried tone to his voice.

"Depends on how you look at it!"

"What do you mean?"

"Well, Sadie's gone and got herself pregnant again."

"Surely that's good news?" Tommie failed to see the problem.

"For fuck sake Tommie, enough is enough! We have five healthy children already and I was more than happy with that. But another one? God I don't know! Do you realise how much dosh it takes to feed these kids every week? The building trade is not what it used to be at all. People out there don't have the money anymore. Do you see what I'm getting at? I can't afford another child."

"Surely it can't be as bad as all that?"

"Jesus, Tommie I'm working every hour that God sends as it is and all I'm doing is keeping a roof over our heads and a bit of food on the table. We have no money for extras."

"Something will turn up Bill. It always does!"

"I hope to Jesus that you are right Tommie. Sadie is like an anti christ at the moment. She won't talk at all and when she does it's only to bite my head off."

"I suppose it is as big a shock to her as it is to you."

"Probably but I suppose we may just get used to the idea. As you said, something might turn up! Maybe with a bit of luck I will win the pools! Anyway, have you anything strange yourself? It's a while since I've been talking to you."

"No, not a lot. Things are as they were." He finished the last of the beer in his glass and raised his hand to order another one.

"No woman then?"

"Lord no." Bill was constantly inquiring about his love life and he wondered at this stage why he bothered. Nothing ever changed there.

"Maybe you are as well off. Look at the pickle I've gotten myself into!"

"But you do love Sadie, don't you Bill?" Tommie paid for his pint and began to sup.

Bill was quiet for a moment and then he looked at Tommie. "Most of the time I do but there are days when I feel like strangling her. Can you understand that?"

Tommie failed to see the logic in what his friend had said but he nodded his head in agreement. There was simply no point what so ever in contradicting or disagreeing with Bill tonight and so Tommie decided to change the subject. He began to talk about the price of cattle and after about four pints he was delighted to notice that Bill's had relaxed his mood.

Half an hour later Podge Hodgins and Eve entered the pub. Podge was rather sour looking but Tommie felt an immediate pulse rush as he glanced at Eve. She wore a cream sweater and a black pair of trousers and looked very fetching indeed. She smiled over at them while Podge ordered the drinks and throughout the next hour Tommie was aware that she kept glancing across the bar at him.

"Well, what have you got to say for yourself." Bill was asking him a question and he found that he was unable to answer. He had been paying absolutely no attention to his pal for the last five minutes. Instead his thoughts had been centered on the corner where Podge had begun to raise his voice. He was arguing with his wife and from where Tommie was sitting it looked like a very heated row indeed.

Suddenly and without any prior warning Podge leapt from the seat and angrily made towards the door. If he had been expecting Eve to follow him he was sadly disappointed as she stood her ground and kept on sipping her drink as though nothing untold had happened. Bill had now been alerted to the situation and grinned slyly as he turned his attention back to Tommie.

"All is not rosy in that camp either by the looks of it. I wonder what she has said to annoy him like that."

"God only knows but what ever it was he was not impressed by it."

"She's been throwing you the odd glance all night. Have you noticed?"

"Get out of here Bill. Sure what does she want to be doing that for?" But he definitely had noticed her eyes on him.

"Maybe she still carries a torch for you."

"Maybe." Tommie was deep in thought.

"Be careful there Tommie." Bill felt that his advice was needed here. "Podge is not a simple man and if you were to go messing around with his wife God alone knows what might happen."

"Don't worry I'm not that stupid." Tommie tried to laugh it off but he couldn't help wondering what exactly he would do if he had the choice.

Bill left at a quarter to eleven and promised to call and see him during the week. After his departure Tommie sat alone and was careful not to glance at Eve. She was looking so sad and forlorn as she sat there alone, slowly sipping her drink and he was fearful that his compassionate side would reach out to her.

He was not prepared, therefore, when she came over and sat beside him and he could feel his heart leap within his chest.

"Hello Tommie." Her voice was sultry and sent shivers down his spine. "Do you mind if I join you? There's no point in two of us sitting alone is there?"

"No, not at all. Podge gone home then?" His heart- beat had quickened and he was hardly able to answer her.

"Ah come on, you know he is." Her gaze was unsettling and she was beginning to make him feel uncomfortable. He realised that she was a little merry and he warned himself to be careful. "Surely you heard him roaring at me?"

"I did actually. What did you say to annoy him so much?"

She was silent for a few moments and then she began to grin. "Can't you guess?"

"No!" How on earth was he supposed to know what went on between her and her husband?

"He accused me of spending my evening looking over at you."

Tommie nearly choked on his mouthful of ale. Jesus, he didn't need this! Podge had noticed that his wife had been making eyes at him across the room and had left in a jealous rage. What next?

"Did you hear what I said." She kept eye contact with him and he found that he was unable to look away.

"Yes, I heard." The words were practically stuck in his throat.

"And?" She fidgeted as she waited for his reaction.

"And what?" What did she expect him to say?

"And what do you think?" She was still grinning and if his heart did not think so much of her he would have walked away at that precise moment.

"Podge is a fool to think that you would have eyes for anyone but him. Did you not explain that to him?"

"No. And do you want to know why I didn't?" He was sure he was going to be told anyway so he remained silent. "Because what he said was true. Oh Tommie, I haven't been able to stop looking at you since I walked in here. I still love you, you know."

"Eve, stop that talk this minute! It's only the drink making you say these things. Of course you don't love me, how could you? Sure aren't you a married woman, for God's sakes, with a good husband and two beautiful children. What would you be doing with the likes of me?"

"It's not the drink, I'm afraid, I wish it were then maybe things might be easier! Oh Tommie, I have never stopped loving you and seeing you again at the market has made me realise that." Her voice was soft and gentle and he found himself gazing into her eyes. "Even after all this time I still dream about you, do you know that? I only married Podge because I knew that I could never have you. Oh, it was fine in the beginning, he was good to me and gave me the security that I yearned, but as time went by I knew that it was more than security I needed."

"Eve, do you think that you should be telling me all this?" His stomach had started to churn at her confession.

"I'm sorry Tommie, I really am but you see I need to talk to someone. I need to talk to you! Sometimes I feel that I am going to go mad and I believe that I would if it were not for the two boys."

"And does Podge know any of this?"

"To be honest I don't know! He knows that I am not happy and I think that he understands that I don't really love him. He knows that I still have feelings for you and that annoys him."

"I can see where he is coming from there!"

"He accused me this evening of making a tart of myself. He told me that I was blatantly staring at you and that it was obvious what I wanted you for. Before he left he told me that you were welcome to me and he hoped that you knew what you were letting yourself in for."

"He didn't mean any of it though, did he?" Tommie swallowed quickly and tried to deal with the mixed emotions that were colliding into him.

"No, I suppose he didn't. He was just angry. If he knew that I was sitting here talking to you now he would go mad. But I am gone past caring. I have no real feelings for him anymore."

"But you married him, for better or worse."

"Yeah, I know, but that was a mistake." She lowered her head and was thoughtful for a moment. When she looked at him again he noticed that there was tears in her eyes and he felt her heartache. He didn't want his Eve to be sad! Reaching into his pocket he pulled out a tissue and handed it to her. He was more than surprised to see her laugh.

"That's what I like about you, Tommie, you were always a gentleman." And as he joined her laughter he felt that the ice had broken between them.

By closing time both of them had drank more than they had bargained for and had related their respective life stories to each other. As Tommie walked her home Eve imagined that she was a young, carefree girl again. She was reminded of the days when she had been dating Tommie and so when they turned at the crossroads she begged for him to take her to his cottage.

"I don't think that that is such a good idea." Tommie was trying to be realistic. "What if Podge were to come looking for you?"

"He won't!" She sounded confident. "He'll be fast asleep by now and I won't even be in his dreams. Please Tommie, just one night, that's all I am asking for! If I had you tonight maybe then I might be able to settle back into my old life again. It's the longing and the wondering that's keeping me awake." She flashed her corn blue eyes at him and immediately he relented. He wanted her just as much as she wanted him and the ache around his loins was growing stronger by the minute.

"Okay then! Just for tonight though" and as she drew her face towards his he kissed her with the passion of a man who had been jailed for forty years.

They ran the last mile, both of them anxious to reach the cottage as quickly as possible and arrived happy but out of breath. Eve placed her hands around Tommie's waist as he opened the door and they both giggled like a couple of silly teenagers.

Once inside closed door Tommie drew her to him again and kissed her passionately. As his tongue probed her mouth his hands began to wander up the front of her jumper. Easing her breasts from her bra he was gentle as he fondled them.

As he began to become more aroused he pulled the jumper over her head, undid her bra and watched, as the ample breasts lay bare before him. He began to tease the soft pink nipples with his tongue and, as he heard her groan with pleasure, he knew that she was powerless against his touch.

Undoing his zip he lifted her onto him and began to penetrate as hard as he could. Her back was against the wall but she was almost unaware of the pressure it caused. As they both climaxed they held each other tight and kissed like two in love. Afterwards they walked to the kitchen and as Tommie lit the fire Eve poured a glass of wine. She was so happy and peaceful that she didn't want the night to end.

They made love again in front of the warm flames and Tommie was forced to admit that he did indeed love Eve. He had crossed over the barrier of denial and now he knew that he wanted her back in his life. He probably should never have let her go in the first place. Oh to hell with the consequences, they both needed each other so how could an affair be wrong?

He walked her home at dawn and promised to contact her soon with a view to meeting again. He knew that now he had tasted her again he could not let her escape. However, deep down he did realise that she belonged to another, she was not his to keep anymore!

CHAPTER TWENTY

April 1994 promised to be a good month. The mornings were foggy and the night's cold but the days were glorious and there was plenty of heat in the early sunshine. The daffodils floated on the gentle breeze and hidden away in the budding woodlands the tiny violets and white anemones gave delight to many a rambler.

Easter was approaching and Tommie was busy as usual. He had had a good calving season that winter, having lost only two of the calves, and had been blessed with some good strong bulls. The winter nights had been particularly tough but now all that was behind him and it was time to let all the stock out into the bright world again. Kevin was his right hand man at this stage and a real treasure. He could always rely on him to finish up the day's work when he himself wanted to get off early. And indeed, there had been many a night when he had arranged to meet Eve.

Three years had passed since the night that he had made love to her in the hallway and not for one moment did Tommie regret his actions. He had continued to see Eve almost every other night and had become besotted with her. Oh, he knew that she belonged to someone else and that she could never be really his but he didn't care. He had let her go once before and did not intend to make the same mistake again. It was hard trying to keep their meetings a secret but as far as he was aware no one had as yet discovered their affair. If Podge found out there would be hell to pay but Tommie felt that he could handle anything that came his way as long as Eve was with him!

To complicate the matter further she had become pregnant a couple of months after their reunion. Tommie was not sure whether or not the baby was his but he loved it as his own. However, as the child developed he grew a mass of brown curls on the top of his head, leaving Tommie with no doubts at all. Hadn't he had the same head of curls when he was a young lad? He was definitely the father and this knowledge made him more determined to raise him as his own.

Eve had called her son Jack, after Tommie's father, and had been delighted at how much he loved the child. Tommie had pleaded with her to leave Podge and come and live with him at the cottage but she had not as yet plucked up the courage to do so. She kept putting off the inevitable and kept promising that they would be together some day soon.

Tommie did not want to pressurise her too much. He knew that she would be with him whenever the time was right and he could live with that.

On this particular April morning he was full of the joys of spring as he went about his business. His sister, Sylvie, whom he had accepted he would never see again, had returned after years and years of silent absence. He had picked her and her husband, Ben, up at Dublin airport and had renewed old acquaintances on the journey down to Dalesport. Sylvie was staying at the Manor with Kitty and, although her visit was short, it was great to see her after so long and realise that everything had worked out well for her.

He had noticed earlier that Kevin had been quieter than usual and he had wondered what had been troubling him. "Probably some girl somewhere" he had mused to himself as he strolled across the meadow. He was surprised to see Kitty running on the headland and what was more she was beckoning to him. It had been over a week since he had been talking to his sister and so he greeted her with a smile. She looked grave and tired.

"Tommie, is Sylvie with you?"

"No, she left a short while ago. Is something the matter?"

"You'll never guess what has happened." She looked at him with round eyes and he noticed that she was rather exhausted looking.

"What's up Kitty? Have you won the lotto?"

"No such luck! No, it's Rosie. She has come back to the land of the living."

"Come back to the land of the living?" He repeated her words as he allowed them to sink into his tired brain. "Jesus Kitty, I don't believe it!"

"As God is my judge, it's true Tommie! I got a phone call yesterday morning to say that she had her senses back and I took the kids to see her last night." That explained Kevin's mood this morning! "She's in good form and the doctors are hoping that this is going to be a permanent thing. She could be home with us before long."

"That's good news, isn't it?" Tommie had only visited his older sister a couple of times since she had been admitted to hospital and suddenly he began to feel guilty.

"Yes, it's great! She was asking for Robbie and I'm expecting him down any minute now. I just said I'd run up and tell you before anyone else did. You might want to go in and see her tonight."

"Yeah, maybe I will. God it's hard to believe! Rosie back with us again! It's been years since any of us have even mentioned her."

"I know but she has been dead to us for so long. We're getting a second chance with her and second chances don't come around that often. We will have to make the most of it."

When she had gone Tommie contemplated what she had just said. She was dead right! When a second chance came along you had to make the most of it. He really had to start putting the pressure on Eve to move in with him. He'd wait, though, until Rosie was home again and settled.

Life was going to be strange for her after being away for so long and he knew that they would all have to rally around and help her out. After all, she had been around for them when they had lost their mother. Oh, she had made some terrible mistakes but who was he to judge anyone? Wasn't he himself conducting an illicit affair with a married woman and just waiting for the arrival of the day when she would leave her family for him. Yes, he would give Rosie all the support that she needed and he certainly would not be the one to cast the first stone.

Tommie entered the hospital at around half past six that evening and slowly made his way to his sister's bed. Rosie was dosing but as soon as she heard him she immediately tried to sit up.

"Hello there, old girl" he was not sure how to greet her and was feeling a little self-conscious. "How are you keeping?" He thought that she was rather fragile but was surprised at how well she looked.

"I'm not too bad now that I have finally awoken." She pulled him to her and weakly hugged him. "God, Tommie, it's so good to see you and I must say you have grown up into a fine man altogether. Mam would be so proud of you."

"You're not looking too bad yourself considering" he had no desire to start talking about his mother. It might just lead to talks about his father and he felt that Rosie was not strong enough yet to deal with that.

"All your curls have disappeared" she looked proudly at her brother and thought that, after Robbie, he was the most handsome man that she had ever seen. "You don't know the hardship that I had to go through each morning to try and brush those curls. I can still see you pulling away from me, complaining that I was taking the head off you."

"That's a long time ago now" he found himself wondering if Eve had the same hardship with little Jack's curls.

"Yeah, I've missed so much." Rosie sighed as he gazed at her hands. "The children have all grown up on me and I hardly recognise them. Kitty brought them along last night to see me."

"Yeah, she told me. They are great kids, you can be proud of them."

"I am, extremely proud. And what about Robbie, do you ever see him?" Her gaze smothered him and he shifted uncomfortably. "Does he come down to the farm often?"

"Yeah, I bump into him every now and again" he decided to answer her truthfully. "He seems to be doing okay and adores the kids."

"Does he ever mention me?"

"To be perfectly honest I don't know. You see I only ever have quick conversations with him. I seem to be so busy all the time so I never have the opportunity to sit down for a proper chat."

"I loved him so much" her voice was sad and he was afraid that she was going to cry. "I never wanted anyone else but, through no fault of my own, I made a mess of my life. I wonder if he will ever be able to forgive me."

"I'm sure he will" Tommie realised that, no matter what she had done to hurt him, she still loved him. Was that because true love never really dies? Did it just lie dormant for a while and await it's opportunity to be re-released. That's exactly how it had been for himself and Eve and he hoped that Rosie would be as lucky with Robbie. "Kitty mentioned that he was going to call and see you so you can have a chat then."

"When? When is he calling?"

"I'm not sure but I know that it's soon!"

As he left the hospital an hour later Eve was on his mind and he felt a real need to speak with her.

As soon as he reached the cottage he made for the phone and rang Hodgin's farm. It was Podge who answered and Tommie placed the phone down without speaking. Ten minutes later he dialed again and this time Eve answered. She sounded anxious and somewhat nervous.

"Did you ring a little while ago?" She was almost snapping at him.

"Yes, but Podge answered so I said nothing. Why?"

"Why? Oh God, you can be so stupid Tommie! He's beginning to suspect that I am up to something. He says that I am always out and about and he has even asked me if I have a man on the side. What if he finds out? What will we do then?"

"Maybe it would be for the best." Wasn't that exactly what he was longing for?

"What do you mean?"

"Look, I'll explain later. Can you meet me in half an hour on the road to Dalesport? Near the grotto?"

"I'll try but you know he is watching me like a hawk."

"Do what you can anyway. I'll hang around till eleven and if you're not there by then I'll know that you couldn't come."

Tommie put down the phone and set the kettle to boil. He was sick to death of all this sneaking about and now that Podge was onto something God only knows when he would get to see Eve. The sad truth, however, was that he had no one to blame except himself. He should have held onto her all those years ago

153

instead of allowing himself to be eaten up with the mistakes of his past. Now he was paying dearly for his own mistake.

Eve was already at the grotto when he arrived and as he kissed her he felt that she was holding back. He noticed that she was constantly looking over her shoulder and after a few minutes he began to become irritated.

"Jesus we can't keep going on like this! Look at you! You're like a frightened rabbit."

"I know and I am sorry but if Podge finds me here he'll kill me."

"Did he see you leave?"

"No, he went off to bed early."

"Well then, settle for a few minutes." He was annoyed that she was so fidgety.

"I can't stay long. I don't want him to miss me again."

"Eve." Tommie was serious now. "Look at you! You're a bag of nerves. That can't be good for you at all. You're going to have to leave him you know. There is no point in putting it off forever. Life is too short and we are not getting any younger. I'm forty now and I have lived too long without you already."

"I know." She brushed his hair with her fingers. "And I will leave him but not just yet."

"Why not?" He couldn't understand what was holding her there.

"He has a few problems with the farm at the moment but as soon as they are solved I'm gone. Can you hold out just another few months, darling?"

"Yes, I suppose I can." Did she detect an air of despondency in his tone?

"You know every time I see you I want to ravage you? Right now I would love to pull you to the ground and make love to you until morning."

"And what would the Blessed Virgin have to say about that?" She pointed to the statute behind her and both of them started laughing.

When the laughter had died away Tommie was serious again for a moment. Then he looked at Eve and smiled.

"Remember I told you about my sister, Rosie? Well, she has come back to her senses. She has woken up at last."

"Oh Tommie, that's marvelous! When did this happen?"

"Yesterday, apparently. The doctors are hopeful that she has made a full recovery. I went over to the hospital earlier to see her and she's in good enough form. The funny thing is that she keeps on talking about Robbie."

"Robbie is her husband, am I right?"

"Yes. She still loves him deeply, you know."

"And what about him? Does he still love her?"

"Hard to say with Robbie. I know that he was deeply hurt when she betrayed him. Can you forgive someone for that?"

"Jesus I don't know! I couldn't see Podge ever forgiving me, could you?"

"No, I suppose not! Does he still love you?"

"Yes, I think so but Podge's love is completely different from the normal run of love. His is of a possessive kind. He hates me talking to anyone else. If he could see me now he would throttle me."

"I wouldn't let him!" He pulled her close and kissed her moist lips.

"I do love you, Tommie Bordoni" she whispered as he caressed her breasts "and we will be together some day soon, I promise you that! You will just have to be patient for another little while."

"I'm not left with much choice am I but I have to remind you that patience was never one of my strong virtues." He was half joking and half in earnest but he would bid his time until she saw fit to leave her husband.

However, over the next few months Tommie saw very little of Eve, much to his disappointment. Podge was keeping her close to him at all times and even on market days he found it impossible to talk to her. He began to fret for her and he could not sleep. She was constantly on his mind and his body ached for her closeness.

Robbie and Rosie's love had been reborn. She had found it hard to cope with life after being shut away for twenty years and so she attempted suicide. She slit her wrists and the doctors had a hard enough job trying to keep her alive. It was while she was recovering that her husband decided that he still loved her and did not want to lose her again. He forgave her all the sins of her past and she had left Dalesport to begin a new life in Meath with him. The children decided to stay at the Manor with Kitty as they each had their own commitments and secretly Tommie was delighted. He did not think that he could manage without Kevin now, he relied solely on him, and would have been soul destroyed if he had lost him.

He went about his business as usual and lived from market day to market day when he could at least see Eve. Seeing her was better than nothing at all! He was surprised, therefore, one night in early July when she called to his cottage, completely unannounced.

"Come on in" he led the way to the warm kitchen. "This is a pleasant surprise, I must say, but how on earth did you manage to get away?"

"Oh, Tommie I had to come. I'm nearly gone mad. I can't bear to be away from you like this."

As he held her in his arms he could feel her tremble and his heart bled.

"Podge has gone to Ballyhale to a farmers meeting and won't be back until around ten. I had to take the chance to come here. At least we can have a few hours together."

Without another word he caught her by the hand and led her to the bedroom. As he undressed her the warm fragrance of her perfume filtered through his nostrils and touched his soul. Their first attempt at love was rather rushed and rough as both had been denied for so long. The second, however, was full of passion and contentment and lasted well over an hour. As they lay naked together Tommie stroked her hair and spoke softly.

"Eve, this is not enough for me anymore. I simply can't live without you, my darling. I want to see you when I wake up in the morning and know that you are there for me when I come in at night. Can you understand that?"

"Yes, I understand what you are saying because it is exactly the same for me. I've been in hell for the last few weeks. Everywhere I go he's after me and I can get no peace at all. He knows that there is someone else but he doesn't know who it is. He won't even allow me to answer the phone anymore."

"Maybe it's time that he did."

"What do you mean?" She sat up and faced him, her full breasts align with his eyes.

Tommie was thoughtful as he gazed at her beauty.

"Maybe it is time that he did know who you are in love with! I think that the moment has finally come to tell him that you are leaving him. The sooner it's done the better! Tell him that we are in love and want to be together. I'll go with you and that way it'll be me who will bear the brunt of his anger and not you."

"Jesus, I don't know. Things are a bit strained at the moment and—"

"For God's sakes, Eve, will you grow up. Things are always going to be a bit strained between you two. What other way could they be when you are having an affair? Maybe you don't want to leave him at all. Maybe you still love him and I'm just a bit on the side for you. Is that it?"

"How can you say that? You know that isn't true. I love you, Tommie. Jesus I have spent nearly all my life loving you!"

"Well then prove it. Leave him Eve and come and live here. Bring Jack with you, please."

"I'll see." Her reply was anything but positive.

"He'll have to be told sooner or later and as far as I can see we're just wasting our lives apart. Tell him and be done with it and we can start our new lives together."

"You make it sound so simple." She stroked his dark hair and wished that she had more nerves.

"It is simple. Will you tell him tonight?" Tommie was sitting straight now, excited at the prospect of having this woman with him every minute of every day.

"I don't know. I'll see what sort of a mood he is in when he gets home."

"I can't wait to have you all to myself. Can't you just see us working side by side? Walking through the woods and making love under the stars?"

"Oh, Tommie, it sounds really lovely and you know it's what I've always wanted although I could never make you see that. But now I'm afraid that I had better be going. It's gone nine and he will be home soon."

"Yeah, I suppose it's for the best! Do you want me to come with you and tell him?"

"No." She caught him roughly by the arm. "I got into this myself and I'll get out of it by myself too. By the end of this week I will have moved in here, just you wait and see."

"I'm looking forward to it. Meet me by the grotto tomorrow at seven and let me know how things are."

"Okay then." She buttoned the last hole of her cardigan and, kissing him, departed quietly. Hastily making her way up the road Eve was not to know that by the time the clock struck midnight that night both her life and Tommie's was to change drastically and not for the better.

CHAPTER TWENTY ONE

She could sense that he was home even before she turned into the lane. A cold shiver raced down her back and her heart felt sad and heavy. Her body began to shake uncontrollably and she was unable to stop it. Joe was in the yard playing with Jack as she approached and the car was parked in the corner.

"Where have you been?" Joe sounded a little concerned.

"Nowhere special. Just out for a walk." She hated lying to her son but knew that she had no choice.

"He's been home for over an hour and he's been looking for you. Going mad he was!"

"And where did you say I was gone?" She was suddenly scared. There'd be hell to pay now!

"I told him that I didn't know. That was the truth! And then he had a go at me and started ranting and raving and saying that you were never here anymore. I think he's losing the plot!"

"Has he calmed down yet?" She did not want to go inside. She had seen Podge lose his temper before and it had not been a pretty sight.

"Don't know! I had enough so I came out her to play with Jack. He had to make his own cup of tea and he didn't like that."

"Where's Pete?"

"He's still helping out on Bergins. He hasn't come home yet."

Eve rubbed her sticky hands together and somehow managed to drag herself through the door. Her few hours alone with

Tommie faded into oblivion as a very angry Podge confronted her.

"Nice of you to come back. Where the hell have you been?"

"Nowhere." She was frightened of him and did not want to anger him further.

"Nowhere!" His laugh was hollow and loud. "You've been gone for the last few hours and you were nowhere?"

"I just went for a walk, that's all!" Why was he so possessive? Was she not entitled to some time alone every now and then?

"I turn my back for one minute and you scuttle off. Where were you walking?"

"I went up around the long field towards the hill."

"Liar!" His clenched fist came down on her and bruised her jaw. "You're a dirty rotten liar. I've been all over this farm and I've seen no sign of you anywhere. Now tell me again where were you." He was roaring now and as Eve rubbed her lower jaw she could feel the pain weave it's way towards her head.

"I told you I went for a walk." She hoped that her jaw wasn't broken. God, she felt like crying. He had never struck her before and she was seething inside.

"With who?" She could see the veins rise on his neck. This always happened when he was furious.

"With no one! I was by myself. Why do you find that so hard to believe."

"I'll tell you why." His face was adjacent to hers and she could feel his hot, smelly breath begin to suffocate her. "Because you are a slut! I've seen the way you look at men. Give them the come on with your baby blue eyes. How many men have you been with since I married you?"

"None! I don't know why you keep saying these things. You're only imagining them."

"Imagining them?" Again she felt the force of his hand across her face. "You mean you can actually stand there and tell me that I only imagined you looking longingly at that Tommie what's his name in the pub that night. Come on Eve give me some bit of credit."

"That was different. I knew Tommie years ago."

"I bet you did! And has he had you in his bed? Have you shown him these?" He caught her breasts and roughly pulled at

160

them. Pain seared through her body and forgetting her fear she began to feel her anger take control.

"Stop it you great bully" she was shouting at him now. "You stop this very minute."

"Don't tell me what to do, you tart." Again he boxed her, this time it was her eye that bore the pressure. "I bet he has, you know. I bet the Lord of the fuckin' Manor has seen your big tits. Bet he has seen this too."

Pulling up her skirt he shoved his finger deep into her vagina and she squealed with the pain. Was this what she had married? Was this why she wouldn't go to live with Tommie? Was this how she had planned to stay for the rest of her life? Well, enough was enough! She wasn't going to spend another night under the same roof as this animal. Let him kill her if he wanted to, anything was better that this.

Looking him straight in the eye she wanted to inflict pain on him and so delighted in telling him the truth. "Okay, you want the truth? Well, I'll give it to you but you're not going to like it one little bit! Yes, I did sleep with Tommie. Yes, he has seen my big tits and yes he has entered my vagina. In fact he had entered it ever before you came along and I can tell you he is a far better lover than you can ever hope to be." She knew that she had gone too far but there was no turning back. He had been asking for it and he had driven her to the edge of her sanity.

"I knew you were a brazen hussy, a good for nothing lazy slut! Well it's time I started to teach you a thing or two." Catching her by the hair he shoved her to the ground and she could feel the coldness of the hard tiles underneath her. Then with an incredible force and without any prior warning he began to kick her roughly.

As the heavy farm boots pounded against her flesh Eve pleaded with him to stop but he was out of control. Not even the sight of her blood lying in little bright pools along the tiles yielded to his motions. As far as he was concerned he was giving her what she deserved and he continued kicking like a lunatic until she had ceased to move. Then, reaching for his shotgun, he ran from the house and made his way towards Dalesport Manor.

Tommie had only just managed to get up out of the bed and was washing his face at the sink when he heard him coming. Realising that Eve must have told him of their love he tried to stay calm and, as Podge hammered on the door, he uttered a silent prayer before answering.

Nothing could have prepared him for the sight that he witnessed in front of him. Podge was like a mad man. His hair was unruly, his eyes wild and froth had begun to form on the side of his lips. To make matters worse he was pointing a shotgun directly at his chest.

"Come outside you, you rich piece of trash" he roared. "I have something I want to settle with you."

"Calm down Podge." Tommie pretended not to be frightened. "Let's talk about this like two adults."

"You know what I want to talk to you about then?" So the bitch had been telling him the truth!

"I presume that it is Eve?"

"You bastard! So it is true, you have been fucking my wife?"

"We love each other. Surely she has told you that?"

"She has told me nothing nor will she ever again."

"What do you mean?" He was suddenly sick. Had this madman harmed the woman he loved?

"Eve will be quiet forever now and you will be too before I have finished with you"

"What have you done to her?" He was more terrified now than he had ever been in his life but still he had managed to raise his voice.

"I've given her what she deserves, dirty piece of filth that she is and now I am here to do the same to you. Think you can come along and steal my wife from under my nose, do you?" He pointed the gun and pulled back the trigger.

Just as he was about to take his finger to the limit Jake, the farm foreman appeared around the corner and, frightened by the sight in front of him let out a piercing roar.

Turning to see what the interruption was Podge lost his bearings for a split second but it was all the time that Tommie needed. He was on him like a lion and he pulled him to the ground. Jake watched in horror as the two men struggled on the path and when the sound of a gunshot was heard ringing through the still night air he closed his eyes against the terror.

Upon opening them again he was delighted to see that it was Tommie who was rising from the ashes and not Podge. In fact Podge lay in a pool of blood, a bullet securely lodged in his chest and his mouth twisted in bitterness.

"Jesus Christ." Tommie was clearly shaken from the ordeal but his mind as ever was on Eve. "He's dead. I've killed him. What's to happen now?"

"What has been going on here at all?" Jake was mystified. "What was he doing here?"

"I'll explain later. Now go and call the guards and tell them what has happened. I'm away up to Hodgin's farm. I'm afraid Mrs. Hodgins is in trouble."

"Trouble? What kind of trouble?"

"Oh, stop mitering and go get the guards. I'll tell you the whole story later." And with that he drove like a lunatic to his loved one.

Joe was standing over Eve's body and Jack was crying on the fireside chair while Pete was nowhere to be seen. She was still motionless on the ground and as he ran to her and held her to him he was grateful that he could at least detect a slight pulse. She had to stay alive- she just had to be! Podge was gone and now they could be together. Nothing could stop them! God, what way was his mind working here at all? He had killed Podge only moments earlier and Eve's life was hanging in the balance and all he could think about was that they had a chance of being together at last! Gripped by a stiffening fear he shook himself and was suddenly shouting. "Call an ambulance. Quickly, call an ambulance."

Joe arose and ran to the phone. He dialed 999 and explained his business as quickly and as clearly as he could. Meanwhile Tommie softly called his sweetheart's name but recieved no response. All the blood that swam around the floor frightened him but he tried to ignore it. He had to be hopeful. Eve wouldn't die! She mustn't!

"They'll be here in ten minutes." Joe was breathless as he made his way back to the kitchen and faced Tommie.

"Who?" Tommie wasn't able to think anymore. His body was weak from the entire goings on.

"The ambulance. Ten minutes! Will she be alright till then?"

"Jesus, I don't know. She's very weak. Can they not get here any sooner?" He started to curse and pray at the same time.

"He did it, you know!" Joe looked at his mother and tried to stop the tears from falling.

"Who?" His mind was still a mess.

"Me Dad. They were fighting. I could hear them through the door. They were fighting over you and then he started hitting her and boxing her."

"Could you not have stopped him?" Was this chap not man enough to have taken his father on? Could he not have done something to aid his mother?

"I was afraid. You don't know him when he's mad. He could kill you." Tommie could hear the frightened quiver in his voice.

"I hope to God he hasn't killed your mother." The tears began to sting his eyes and he looked towards the door.

"Do you love her?" The question surprised him.

"Why do you ask?"

"I think that she loves you. She said you were better than him any day!"

Looking at this boy who should be a man by now, Tommie was moved. He was the spitting image of his father but clearly had more nature in him. He was perhaps a little childish for his years but could he not have made an attempt to save his mother? Was there nothing that he could have done to prevent all this?

"Yes, I do love her Joe. I always have you know but I was just too stupid to admit it to myself. I could have had her years ago but I didn't want her. Now look at what all my selfishness had caused. If anything happens to her I won't be able to live with myself."

"She'll be okay. You'll see." Tommie was touched as Joe laid his hand on his shoulder and he knew that the lad had suddenly taken the first step towards maturity.

Just at that moment the ambulance pulled up outside and Eve was rushed to Ballyhale hospital at top speed. Tommie sat in the back beside his loved one and cried silently as he held her hand throughout the hurried journey. Pete had returned from his days work only moments before the ambulance had arrived and he had been truly upset by the incident. Tommie had not the energy to console so he had left the job to Joe.

Two hours and several cups of coffee later he was frantic in the waiting room as he awaited news of her condition. When at last the doctor finally came to him he was a bag of nerves and had no nails left on his fingers.

"You must be her husband?"

He had better let on that he was otherwise he might get no information. Hospitals were strange like that! He nodded.

"You're wife is a strong woman but she has had a lot of surgery which has considerably weakened her. She was in a pretty bad state when she came in here, I needn't tell you! Her jaw is broken in two different places and her ribs are cracked. Her hip had been dislocated and her left arm fractured. She has also lost the baby that she was carrying. That accounts for all the blood. Now we have mended her bones but she is still asleep. We do not know if she is suffering from shock or if she has had some internal damage to her brain. We have done a brain scan and are awaiting the results. We should know something then. She hasn't awoken yet and that is a bad sign. She is weak and all that loss of blood weakened her even further. The next few days are going to be crucial. Now, what I want to know is what happened to her."

"She was beaten up!" Tommie was obviously in shock. His lovely Eve was fighting for her life and there was nothing he could do to help her. And she had lost a baby! Was it his?

"Who beat her up?" The doctor's voice was stern as he looked at Tommie.

"Her husband." He almost whispered his reply as the tears began to choke him.

"But I thought you said that you were-"

"I know! I lied! I am her lover. It is my fault that she is lying there."

At that precise moment a nurse walked into the waiting room and looked from one man to the other. Excusing her interruption she turned to Tommie and asked him his name. Confirming that it was he whom she was looking for she explained to him that Sergeant Molloy was at the front desk and wished to speak to him. He made his way to the reception desk and looked nervously as the Sergeant greeted him. It was only as he neared him that he noticed the handcuffs.

"Tommie Bordoni, you are under arrest for the murder of one Podge Hodgins. You have the right to remain silent. Anything you say can and will be held against you in a court of law. You have the right to-" He heard no more. All he could fathom was that he was been jailed for Podge's death and when Eve woke up he would not be there for her. This had turned into a nightmare and there was nothing he could do. Absolutely nothing at all!

CHAPTER TWENTY TWO

"You have a visitor." The stocky officer's impartial voice echoed through the cold, grey walls of the prison, startling Tommie in his lonely cell. "You will be given twenty minutes to talk to her and then you will be returned to your quarters. Please note that there is to be no touching and no shouting and mind, I will be watching you closely! Now away out with you."

Kitty was sitting quietly at a round table when he entered the visiting room and she jumped up as soon as she saw him. He had been in the cell for two days now and this was the first time she had been allowed a visitors pass. Her heart turned over as she watched him approach, his eyes black from lack of sleep and his face unshaven and grave.

"Tommie" she stood up as he neared, delighted to see him but at a complete loss for words. "How on earth are you keeping?"

"Oh Kitty! It's awful in here, shut away from the outside world. I don't see the light of day at all."

"Tommie I'm so sorry, I know it must be terrible for you. What happened at all? I've heard so many different versions and at this stage I don't know what to believe."

"It all happened so fast Kitty, I hardly had time to think. Podge Hodgins pulled a gun on me and when we started to wrestle the gun went off. It killed him and here I am awaiting trial for murder."

"But why did he pull the gun on you in the first place. What was he doing up at Dalesport? I don't understand it!"

"He heard that I was having an affair with his wife." He kept his head down as he spoke, too terrified to look her straight in the eye.

Kitty listened attentively and then threw back her head and began to laugh quietly. "His wife?" She finally found her voice. "But that's ridiculous, isn't it? Where on earth did he get that notion? Sure everyone knows that you hate women and wouldn't touch one with a forty foot pole."

"It was true!" He continued to stare at the table in front of him and knew that there was the point in denying it. The truth would eventually come out and, anyway, hadn't he been denied of Eve for far too long already?

"You mean to tell me that you were actually having an affair with her?" Kitty could hardly believe her ears and was unable to refrain from keeping the surprise out of her voice.

"Yes." Still his head was bent.

"Oh, Tommie, Tommie have you lost your mind altogether? What ever were you thinking about? Are there not enough single women in the world out there without becoming involved with a married one? You of all people should know better than that after all that has happened around here! Sure what else could you expect only trouble?"

He didn't need this lecture. Things were bad enough and he couldn't take much more.

"You don't understand, Kitty, you couldn't possibly understand at all. You see, Eve is not just another woman. Eve is the one and only love of my life and we go back a long, long way. I dated her before she married Podge but I was stupid enough to let her go. It was the biggest mistake that I have ever made and I'm paying dearly for it now. Now, stop rabbiting on! It won't change a thing. Just tell me have you heard anything about her? Has she awoken yet?"

"I don't really know, Tommie. The last I heard was that she is still in a coma." She was immediately sorry for lecturing him but felt that it needed to be done. He was the last person on earth that she would have imagined to be in these circumstances.

"I need you to do me a big favour. Go to the hospital and find out exactly how she is. I want to know all the details. Will you do that for me?"

"Yes, yes of course I will. I'll go over there on my way home. God, Tommie, you really do love that woman, don't you?" She had never seen him this way before.

"Yes, Kitty, I love her with all my heart. She means everything in the world to me and if anything happens to her-" He paused for a moment, his emotions in tatters. "If anything happens to her I don't know what I will do."

"She'll pull through Tommie, just you wait and see." What else could she say? "What about you though? Do you think that you will be found guilty?"

"I don't know. It was an accident. I never meant to kill him, it was the last thing on my mind, but it all depends on how the jury look at it."

"Rosie is coming down tomorrow and she is bringing a lawyer with her. She says he is the very best so he will be able to get you through this."

"I hope so" but he wasn't convinced. He had a bad feeling in his bones and he was finding it hard to shake off.

Kitty called to the hospital on her way home as promised but was not allowed to visit Eve. She was told that she was still in a coma and only immediate family was allowed to see her. Remembering the horror of Rosie's coma Kitty prayed silently as she returned home. Eve may have been instrumental in Tommie's downfall but did that entitle her to lose out on her own life? She didn't think so!

It took about two months for Tommie's trial to be heard at the Central Court in Dublin and by that time he had nearly lost his mind in prison. His picture had been all over the news and sprawled across the pages of the local newspapers and, as he sat nervously in the dock awaiting sentencing, he felt like a wanted criminal. There were people out there who were plundering and murdering every day of the week and the guards couldn't catch them while he was only acting in self defense! To make matters worse the jury who had been assigned to his case were all of an older race and were harsh and serious throughout the entire trial. He thought that they looked anything but favourable but he could not allow himself to give up hope. It was all he had to hold onto!

As he finally stood in the dock to hear the verdict the beads of sweat on the brow of his forehead and palms of his hand made him uncomfortable. He had aided the death of a man because of an illicit affair with his wife and, because he was of a higher class, was not confident of release. He waited with bated breath for his fate to be established.

"We, the jury, find Tommie Bordoni guilty of the murder of one Podge Hodgins on July 18th of this year."

His world came crashing around him in that instant and he heard no more. Glancing towards the crowd he noticed Rosie and Kitty and both were crying. Jake was also there and his evidence, which should have swayed the jury, seemed to have had the opposite effect.

"Not intentional, Ten years, Mountjoy prison. Good behavior, out in seven." His head had started to spin and he was only vaguely aware of what the judge was saying. He hardly remembered being led down the stairs in handcuffs and being roughly thrown into a prison van. The cameras and journalists flashed before him as he was driven away and within half an hour he began the first of his ten years in Mountjoy.

Eve spent two long weeks in a coma and was totally unaware of the tragedy that had befallen Tommie. The brain scan had been successful! As soon as the swelling had subsided it was clear that there was no permanent damage and so it was entirely up to herself to dispel the darkness that had enveloped her mind. Her bones began to knit together again and the swelling around her eyes had healed. However, even when she did return to the normal world she had a long, long road in front of her. It would be a while before she would walk without the aid of a crutch and her jaw would be painful for many a month.

It was on the Thursday of the second week when she finally decided to come back to the land of the living.

Joe was sitting at her bedside reading the daily newspaper and became highly excited. He leapt from his chair and immediately alerted the doctors. Three of them arrived in the ward and Eve thought that they would never get through examining her. She was tired and weak and in no mood to be pulled around. Besides, there were so many questions she wanted to ask Joe and she was impatient for answers. That tragic night was uppermost on her mind and she could still feel Podge's boots on her body.

Eventually the doctors left and Eve turned slowly to face her son. All her injuries had been explained to her and she knew that she was a mess but she didn't care. Her main priority was Tommie.

It was Joe, however, who spoke first.

"You gave us quite a scare, Mam. I was beginning to think that you were never going to wake up. You've been asleep for ages!" He held her hand as he spoke, thrilled that his mother was at last able to respond to him again.

"Oh, Joe! How lovely to see you! How is Pete? And Jack, is he here?"

"Jack's fine, Mam and so is Pete. Mrs. Daly down the Mill Road takes him during the day and Pete and myself have him in the evenings. He misses you a lot. Thank God you woke up. We thought that we had lost you too."

"Too? What do you mean too? Was has happened, Joe?" Had something happened to Tommie?

"Oh Mam, I'm afraid it's Dad! I'm so sorry to have to tell you this but he's dead, Mam, he's dead!" His voice quivered as he spoke but he needed to be strong for her sake. After all he was the man of the house now!

"Dead?" She tried to sit up in the bed as her mind attempted to piece the facts together. "What do you mean dead? He can't be dead, sure he was a strong healthy man! How did he die? When did this happen?" Her heart was racing faster than normal and her blood pressure began to rise.

"He's dead alright, Mam! He died the night that you were admitted to the hospital, the night you two had that awful row. He was buried last week in the same grave as Granddad and there was a great crowd at the funeral. He didn't die from natural causes though! I'm afraid that it was Tommie, Mam. Tommie killed him."

"What do you mean killed him?" This was worse than she could have ever imagined.

"Do you remember anything of that awful night?" He needed to know before he went any further.

"Yes, yes I do" her tone was sad as she looked at her hands. "I remember your father losing his head because I went for a walk and I remember him kicking me on the floor." She sighed and knew that she did not want to remember anymore.

"Dad lost the head completely that night and I think he meant to kill you too!" Joe rubbed his hands along her shoulders in an effort to comfort her. "Thank God he stopped before-" He wiped his eyes before continuing. "Anyway, he left home with his shotgun under his arm and went over to the Manor. He was wild looking, mad even and he intended to shoot Tommie. I don't know what happened but he ended up dead himself. Why did he want to kill Tommie anyway? Why did he hate him so much?"

"Oh my God, this is terrible, how has it all come to this at all?" She placed her head in her hands and tried to come to terms with what she had just been told.

"He must have been gone mad, altogether Mam! Turned himself into a lunatic, I'd say!"

"Joe, don't be too hard on him! It's my fault as much as his! It was plain old jealously that drove him over the edge and there was nothing that he could do to control it. He was a very possessive man!"

"Jealousy?" Joe fought to understand. "Jealous of you and Tommie?"

"Yes, he found out that I was having an affair with Tommie."

"Why, Mum? Why did you have to go after him? Were you not happy with what you had?"

"Oh Joe, I don't know, it's too hard to explain. I suppose you could say that I have always loved Tommie. Even when I married your father it was Tommie that I really wanted. I should never have married Podge. I should have known that Tommie would come back. But I was young and foolish and all I wanted to do was get married."

"Did you not love Dad at all then?" he was doing his best to try and understand the situation with an open mind.

"You know, I did in a strange sort of way. It was nothing like the love that I have for Tommie though. It was more respect I suppose than love."

"He beat you up real bad, didn't he? People are saying awful things about him."

"Don't listen to them at all, son. People will always talk, they know no better! It's only human nature after all! Your father was a good man at heart. He was a hard worker and he loved you and your brothers with all his being. Don't listen to the idle gossip and don't think bad of your father. Remember the good times that you all had together, that's the way he would have wanted it. Now tell me, how is Tommie? Has he been in to see me at all?" She felt no sorrow for the loss of her husband's life but she hoped that her son would not notice.

"Oh Mum, it gets worse!" He wondered if she could cope with any more. "Tommie hasn't been in nor won't be for a long while."

"Why ever not?" She couldn't understand it. Surely he didn't want to stay away, not now anyway?

"He's in prison." There he had told her all the awful truths and now he would have to help her deal with the grief.

"In prison? Good Jesus, whatever for?" She was finding it hard to take it all in.

"For killing Dad." It was almost a whisper.

"Jesus Christ, I don't believe you! Surely Tommie didn't mean to kill him! He's not that sort! Sure it must have been an accident. How long will he be there?"

"His trial hasn't come up yet. He'll be kept there until then anyway."

"I aim to be better for that trial, Tommie will need me. Give me a mirror there until I see how bad I look."

Eve, however, wasn't well enough to attend the trial. A series of infections set into her hip and she was confined to the hospital for another three months. She read about the sordid affair in the papers and cried for days when Tommie was sentenced. After the grief subsided she swore that as soon as she was well enough she was going to fight his case. Tommie was innocent; he had been trying to save himself. Self defense, that's all it was! He had not meant to kill Podge and therefore he should not be punished for it. He had been a victim of a bad jury and she was going to do everything in her power to free him.

CHAPTER TWENTY THREE

It was a cool but dry day in late October when Eve finally walked out of the hospital. Aided with a crutch, she was still a little unsteady, but was more than thrilled at the thought of going home. She had been in the hospital for a little over three months but it felt as if she had been away for years. She couldn't wait to see her home again and attempt to settle back into a routine life. Things would certainly be different now that Podge was no longer around and she hoped that she could manage to pay off the farm debts on her own.

Life wasn't going to be easy and she still had Tommie to see to. Come hell or high water she intended to get him home to Dalesport and she was actually looking forward to the fight. Joe and Pete helped her into the car and Jack nearly knocked her over with hugs.

It took her over two weeks to obtain a visiting pass to see Tommie and she went to great lengths to dress herself on the morning of her visit. She was both excited and anxious as she boarded the train to Dublin but the thought of seeing her lover sustained her throughout the journey.

An old man sat in the seat opposite her and the smell of tobacco from his pipe wafted all over the carriage. She closed her eyes as she inhaled it, somehow comforted by its sweet, aromatic essence.

"Grand day for a train ride" he took the pipe from his mouth as he addressed her.

"It's not too bad at all." She smiled at him, glad of the opportunity to talk.

"Going up to the big smoke for the day?" He looked her up and down and noticed how neatly she was dressed.

"Yes, I am!" She prayed that he would not ask her for her final destination.

"I'm heading that way myself. Got an appointment in the eye and ear hospital. I'll be there for the day. You from Dalesport?"

"Yes, I live a little outside- in the country." She knew that he wasn't local, she had never seen him before.

"I'm from Baile Beag meself, five miles from Dalesport. Have you heard of it?"

"I have actually but have never visited it."

"Grand little place it is too" he puffed at his pipe again. "You should visit it some day."

"Maybe I will" she actually managed a smile.

"Terrible business that with your man from your place. You know the lad that killed his lover's husband? It was all over the newspapers! What happened there at all?"

For a moment Eve thought to deny any knowledge of the incident but then she wondered why she should. She was not ashamed of what Tommie had done and she certainly was not going to sit back and let his innocence be questioned.

"It was self- defence, you know! If Tommie had not acted in the manner that he did then he would have been the one to end up in the graveyard."

"You knew him then, this Tommie bloke?" he was all ears now, delighted with the opportunity of a bit of gossip.

"Yes, yes I did!" She paused for a moment as she regarded his eager face. "In fact I am the woman with whom he was having the affair."

"Sweet suffering Jesus!" He almost choked on the smoke but managed to steady himself. "God, it's a small world isn't it? I'm sorry, I would never have opened me big gob if I had known."

"It's okay, really, I don't mind. In fact it's good to be able to talk to someone about it."

And so she spent the rest of the journey explaining her affair with Tommie and as she alighted from the train she knew that she had convinced the old man of her lover's innocence.

She hailed a taxi at Heuston station and prayed for guidance as she was driven through the busy city. Standing outside the tall, grey building that was Mountjoy prison she couldn't stop the shivers that were enveloping her body. The building was as bleak on the outside as she imagined it would be on the inside and she dreaded the thought of entering.

Nervously she made her way to the door and, after being checked by the officers, followed the crowd to the visiting room. Looking around she felt that most of the surrounding people were rather tough looking and certainly belonged in a prison cell. Not Tommie! He was so gentle and should be farming the land that he loved so much. It just wasn't fair!

No amount of forward planning could have prepared her for what was to come. She had been expecting Tommie to have failed a little- prison life always did that to a man- but what she saw shocked her to the very core. He was only half the man she had remembered! The weight had fallen from his bones and he was gaunt. His body was bent forward and he had aged at least ten years. His eyes were sad and even though he smiled upon seeing her it did nothing to improve his appearance.

He sat down slowly, careful not to touch her. She longed to cradle him in her arms, to lay him to her bosom and assure him that everything would be aright but she knew that it was against the rules. Instead she tried to be cheerful even though her heart was breaking.

"Oh Tommie, I'm so sorry that it has come to this. How are you keeping?" How was she to refrain from touching him?

"Eve, my little Eve, how good it is to see you. Thank God you are well and strong again. I don't know what I would have done if anything had happened to you. I've been lying awake in my cell just picturing your face before me. It's the only thing that keeps me going. And I'm so sorry about Podge, I never meant anything like that to happen."

"I know you didn't Tommie, I know you didn't. Podge was an obstinate man and always acted on impulse. I know that I shouldn't be saying this but thank God it was his body that the bullet sped through and not yours."

"Oh Eve" his eyes filled with tears. "How are we going to get through this?"

"Is it really bad in here?" She knew the answer but needed his confirmation.

"Yes! It's awful! It's even worse than awful. You have no idea!"

"But why on earth were you convicted? Surely be to God they must have known that it was an accident! It wasn't intentional, was it?"

"Of course not, how can you even ask me that? The jury took a hard stand because I was playing around with a married woman. A married woman with children at that! You know the score yourself- the rich man messes with the poor farmer's wife and ends up killing him. Where's the sympathy to lie there, I ask you? I never had a chance of getting off and now I have all these years ahead of me to serve. It's worse than anything I could ever have imagined."

He bent his head for a few moments and an uncomfortable silence followed. Suddenly he shook himself and was looking at her again.

"How are you keeping anyway? Kitty has kept me informed of your progress."

"I'm not too bad now. Still a little stiff but I will survive. I finished with the crutch two days ago but I'm getting steadier on my feet all the time. I miss you so much you know."

"Yeah and I you." If only he could touch that soft, tender skin!

"I'm not going to leave you here to rot, Tommie! I'm going to do everything in my power to get you out. I will find a good lawyer and try to get you a retrial. But first you must tell me exactly what happened that night."

"Oh Eve! It's no use! I have ten years ahead of me in here no matter what way you look at it and nothing is going to change that. You'll be only wasting your time."

"I asked you once before to trust me but you couldn't find it in yourself to do that. Don't make the same mistake twice!"

"Okay, Eve, I will trust you! Of course I will trust you!"

"That's it Tommie, you can't afford to give up hope. It's all we have to hang on to! Now, if it's not too painful I would like you to tell me exactly what occurred on that dreadful night."

"Well, Podge came to the door shouting the odds. I was sure that you had told him about our affair and that he was

177

coming to give me a hiding. However, I quickly realised that he had a shotgun in his hand and that he was pointing it at me. He had his finger on the trigger and I needn't tell you I was terrified. I was sure that I was done for, my entire life flashed before me in a matter of seconds. He had a mad look about him; he was capable of doing anything but just as he was about to release the trigger Jake came around the corner. Podge lost his concentration for a moment and I tried to take the gun off him. He struggled with me and the gun went off. The rest is history."

"You see it was self defense, I knew it all along. I could never picture you killing anyone intentionally; you haven't got it in you! What you need is a new trial and a new jury and you'll be out of here in no time."

"Oh I don't know. Jake has already told the true story and it made no difference."

"Leave it to me Tommie." She smiled confidently at him and, looking quickly around her, she touched his cold hand. A surge of hope suddenly overwhelmed her and she felt good. "I'll have you back where you belong in no time, don't you worry!"

She had to get him out of here no matter what the cost- she had no choice! Looking at him now she didn't think that he would survive two years in here let alone ten. She was his only chance of survival and, after all that they had been through together, she wasn't going to let him down. She'd go looking for a lawyer first thing tomorrow and in six months Tommie would be back at the Manor, farming the land that he loved so much. The only problem was that she knew she couldn't do it all alone. She needed help!

CHAPTER TWENTY FOUR

Even though she hated saying goodbye to Tommie Eve was glad to leave the cold, bleak prison behind and make her way out into the afternoon sunshine. Hailing a taxi she made her way back to Heuston station, feeling miserable and so alone. The very sight of Tommie had frightened her. That fine, handsome man that she had once known and fallen in love with had disappeared and had been replaced by a sad dejected individual. His spirit was broken, she knew that, but it had been his eyes that had frightened her the most. They were practically sunken into his face and had stared wildly. Oh God, how it pained her to see him in such anguish. He had never even mentioned his farm and that was most unlike him.

She wondered who was managing the estate and told herself that, if she was going to be part of his life, it was up to her to find out exactly what was going on. She would go to Dalesport Manor and see what was happening up there.

As the train swept from the city and made it's way down the winding track towards the countryside she braced herself for the experience. She had never met any of Tommie's family and did not know how they would react to her. Would they blame her for the trouble he was in or would they be willing to help reverse his charges? She simply could not tell but she certainly felt that the time had come for her first encounter with them. After all she was no longer the mistress in the background anymore! She was going to marry him as soon as she had him out of prison and she would be living at the farm so they might as well get used to the idea. Eve had it all worked out in her mind but first she had to rescue her love.

She caught the six thirty bus from Portlaoise train station and in less than twenty minutes had arrived in Dalesport. The village was quiet as she walked through it and hurriedly took the country road to the farm. Her knees began to shake uncontrollably and her heart was beating so fast that she was sure she would have an attack. As she approached the Manor door she suddenly felt that she had already lost some of her earlier resolve. But she was here now and there was no way that she was going to turn back.

Praying silently Eve rang the great doorbell and listened, as it's sharp tone pealed down the hallway. Within minutes she heard a scuffle behind the oak door and a beautiful young girl with long dark hair and a wonderful smile opened it. She nodded at Eve and asked her what her business was.

"I was wondering if I might see Kitty please." She took a deep breath as she waited for the reply and wished that she did not feel so conscious.

"Yeah, she's in the kitchen, I'll run in and get her for you. Who will I say wants her?"

"Just tell her that I am a friend of Tommies."

At the mention of her uncle's name Sarah's smile faded and she was clearly upset. She looked Eve up and down and then ran off in search of her aunt. Eve paced the porch for several minutes as she waited for Kitty to appear and had almost given up hope of her ever arriving.

Kitty was rather sour looking and not a bit friendly.

"Sarah says that you are looking for me. How can I help you?"

"I'm a friend of Tommies and I-"

"What sort of a friend might you be? You're not a reporter are you? I'm sick of you guys hanging around here. Haven't you got enough information at this stage? It's time you left us alone."

"I'm not a reporter." She could understand why this woman was so upset.

"You're not? Then who the hell are you?" Kitty started to stammer as the confusion set in.

.

"I'm Eve, Eve Hodgins. I'm a friend of Tommies." The words were uttered quietly as Eve waited for a reaction.

However, Kitty was speechless for a moment and simply gazed intently at this woman in front of her. So this was the one who was responsible for all their troubles! This was the one who had made Tommie forget all about his hatred of women and cause him to fall in love! Well, she certainly was beautiful, she'd give her that, but was that enough? Kitty didn't think so and wanted nothing to do with her at all.

"So you're Eve." She finally spoke. "And what may I ask do you want here?"

"Can we talk? Inside?" Eve had been expecting the meeting to be tough but she had been unprepared for the cold bitter tone that was affronting her.

"I don't think so." Kitty was not even trying to be friendly. "I have no desire to talk with you after all the trouble you have caused!"

"I can appreciate that but please just give me a few moments of your time!" Eve was practically begging at this stage as she knew that she needed help if she was going to be able to do anything for Tommie. "I've been to see your brother and to tell you the truth I am very worried about him. Please let me in. You don't have to like me but I think that you will want to hear what I have to say."

Kitty thought for a moment and then decided that she had nothing to lose. She seemed to be okay, despite the fact that she had ruined Tommie and she did wonder what it was she wanted.

"Alright then, let's go to the study." She walked down the hall and expected Eve to follow. She wouldn't spend long talking to this woman and she certainly wouldn't be civil to her. How could she, after all the hardship she had caused them?

Eve was in awe of the splendor of the house as she followed close behind Kitty. She had never seen a hall so large before and the study was so ornate that it took her breath away. It was hard to credit that Tommie was the owner of all this wealth. He was such a down to earth chap!

Kitty silently indicated a chair and she sat. She was about to refuse the glass of wine that was offered but decided at the last minute to accept. God knows she could do with something to help to settle her nerves. She was completely in shatters! The experience at the prison had been anything but good and now she was wondering if it had been a foolish idea to come to the Manor. Kitty was not a bit accommodating and, although she had not directly said as much, Eve could sense that she did not like her.

"Well, what is it you have come to say?" Kitty placed her wine glass on the desk and looked at Eve with wide eyes. It was easy to see how Tommie had been so enchanted with this creature. She was beautiful, yet fragile in a quaint sort of way. It was such a pity that she had been married.

"I don't know how much you already know about me. Has Tommie mentioned me before?"

"No, he never said a word. The first we heard of you was when this awful tragedy happened." Kitty stared at her as if she was a leper and although Eve quivered under the gaze she did not allow herself to be intimidated.

"I have known Tommie for a long time. I was very young when I fell in love with him. I went out with him for a while but he never wanted to get serious. Said he couldn't trust women." She paused and sipped from the glass, her lips practically dry from the dust of her journey.

"Yeah, that's what he always told us. Said he'd never marry so we assumed that he never bothered with women." Kitty was suddenly lost in thought. "But there was someone once now that I think of it. It was a long, long time ago! He had a woman up in his cottage for a couple of weeks. That was never you, was it?"

"Yes, yes it was me. I had a misunderstanding with my father and I moved out. I had no where to go so Tommie let me stay with him for a while. We became lovers and he couldn't handle that so I had to leave. He hurt me so much that I swore I would never speak to him again. That was when I met Podge and married him."

"So you actually married Podge on the rebound from Tommie? Is that what you are saying?"

"I suppose!" Eve held the glass to her lips, fearful of looking at the angry woman in front of her.

"That wasn't a great idea, was is? And were you not happy with Podge? Why did you feel that you had to come after

Tommie again?" Kitty still could not give her the sympathy that she deserved.

"I was happy with him for a while but Podge was a possessive man. He actually smothered me! And I didn't come after Tommie, as you put it. We just happened to bump into one another and we both realised that we were still in love. You have to believe me when I tell you that I never meant for any of this to happen. I loved Tommie with all my heart- I never wanted anyone else. I still love him dearly and I mean to marry him when he gets out. He kept on asking me to leave Podge but I kept putting him off. I knew that something bad would happen but I didn't think that it would be as tragic as this. Podge was a hard man but he didn't deserve to die. He made the mistake of falling in love with me and I couldn't return the love that he needed as I had already given it to another. Can you understand any of what I am telling you?" She looked hopefully at Kitty, her large eyes willing her friendship.

"I suppose!" Kitty had listened intently and was now beginning to soften. After all, what wrong had she done? She had fallen in love with her brother and if Tommie had loved her back then she couldn't have been all that bad. "You said that you saw him today?"

"Yes, I went to the prison. It was my first time to go there. I haven't seen him since that awful night. I was in hospital for a long time and it took me ages to get a pass into the prison."

"How did you find him?" She hadn't been to Mountjoy for a week now and wondered how her brother was coping.

"Oh, Kitty, he's not good, not good at all. That's why I came here tonight. I thought that you might be able to help me. That prison had broken his heart and he is so very thin. He won't last long in there at all, of that we can be sure."

"I know!" She also despaired for her brother. "But there is nothing we can do about it. It's out of our hands."

"I don't agree with you entirely" Eve was feeling a little hopeful now. "I intend to try and overturn the verdict he was sentenced with. He did not murder Podge, not intentionally anyway, we all know that! He was trying to save himself. I don't know why he was found guilty the first time but we have to do something to rectify this whole sorry matter. Would you be willing to help me?"

"What do you suggest we do?" Kitty was interested in this woman's spirit.

"Well, I'm planning to see a lawyer in Ballyhale tomorrow. I'm going to get an appeal and make sure that he gets a fair jury this time. I will do this on my own if I have to but I would prefer if you could come with me."

"Do you honestly think that it will do any good? We were meant to have the best lawyer that money could buy the last time."

"That may be so but it is definitely worth a try. What have we got to lose and I know that I have to try and do something. I can't stand back and watch the life fade from him. He needs help!"

"Well, if that's what it is going to take then I will certainly come." Kitty could not believe the enthusiasms of this woman and knew that she must help her. "But do you really think that there is hope?"

"Of course! As long as we work together we will get him out. We have to! He's not going to survive in there and we can't just hang around and watch him shrivel."

"You're dead right, you know! What time tomorrow do you intend to meet this lawyer?"

"I'm going around ten. Would that suit you?" Eve was clearly delighted with Kitty's co- operation.

"I'll be ready. And Eve." She was gentle now. "I'm sorry for being a bit harsh on you when you first came in. It's just that I am so upset over this whole thing."

"It's okay, I understand. I probably would have reacted in the same manner if I had been in your shoes. This terrible business has upset us all but we will soon put things right again. Now, how is everything else here? The farm managing alright without him?"

"Yeah, Kevin, Rosie's young lad, is great and the farmhands have all taken on extra chores. We want to continue making a profit so that he will have something to be proud of when he comes out."

"He'll be thankful to you all for that. Oh, Kitty, we have to get him out, we just have to. You know he never even mentioned the farm today and sure isn't that what he lives for! We have a few hard months ahead of us but it will be worth the hassle in the end."

"Let's hope so, let's hope so." Kitty was not as optimistic but she would pray.

Fintan O' Meara looked out from underneath his thick rimmed glasses and scratched his balding head as he surveyed the two serious looking women who were seated at his desk. He hadn't wanted to meet them, hadn't wanted to handle their case but the younger one had been so insistent. He simply couldn't understand them at all. Justice had been served but here they were looking for him to take out the files again and have another read. What in the name of God was the point?

"Ladies," he was trying not to sound too dour. "Do you really think that you can achieve results here? It will be a long, long battle because, as you must know, the courts are reluctant to delve into cases that have already been put to bed. It's going to take everything that you have to get this one reopened. You will need to come up with some new evidence before a re- trial is even considered. You may find that you will be unable to cope with it all."

"Mr. O' Meara." Eve looked him straight in the eye. She was determined that his pessimistic outlook was not going to disillusion her. "I have a feeling that you under estimate our intelligence here. We are well aware of what is ahead of us and we will come up with the new evidence. We know that it is not going to be easy but how easy do you think that it is on Tommie, sitting in that prison cell, day after day? He is innocent and we want him released. Now, I heard that you were the best that there is but if you feel that you are not able for the job then we will not waste any more of your time." She nodded at Kitty and pretended to arise.

"Let's not be so hasty." O' Meara pushed the glasses further onto his nose and picked up his pen. "You have heard correct! I am the best, the very best, and you will travel a long way before you will find anyone better. And I will help you but I have to warn you, I don't come cheap."

"Money is not a problem. I have my own farm and can come up with your fee in the morning." She secretly wondered where on earth she would even begin to look for the money but she was not about to be swayed.

"No, Eve." Kitty spoke for the first time since she had entered the office. "We will raise the money from Tommie's farm. It's only fair."

"Kitty." Eve caught the woman by the hand. "I want to do this for Tommie. Please let me pay."

"If you're sure." What right had she to take the privilege away from her? The more she saw of Eve the more astounding she appeared to be and she was glad that Tommie would have her when he came out, whenever that would be!

"Well, that's that solved. Now, Mr. O' Meara, where will we begin?"

"You can start by telling me the story from the beginning and giving me a run down of this new evidence. Don't leave anything out and mind you tell me nothing but truths. It will take a long while to organise the appeal but we'll get one. I will have to get a copy of the trial, of course, and go through it with a fine tooth -comb. Perhaps I will be able to come up with something that was over looked the first time round. Say nothing to Tommie about any of this until we have a date. We don't want to give him too much hope just yet."

Between them they related Tommie's story to the lawyer and he jotted everything down in shorthand in his wide notebook. Eve was introduced as the new evidence. Hadn't Podge told her that he intended to finish Tommie off as soon as he had dealt with her? He agreed that it was a definite case of self-defense and gave them the much sought after hope that they needed. When they departed from his office both of the women were in a lighter mood and went to the coffee shop and became better acquainted.

Over the next few weeks they had a path worn to and from the lawyer's office and no stone was left unturned. Podge's last moments at Tommie's farm were relived over and over again and Jake had been persuaded to act as witness once more.

It was agreed that Eve would take the stand this time and relate her version of the story. She had to obtain hospital reports for evidence but had no bother in locating them. As yet they did not have any date for the retrial.

CHAPTER TWENTY FIVE

It was a cold wet day at the beginning of December and Tommie had already spent four and a half months in prison. Time was literally crawling by and he felt that he had been locked up forever. He was constantly depressed and hated everything about prison life. He hated the damp, musty smell of his cell and he hated the food that was dished out to him. He hated the long cold nights and the loneliness that accompanied them. But above all he hated the other inmates. He found them rather a tough lot-they were so uncouth and rough and constantly sneered at him. If it wasn't for Eve's visits he felt that he would be gone mad altogether. Thank God that Podge had spared her life! He wouldn't be able to get through any of this without her!

Sitting on the side of his hard bed he allowed his mind to wander as he tried to conjure up her face. He always did that when he was feeling low and the very image of her beautiful smile brought warmth to his heart. Why, oh why had he pushed her away all those years ago? He would never forgive himself for that! He should be married now with five or six young lads running around the farm. The farm! Oh, how he missed the open fields and the heady smell of his animals. How was he supposed to survive another nine and a half years in this place? It was going to be tough and he wondered if he would make it.

Just at that moment he heard the key turn noisily in his cell door. What was wrong now? It was too early for dinner and yard patrol was not for at least another hour. Maybe he had a visitor! He knew, however, that visiting was already over and the prison had strict beliefs about adhering to their rules.

The prison warden nodded at him as he shoved a big man roughly into the cell.

"This is Ger Rodgers, you're new cell mate. He has come to stay with us for the long duration and will be moving in here with you for a few weeks. We have to get a cell ready on the west wing but it seems to be taking longer than was anticipated. Burst pipe, I think they said was holding up the show! Anyway, Ger, this is Tommie here. I'll leave the two of you to get acquainted."

Tommie nodded at the man in front of him but his heart wasn't in it. He didn't want anyone else sharing his cell. He had been lucky up to now and he had hoped that it would have stayed that way. He valued his time alone when he could think of Eve and he didn't want his privacy invaded. But what choice did he have?

Ger grunted and jumped onto Tommie's bunk. He was a stout man with beady eyes and a dirty, black beard. His breath smelt bad and his hands were like shovels. Tommie felt uncomfortable in his presence but no one was going to take procession of his bed.

"I sleep in the top bunk." He mustered up his courage and tried a smile. "I'm afraid that you may settle into the bottom one!"

"I want the top one." He was like a child. "Can't be doing with all that stooping to get into the bottom one. You may swop around. Of course we could both sleep in the same one, if you'd prefer that." His laugh was eerie and portrayed the sort of man that he was.

Feeling suddenly unnerved Tommie shivered with unease and agreed to take the bottom bunk. He did not want to annoy this fella any more than was necessary. He had that look about him- a look that Tommie could not exactly pinpoint but a look that smelt of trouble. He knew that his new cellmate was certainly going to make his days behind bars all that much more unbearable.

"What are you in for, anyway? Kill the wife did ya?" Ger was sitting on the bed now, his big legs dangling awkwardly over the side.

"What do you want to know that for?" Tommie did not wish him to know any of his business.

"Curious, that's all. You needn't tell me if you don't want to, that's your privilege. I'm here for life meself! Killed two men I did and the funny thing is that I have no regrets. I knifed them until they couldn't cry anymore. You should have seen the blood that spurted from their bodies, bright red it was and I got meself covered in it! Still, they deserved everything that they got! Caught them I did, doing it behind me back! In me own bed, if you don't mind. What do you make of that?"

Tommie had lost the drift of what Ger had been saying as he had been pondering on the ruthlessness of this man but he knew that he had to feign interest.

"What do you mean?" It was all he could say.

"Me boyfriend, ya twit! I caught him in my bed with a lover. Ten years we were together and I never suspected a thing. I was so sure that he loved me but he had been playing the field behind me back the whole time. Thought he'd get away with it too, more fool him! He won't need a lover anymore, though, I've made sure of that!" He laughed a low, evil laugh, the sort that would make your blood curl.

Tommie stared hard at this cruel, devious man in front of him and began to wonder if in fact he was human at all. How could he laugh like that at the thought of the horror he had inflicted on those other creatures? And into the bargain he was a homosexual! He'd never sleep easy in his bed at night knowing that this beast was in the bunk above him. Mother of God, he'd have to get him moved, somehow.

"You're gone terribly quiet all of a sudden. Did I shock you or have you never seen a faggot before? That's it, you've coped on that I'm a queer and you think that I'm disgusting. But let me tell you something for nothing. Once you have sex with a man you will never want a woman again as long as you live. It's what you call real sex and sure maybe you know what I am talking about, maybe you have already done it!"

"Done it?" Tommie's stomach was sick at this stage. "Of course I haven't done it, what do you take me for?"

"Ya don't know what you are missing, me dear man! Hey, I've got a brilliant idea, why don't I show you what it's all

189

about?" He jumped suddenly from the bunk and landed heavily on the floor opposite him.

"The hell you won't." Tommie's body actually shook at the very idea and he took a step back. "Don't you dare lay as much as a finger on me, have you got that? You leave me alone and I will leave you alone, understand?"

"Scared are you? Not half the man that you thought you were? Don't you think that it would be a great way to pass the time in here? You've a lovely bum, by the way. Made for it, you were!" Ger made a move towards him and Tommie backed all the way over to the bunk.

"Leave me alone you fuckin queer or else you'll be sorry."

"I'll be sorry, will I?" Ger was grinning now, his mind playing all sorts of tricks with him. "I don't think so!" He caught Tommie's wrist roughly and pulled him to him. "How about a kiss for starters?"

As he felt the beard along his cheek Tommie automatically panicked and drew a kick at his perpetuator. He came down hard on Ger's shin, causing him to cry out.

"You stupid little fuck" his eyes were alight and he was clearly riled. "No one messes with Ger and gets away with it. I'll have to make you sorry for that, make you see the error of your ways!" and with that he hit him hard across the face. Tommie was thrown against the bed for a moment, his face stinging with the impact of his cell mate's big hand, and in his weakened state he found it hard to catch his breath.

Seizing the opportunity Ger leapt on him like a tiger and pinned him to the hard bunk.

"I'll teach you not to mess with me, you stupid little creep!" he was actually talking through his teeth and his pent up anger gave him all the strength he needed.

Turning Tommie over on the bed so that his head was spread on the blankets he ripped his trousers from his limbs. Immune to the screams and struggles Ger undid his zip and within a matter of moments he had penetrated Tommie from behind.

"Stop your squealing, you fuckin Mammy's boy," he yelled as he penetrated further. "How do you expect me to enjoy the ride with all that bleeding whimpering?"

Showing no remorse or compassion what so ever Ger shoved until he was satisfied that he had fully entered and then he began to push with all his might. Poor Tommie was absolutely powerless underneath him and when Ger reached his orgasm he laughed contently and climbed off.

"See how easy it is, you big fuck" he grinned as he pulled up his trousers and redid his zip. "I know that you enjoyed it too, so don't go denying it! You'll be begging me for some more of that before the night is out, you mark my words."

Tommie remained motionless on the bed, too humiliated and sore to move. The pain that had raked his body had sent him into oblivion and he had found it unbearable. He was completely shattered from the stress of the entire trauma but he knew that he needed to get out of there. He tried to move from the bed, to shout at a warden for aid, but he collapsed onto the floor. Without prior warning his chest began to feel tight and he was having difficulty breathing. He was in fact suffering a mild heart attack and, as he gasped for air, he honestly didn't care whether he lived or died.

Ger looked at the lifeless man on the floor before him and became frightened by the colour of his face. He knew that Tommie was anything but well and, because he did not want to be in the same cell as a dead man, he automatically began to scream for a prison officer. He felt no remorse for what he had done. Why should he? After all it was only a bit of fun and if Tommie had not been man enough to be able to take it, well then that was his problem. He was a waste of space and the sooner he was removed from his sight the better!

The prison warden arrived within minutes, after being terrorised to the core by Ger's demanding screech, and shook his head as he stared at the sight in front of him. Tommie was so still that it was hard to tell if he was dead or alive but he knew that the new prisoner had caused the upset. He was an evil, evil man and the sooner he moved to the west wing and out of his sight the better.

"What the hell has been going on here?" He looked at Ger and tried to keep calm.

"He's fainted, the stupid dope!" Ger was smiling, the knowledge that he had abused this man was still warming his soul. "I gave him a bit of pleasure to try and cheer him up and he fainted. Can you credit that?"

"What sort of pleasure are you talking about?" he hoped that his imagination was wrong.

"You know yourself!" Ger definitely had no regrets. "The sort of pleasure that only a man can give you. Anyway, take him to hell out of here before he dies! I couldn't settle here if that happens!"

Tommie was immediately taken from his cell and rushed to the prison hospital. He was placed on a heart machine and given sedatives to prevent his being from shaking. His condition was not that serious but he spent three full days between sleep and wake. His mind was a total mess and every time he closed his eyes he could feel Ger's breath on him, feel him do that awful thing that he had done and he began to hate his body. Another man had abused him and there was no getting over that. He prayed that no one would ever find out about the vile act. He'd kill himself rather than have that happen!

Eve visited the prison on the second day of Tommie's illness and was informed at the desk that he was unable to receive any visitors for at least a week. She was not happy with the verdict!

"I've come a long way to see him and I want to know why you are not going to allow me to do so. I have my visitor's pass and everything here." She fumbled in her pockets and brought out the pass.

"I'm not questioning any of that, my dear." The man behind the desk had a kind voice. "I'm sure everything is in order but you see, Tommie has suffered a mild heart attack and is in the hospital. Visitor's might just upset him at the moment and we want to keep him quiet until we are sure that he is alright."

He did not mention anything about the rape; prison officials did not want this information to leak out as there would be all sort of inquiries and God alone knows what the end result would be. Anyway this woman in front of him seemed distressed enough as it was.

"Oh, my God! Will he be alright? Was the heart attack serious? What brought it on? Could you not have telephoned me with this information? God, I wish I could see him!"

"Don't fret yourself, madam, Tommie will be alright. We rang his sister yesterday and hoped that she would pass on the news to you. The attack was only a minor one and he is pulling through. We are keeping him monitored just in case he has another one but to be honest we are not expecting it. He is young and strong and his body will put up the fight. Go home for now and come back early next week. You should be able to see him then!"

Eve couldn't stop the tears from falling as she sat on the train and was glad to reach her destination. All sorts of terrible thoughts were going through her head and she prayed to the Lord to give them a break. They had been through enough already and all she wanted now was to live happy ever after with the man that she loved. Was that too much to ask?

She had just entered the hall when the telephone rang. It was O' Meara.

"Eve, are you sitting down, my dear? I've just got word this very minute of a date for the retrial. It's set for Wednesday, the eighteenth of December. If everything goes according to plan we should have Tommie out, home and dry for the Christmas!"

"Oh, my God, that would be fantastic!" She allowed the tears to fall again. "The sooner all this is behind us the better! I've just come home from the prison and Tommie is in the hospital there. He has suffered a mild heart attack, nothing too serious according to the man behind the desk but how do we know? I wasn't allowed to see him! Oh, Mr. O' Meara, I'm so worried about him, we just have to get him out of there as soon as possible!"

"And we will, we will! We have a good defense lined up this time and you will be able to relate your side of the story. Eve, you will have to try and hold yourself together and be strong. We have a lot of work to do over the next few days so I can't allow you to fall apart. Tommie will pull through so you don't be worrying! As soon as the wardens let him know about the trial his heart will become light again and will aid to his recovery. Now, I'm going to ring Kitty and tell her the good news and I want to see the two of you in my office first thing in the morning."

"We'll be there," She tried to pull herself together as the lawyer had suggested. "And, Mr. O' Meara, thanks a million for everything."

Eve felt better as she brewed a strong cup of coffee and decided to make her way over to the Manor. She needed to talk to Kitty and she could collect Jack on the way.

Kitty was delighted to see her and immediately threw her arms around her. "Can you believe it Eve, the retrial has been set. It didn't take that long after all!" she was clearly on a high and hopeful of a good result. "We'll get him out this time, I can feel it in my bones."

It was then that she noticed the small boy at Eve's side. "And who may I ask is this?"

"This is Jack, my youngest. Say hello, Jack."

The child muttered his greeting and then hid behind his mother's back.

"Jesus, Eve, I shouldn't say this but that boy is the spitting image of Tommie when he was a lad. He even has the exact curls on top of his head. It's uncanny!"

"No, it's not uncanny at all, Kitty! I was never sure at first who his father was but, in the last few years, there seems to be no doubt at all in my mind. Tommie is Jack's father!"

"I can't believe it at all!" Kitty placed her hand over her heart. "Tommie has a son. My God, does he know?"

"We have never actually admitted it to one another but I'm sure deep down that he is aware that the boy is his. All the more reason to get him out of the jail! Did you know that he has suffered a mild heart attack?"

"The prison warden rang me yesterday evening. I was going to tell you but I kept putting it off. I didn't want to worry you!"

"I was up there today but I was not allowed to see him. I hope he will be alright!"

"He will," Kitty rubbed her hand. "And we will have him home for Christmas, just you wait and see. Now I have a bottle of red wine in the study, I think that we both deserve a glass, what do you say? And we will see if we can find something nice for this little chap here!"

"Sounds good to me!" And as she followed Kitty to the study Eve's heart began to feel a little lighter than it had been for months.

CHAPTER TWENTY SIX

After spending a week of recovery on a hard hospital bed Tommie physically began to feel a lot better and he was soon deemed fit enough to be sent back to his lonely cell. Terrified of what lay ahead he had pleaded his case with the governor and begged to be given a room of his own. There was no way that he could even contemplate sharing with Ger again and he broke out in a cold sweat when ever he thought of the horrors he had experienced at the hands of that criminal.

The governor did not even put up as much as an argument as he wanted to keep a lid on the entire incident and ensure that it's like never happened again. He had the good name of his prison to uphold and he wasn't about to let scum like Ger bring it down! And so Ger was moved to the other side of the building, even though the burst pipe had not been properly mended, and warned to behave.

However, while his heart may have begun to function healthily again Tommie's mental state was far from being right. No matter what way he looked at it he found the abuse hard to digest. His manhood had been depleted and he was still very sore and emotionally in tatters. He felt that he would never get over the ordeal and even when he heard about his retrial he found it impossible to muster up any form of excitement. While he prayed daily for his release he was far too terrified to sink any lasting hope into his future.

And he was absolutely dreading Eve's next visit. How was he supposed to face her again after what had happened to him? He wasn't a proper man anymore and he was sickened at the thoughts of any physical contact with another human. He wanted to be left alone to die, to fade into oblivion and forget all about the horrors and heartache that life had thrown at him. Was this how Rosie had felt when she had attempted suicide?

He was in the dining area that evening, sitting alone at a table, when Ger walked in. (Even though he was housed at the far end of the building there was a communal dining room, specifically for the benefit of the wardens.) His smug appearance sickened Tommie immediately and he turned to face the other way. This was the first time he had encountered him since the attack and he couldn't bear to be in the same room as him. Ger, however, was a horse of a different colour and he came over, placed his tray on the table next to Tommie's and brazenly sat down beside him.

"Tommie, me ole ride, how are you? Ya gave me a terrible fright, let me tell ya, but it's nice to see ya back among us again!" His grin was leery and lecherous.

Tommie completely ignored him.

"Ah, come on now! There's no need for ya to be like that, is there?" He turned to a group of men who were eating at the next table and managed to catch their attention. "Hey, what do yous lot think of this? This chap here won't talk to me today, he won't even look at me at all and I'm not kidding yous the other week he was in his cell looking for a ride off me!" He laughed a dirty laugh and Tommie winced as all eyes began to focus on him.

"If any of yous want a quick ride, Tommie here is your man." Ger was delighted with his audience and intended to make the most of it. "He's got a grand little arse and a firm, strong body. Ya won't go far wrong with him." Again he let a dirty laugh escape his lips and suddenly it seemed that the whole room was laughing.

Aggravated beyond control Tommie forgot all fears and stood up to deal with this fella. His blood was boiling and his heart pounding and he had never before felt so irate. He knew that in his present condition it was not proper to let himself get so angry but he couldn't help it. This fella was the lowest scum on the earth and needed to be taught a lesson. He tightly closed his fist to box him and that was when his reason started to kick in.

If he was involved in any sort of a scrap, no matter how small, it might affect his trial. Whatever little hope he had of escaping from this hell- hole he needed to cling onto it. His slate had to be immaculate if there was to be any chance at all of release and he knew that if he didn't get out of here soon he would kill himself, he would have no choice! No, he wouldn't stoop to Ger's level. He'd say nothing, let the fucker have his moment while he quietly left!

With his fist still tightly clenched Tommie took one look at the man that he hated more than life itself and quickly turned and walked from the room. His appetite was completely gone now anyway and as he made his way back to his cell he was aware that the entire dining room was laughing at him. He heard Ger make some chicken noises and refer to his 'grand arse' again but he didn't care. In fact he didn't care about anything anymore!

As he sat in the lonely confinement that was now his home Tommie's mind drifted to Dalesport and in particular to his father, Mr. Ken Harrison. He had wanted to make that man so proud of him, to be so successful and ambitious but what must he think of his heir now?

"If you can see me, Father." He looked towards the ceiling, hoping that Harrison had managed to finally escape purgatory and end up in heaven. "Know that I tried to do all I could to please you. This business with Eve and Podge just spiraled out of control and there was nothing I could do about it. But you can help me now. You can intervene to the Lord there beside you and ask him to get me out of here as quickly as he can. I need to get back to my farm, the farm that you left me, the farm that we both loved with passion. It's all I know in life. If the Lord is not able to rescue me for one reason or another then will you please ask him to come down and take me up there to you. I'm sick of it all and I don't think that I can cope anymore!" Blessing himself Tommie lay down on his narrow bed and cried like a child as a result of the depression that had enveloped his life.

Eve came to see him the following day and, although he tried to be cheerful for her sake, he was finding it rather difficult. He was not even able to look her straight in the eye!

She, on the other hand, was on a high over the retrial and kept rabbiting on and on about his release. He wished that he shared her confidence!

"Imagine, you'll be home for Christmas and we will make it the best one ever. We can get married early in the New Year and start our life as husband and wife. Don't you see it is all coming together now, Tommie, at long last, and I just can't wait!"

He glanced at her and a deep sadness gripped him. How could he tell her that he no longer wanted to get married? That he no longer wanted to feel the closeness of another body near his? Would she still want to marry him anyway if she knew what had occurred?

"Tommie, are you alright? What ever is the matter?" Eve was becoming anxious at his lack of response and couldn't understand why he was so sad. "Aren't you excited at the prospect of getting out of here?"

He looked into her lovely face and could feel the tears well up behind his eyes. He didn't deserve this perfect creature at all and she certainly didn't deserve all the hardships that he had put her through. Oh, if only he had held onto her the first time around or, better still, kept away from her altogether that night in the pub! Look at the way her life had been messed about! He had wanted her, then he didn't want her and then he wanted her again. He had killed her husband and here she was trying to free him and talking about their new life together. Maybe he deserved to rot in prison after all!

"Tommie, please say something, you are starting to frighten me!" "Eve longed to reach out to him but held back. His apathy was beginning to break her heart.

"Oh, don't pay any attention to me, this place is getting me down, that's all. The sooner this trial comes up the better."

"Won't be long now. Just another week or so! Hang in there Tommie and brave it out. We'll have you out of here in no time, I promise."

This time she did reach across and stroke his arm and was surprised when he flinched. It was not like Tommie to pull away from her but she knew he still loved her, didn't he? Nothing was ever going to stop him from loving her again! However, when the bell rang a few moments later, signaling the end of visiting, she was not quite so sure of anything anymore and ran from the building in a flood of painful tears.

She continued to cry on the journey home and wondered what had happened to the Tommie she had once known. Perhaps when he was released and had returned to his farm things might start coming right again! They had to- she was looking forward to it so much!

CHAPTER TWENTY SEVEN

"Tommie" O'Meara looked at his client from underneath his thick glasses and wished with all his heart that he could catch him in his hands and give him a good shake. "Can you please show a little more enthusiasm. I am here for the sole purpose of getting you out of this prison but anyone looking at you would think that you do not want to leave at all. Is that the case? Do you not wish to leave here?"

"I'm sorry!" Tommie viewed the man with respect and wished that he could show more interest. "I'm feeling a bit down at the moment but let me assure you that I do want to leave this place. I hate it here and the sooner I can go out those front gates the better."

"Ah good!" O' Meara opened his file. "Now that I know where we stand I will continue. Eve, your girl friend, has already explained your case to me and I have the details from the last trial but I still need to hear your side of the story. Can you relate that to me?"

And so Tommie retold the story of his fateful night and wondered if he would ever be free of it. He had killed Podge in self-defense but would it have been better if he had been the one to die? O' Meara was not given to bouts of self -pity, he felt that they served no purpose what so ever, and so he quickly brought him back to the present.

"Good, your story tallies with what has already been recorded. No discrepancies there good, bad or indifferent! That's the way we want it. Now my intention is to shape your tragic tale into a poignant love story, a sort of Romeo and Juliet affair. I want the jury to be completely bowled over by the passion that you two shared over the decade and thus instill sadness into their hearts at it's tragic end. By the time I am finished with them they will see no other option available but to reunite the pair of you. Everyone loves a good romance and I can assure you that your love will be so pure and undying and they will all be reaching for the tissues. They will not want you separated any more!"

"Let's hope it works out that way" Tommie actually managed a smile and had to admit that O' Meara was good.

"Now, were you ever accused of any previous crimes?"

"No, none!" Sure hadn't he always minded his own business!

"Good, good, and had you ever threatened Podge before that night?"

"No, I spoke to him at the markets but it was always just silly banter. We never argued! To be honest, I never knew him that well."

"So you could say that your character was flawless?" O Meara was delighted with the way this conversation was going and was becoming more and more confident of a victory.

"No body is ever flawless" Ger's heavy body staggered before his mind. "But before I was admitted to this awful place I was indeed a hard working man who went about his business and paid no heed to anyone else. My only crime was to fall in love with a beautiful woman and I have certainly paid the price for that!"

"I like that, I like that" O Meara began to scribble frantically. "I'm going to use that in my opening speech. I will say that the only crime that my client had committed was to fall in love with a beautiful woman and sure aren't we all guilty of that?"

Tommie smiled again and for the first time in a long, long time he felt that Dalesport was closer than he had ever hoped to imagine.

The eighteenth of December was bitterly cold but the day was fine and dry. The frost had cleared away early and a low, watery sun hovered in the wintry sky. Tommie was both excited and nervous as he was led into the dock at the central court, dressed in a suit again and feeling almost human, and as he looked around he could see the anxious faces of Kitty and Eve. Rosie

201

and Robbie were also there with their three children Kevin, Sarah and Jack and looked every bit the content family unit that they were. Jake sat beside them, his old tweed hat held in his hand and Bill sat up at the back with Sadie. It gladdened Tommie's heart to see his old pal. Oh God, he hoped that he would be able to go home with them! Was it too much to set his heart on?

O' Meara began his opening statement and Tommie had to hide a smile as he heard his lawyer state that his only crime was to fall in love with a beautiful woman. "Stand up all of you who have never committed this crime" he stared at the gathering and noticed that, although there was a lot of shuffling and looking around, they all remained seated. It was a good start!

Tommie glanced over to where the jury was seated and was delighted to note that, this time, they seemed to be a mixed bunch. Maybe he did have some hope after all!

Eve was the first to be called to the witness box and all eyes fell on her as she left her seat. She was nervous but determined and had dressed herself in a fetching black suit. Tommie's heart skipped a beat as he gazed at her and prayed that he would somehow be given the will to touch her again.

She was sworn in and then O'Meara began his questions.

"State your name for the record please."

"Eve, Eve Hodgins." She squeezed her fingers and wished that she were not so nervous.

"And what relationship were you to the deceased?" O' Meara did not delay.

"Podge was my husband!" She could hear the sigh from the jury but choose to ignore it.

"Eve, I understand that you have had a love affair with the accused. Is that correct."

"Yes, yes it is." She smiled across at Tommie and looked more beautiful than ever.

"How long have you known him?"

"Oh, I've known him a long time, seems like forever! I met him the night of his twenty fifth birthday."

"And you dated him when you were both single, is that correct?"

"Yes." She continued to smile at him, the love in her heart evident for all to see.

"Why did you break up with him?" O' Meara was pacing up and down in front of her.

"Tommie did not want to get serious. He had been hurt by women in his past and found it hard to trust them." She fiddled with her fingers again as she remembered the heartache of their separation.

"When you say women, do you mean former girlfriends?"

"No, not at all! His mother and sister both had affairs."

"Do you know any of his other girlfriends?"

"No, Tommie did not go out with that many girls."

"So you could say that you were his one and only love?" This was going nicely and the lawyer was satisfied.

"Yes." She looked straight at the jury and knew that they were tense.

"And were you sad at that separation?"

"Yes, I was heart broken! I begged him not to leave but he couldn't be swayed."

"And did you stop loving him after he had left?"

"No! I have never stopped loving Tommie."

"Does that mean that you still love him now?"

"Yes, more than ever! In fact it is safe to say that Tommie is the only man that I have ever loved!"

"But you married Podge Hodgins, the man whom Tommie allegedly killed."

"Yes. I was married to Podge for over fifteen years."

"Why did you marry him if you were still in love with Tommie?"

"Tommie had told me that he would never marry and I believed him. Podge, on the other hand, was always chasing me and at that particular period in my life I needed someone. I married Podge for a home and security."

"And were you happy with him?"

"For a long time I was. He was good to me but then he began to become possessive. He wouldn't let me speak to anyone or let me out of his sight for too long."

"Did you betray his love?"

"Yes, I'm afraid that I did! I started having an affair with Tommie."

"And before Tommie? Had you betrayed him with anyone else?"

"Good Lord, No! I would never have done that."

"But you did it with Tommie?"

"Yes, Tommie was different. Like I said I have loved him all my life and every day I thought about him. When we met up again I couldn't resist him. I was unhappy with Podge and Tommie was everything I've always dreamed of. Looking back I know that I should never have married. I should have waited for Tommie to change his mind but I was young and foolish."

"Tell me what happened on that fateful July evening, the night your husband died."

"I met with Tommie in Dalesport. I was planning to leave Podge and live with the man I adored. Podge was at a meeting in Ballyhale and wasn't due back until about ten. I made it home at around a quarter to but he had arrived home early. He asked me where I was and wouldn't believe that I had been out walking. He hit me across the face, his fists actually broke my jaw, and told me I was lying." She paused to catch her breath and was aware that there was not a sound in the courtroom.

"Go on!" O'Meara bade her to continue.

"He asked me if I had been out with a man and he called me a liar and a slut. He hit me several times and pulled roughly at my breasts. He hurt me and then he shoved his finger deep into my vagina and asked me if Tommie had been there before."

The crowd gasped as they pondered the horror of the situation and Tommie bent his head in disgust.

"I had enough at that stage. I couldn't take it anymore. I told him I had had sex with Tommie and that I was in love with him and that was when he rightly went mad. It wasn't because he loved me. It was because he couldn't bear for anyone else to have me. He pulled me to the floor and kicked me with his boots. He stayed kicking until I was senseless and had to be taken to hospital. I suffered multiple injuries and had slight damage to my brain. Worst of all I lost my baby, Tommie's baby." She wiped her tears from her eyes and found it hard to continue. The sooner it was over the better and as she glanced at Tommie she knew that the news of his dead baby pained him.

204

"Let this hospital records indicate that Ms. Hodgins is telling the truth." O'Meara waved them in front of the jury before handing them over to the judge.

"Now, Eve." He continued. "Do you know what happened next?"

"I was in a coma for a while and when I woke up I heard that Tommie had been jailed for the murder of Podge."

"And how did that make you feel?"

"I couldn't believe it. I knew that there had been some sort of mistake. Tommie would never harm another soul. He is too sweet and kind for that sort of thing. Ask anyone who knows him."

"Here, here." It was a cry from the crowd and when Tommie looked up he realised that it was Bill who was shouting. The judge was not impressed.

"Silence, please, or I will have you in contempt of court." Sadie nudged her husband and the session continued.

"So you do not think that Tommie killed your husband? But he was with Podge when the bullet was lodged in your husband's chest."

"Yes, but Podge set out to kill Tommie, he told me that he would finish me off first and then he would deal with Tommie. He couldn't let him live when he knew that he had already been with me! Anyway, there was a struggle and the gun went off. It was an accident, pure and simple. Tommie did not mean to kill Podge. It was self defense."

"He has already been convicted of the murder."

"Tommie is not a murderer. I'd lay my life on that. I wasn't at the first trial because I was in hospital but it is my opinion that he didn't receive a fair one. He should be set free and allowed to go home to the people who love him. He does not belong in a prison and has become a broken man since he has been committed."

"And you still love him."

"Yes, with all my heart." Her voice was so sincere and O' Meara knew that she had managed to touch the hearts of the jury.

"Thank you Eve, I have no further questions." He smiled as he walked back to his seat.

Paul Tobin was the solicitor for the state. He was an elderly man and it was his firm belief that Tommie should remain in prison. He had had an affair with another man's wife and for that alone he should be punished. He'd nail him today, if he got the chance!

"Hello, Eve." He greeted her. "So you had an affair with this man while you were still married."

"Yes." She did not like the look of this man and was scared at what lay ahead but she knew that she had to be strong for Tommie's sake.

"And do you not feel guilty for that? Did you not promise to love honour and obey until death us do part?"

"Objection, your honour." O'Meara shot up from his seat. "Eve is not on trial here."

"Sustained." The judge looked at Tobin with squinted eyes. "We have already established that these two had an affair."

Tobin looked demure for a moment and then continued.

"You say that you still love Mr. Bordoni. How can you love a man who has murdered your husband?"

"Tommie did not murder Podge."

"How can you be so sure? You said yourself that you were in a coma and therefore did not know what was going on."

"I know Tommie. He is not capable of that."

"Do you intend to marry him when he is free?"

"Yes." Her reply was definite and as she looked into the crowd she could see Kitty smile at her. Kitty who had been so hard on her at their first meeting but had recently become her best friend. She gave her the strength to keep going!

"Maybe that is why you want him out. Maybe you told him to get rid of your husband so that you two could be together."

"That is ridiculous. I may not have loved Podge but I wished him no harm. He is the father of my children after all and I would not take him from them. He was a good man in his own right and did not deserve to die. Anyway, what makes you think that Tommie would ever kill him just because I told him too."

"But you said that you two were in love, won't a man do anything to please the woman that he loves?"

"You have a very warped view of love, Mr. Tobin. You may be willing to please the woman in your life in that manner but

Tommie is made of harder stuff than that. There is no way that he would go out and kill a man just to please me!"

As a titter arose from the crowd Tobin began to feel a little foolish and suddenly declared that he had no more questions. Eve felt triumphant as she made her way back to her seat and she winked at Tommie as she passed.

The rest of the trial also went in Tommie's favour. Kitty was called to the stand and gave a character reference which confirmed Eve's description of Tommie's mistrust in women.

Jake was called upon at twenty past twelve and it was not a minute too soon. He had been sitting there all morning, chewing his nails and praying for his moment to come. His patience was wearing thin and now, as he shuffled his way up the courtroom, he was not in the slightest bit nervous.

"Jake, I understand that you were at the scene of the shooting on the evening in question" O' Meara spoke gently to the old man.

"That's right I was there!"

"How long have you known the accused?"

"Since he was a babby! I worked for his father before him!"

"And how would you describe him?"

"He's a grand fella, a hard worker and a great employer. He's the best in the world, really."

"And do you think that he killed Podge?"

"As God is me judge, he didn't. Sure wasn't I looking on!"

"Describe to me what you saw happen that evening."

"Well, I had been up in the far field looking at the cows and I noticed one of them was a bit lame. I said to meself that I'd alert the boss to the matter, just it case things had disimproved be morning. You never can tell with a lame foot. Anyways, I make me way to the cottage and I hear a lot of shouting going on. I was wondering what the hell was the matter because Tommie here had never risen his voice to anyone before. He's not a violent man, do ya see. Here I see him at the door of the house and what looked like a madman in front of him with a gun. He had his finger on the trigger and was about to release it."

"Who had?"

"Who had what?"

"Who had their finger on the point of release?"

"Podge, do ya see, only I didn't know he was Podge at that time. I had never seen the man before."

"What happened next?"

"Well as soon as I realised what was going on I screamed and he looked over in my direction. He was startled, I think, and Tommie saw his chance to save himself. He jumped on him, just to get the gun away mind, and the pair of them fell to the floor. The gun went off, accidental like, and the bullet hit Podge instead of Tommie. It was self defense, I swear to you and this man here," he pointed to Tommie, "should be at home with his family instead of behind bars. That's all I have to say on the matter!" He took a deep breath and smiled over at the jury, proud of his morning's work.

"Thank you, Jake, I have no further questions" O'Meara turned towards his desk.

Tobin was quick to get up off his seat and make his way to the box.

"Jake" he looked fiercely at the old man, almost terrifying him. "You said that you worked for Tommie's father. What was he like?"

"He was a grand man too."

"Rumour has it that he had an affair with several women, a bit of a ladies man, you might say. Do you think that his son might have inherited those traits?"

"Mr. Harrison was a grand man, as I have just said and what he did in his spare time, well that was his own business. But Tommie was a different kettle of fish altogether. I have never seen him with any other woman, apart from Eve here and I only ever seen them together the once."

"Right!" Tobin scratched his head and knew that he would have to try a different approach. "You said you were there the evening of the shooting. This man" he pointed to Tommie "has already been convicted of murder. Did you got give your evidence at the last trial?"

"I did!" Jake looked a little uncomfortable.

"And if what you say is true why did the jury not believe you? Why was he put down?"

"I can tell you something, me dear fella, there is no question about the truth in what I am after saying! I have sworn on the bible and I have me beliefs, you know. I would never fly in the face of our Lord" he bowed his head and blessed himself hurriedly "and utter falsehoods on his holy word. What kind of a man do you think I am at all? As to why the jury did not believe me, I honestly do not know! I think that they were out to get this man from the beginning, he being so well off and all and after all the news that was printed about him in

the papers I think that they were under pressure to send him away. But I swear to you all, I saw what I saw with me own two eyes and I don't need any glasses. Tommie was only fighting for his life and it is regretful that a man had to die in the process but there you are."

The judge's hammer came down hard on the table at around ten to one and he bid the jury leave to consider their verdict. O' Meara's finishing speech had far-outshone Tobin's and he was nicely confident as he took his clients to lunch in Jurys.

Eve was also smiling over dinner. She was one hundred percent sure that Tommie would be released and she couldn't wait to return to the courtroom.

"It's looking good for him, isn't it?" she directed her question at O' Meara but it was Kitty who answered.

"Don't get your hopes up yet, Eve. God only knows what will happen."

"Do you think Tommie will come home with us?" Sarah had seen the hope in Eve's wide eyes and prayed that everything would work out right for her. She herself was madly in love with Steve, a local doctor and planned to marry him in the not too distant future. She didn't know what she would do if he were ever taken from her.

"I hope so, Sarah, but we may wait and see!"

"He'll come home" Rosie seemed to have more confidence than her sister had. "I can feel it in my bones."

"That's a good sign so!" Robbie joked as he gazed adoringly at his wife. "When Rosie feels it in her bones it usually works out okay."

"I hope it works out okay this time!" Eve had noticed the look and had suddenly become envious. When would Tommie ever be able to look at her like that again?

At two thirty O'Meara's phone rang and he was requested to return to the courthouse. The jury had returned and was ready to give their verdict.

"We have to go back" he looked at the anxious eyes that were staring at him. "The jury are ready."

"That was quick" Eve wiped her mouth with a tissue and made to get up.

"Yeah, I hope it wasn't too quick!" Kitty was gripped with nerves and didn't even want to contemplate how she would feel if the verdict went wrong.

"I don't know" O'Meara straightened his glasses. "Usually when they have only been out for a short time we get good news. Anyway, we had better hurry back and face the music. Tommie will be relieved to see us."

They hurriedly left the hotel and anxiously ran the distance to the court. Eve's palms were sweating and Kitty's stomach was as sick as a dog. She was sorry that she had eaten anything at all.

Tommie was led back to the docks and his face was so pale and worried looking that all their hearts bled for him. Eve began to pray silently and kept her fingers crossed. She knew that she wouldn't be able to face him if things went wrong. Rosie held onto Robbie's supportive arm for dear life while Sarah hid her head in Jake's shoulder.

"What say you the jury, in the case of the state versus Tommie Bordoni?" The judge's voice seemed to bellow around the room. He was anxious to wrap it up and he had another trial starting shortly. "Do you have a verdict?"

"Yes, we do, your honour."

"Well, then, let us have it."

A small man, with a receding hairline, carefully unfolded the piece of white paper that he had in his hand and began to read. Tommie's heart stopped for a moment and Eve caught Kitty's hand and squeeze for all she was worth.

"We, the jury, in the case of the state versus Tommie Bordoni, do hereby find the defendant not guilty of the murder of Podge Hodgins."

"Not guilty, not guilty." Eve was screaming and frantically hugging Kitty. She waved at Tommie and found him to be in shock. He couldn't believe it. He was free! He could go home, it was more than he could ever have dared hope for!

"Silence, please." The judge had to have the last say. "Are you all in agreement here?"

"Yes, your honour!"

"Well then I am ordering that this man be released from prison immediately but he will serve two years community service. A man has died here, accidental or not, and the price has to be paid. We can decide exactly what this service is to be at a later date. Now, all stand. Court is dismissed."

As the hammer came down on the hard wooden desk again Eve ran from her seat and threw her arms around her love.

"I knew you'd get out," she whispered to him and kissed him on the mouth. She was surprised at his lack of response but told herself that this had been a very traumatic experience for him. But he was free now and their lives would begin from this moment.

As the crowd came forward to congratulate Tommie Eve made her way towards O'Meara. She shook his hand until he was sure that it would fall off and she thanked him for his help. She told him to send his bill to her straight away and she would pay it. She had previously sold off five acres of her farm to clear her debts and she had enough put by to pay the fees.

She invited him to join them for drinks in the Shellbourne before they made their merry way back to Dalesport.

CHAPTER TWENTY EIGHT

Tommie jumped suddenly and subconsciously pulled the cotton sheets away from his warm, sticky body. His bare back was wet with beads of sweat and his heart beating faster than an express train. Sitting up quickly he cautiously looked around the darkened room and was delighted to discover that he was in fact in his own bed; in his own room away from the rest of the world. Oh God, he had experienced yet another horrendous nightmare and, if he were to be perfectly honest, he had to admit that they were definitely getting the better of him.

It was almost two weeks now since his release from Mountjoy and in all that time he still hadn't managed a full night's sleep at the cottage. Oh, he went to bed exhausted after a hard day's work and longed for sleep to overtake him but it was not to be. Every time he shut his eyes it seemed that Ger was coming towards him. He could still see those evil eyes, still smell the nauseating sweat that had clung to his clothes and still feel the pain of the penetration. The penetration that had depleted his manhood and ruined his life! It was all becoming unbearable and was driving him mad.

He knew that he should seek professional help. He couldn't cope with much more of this alone but was far too embarrassed to talk to anyone about his ordeal. What would he say? What would anyone think if they knew what had happened to him? Oh God, why had he not been strong enough to stop that mad man?

During the days he found that if he kept himself extremely busy he would never give Ger as much as a second thought.

212

He was delighted to be back on the farm, back on the land that he loved with all his heart and he had a lot of catching up to do. Kevin had done a good job while he was away and had rewarded him with two young heifers of his own but there were things that he needed to do himself, things that not even Kevin would have noticed needed doing.

Stretching across the bed he switched on the bedside lamp and rubbed his eyes in desperation. His body was still shaking but he was calmer now and was beginning to become cold. He decided to dress and go to the kitchen. A cup of tea was what he needed to pacify himself and with a bit of luck the stove might still be emitting a bit of heat.

The kitchen was indeed warm and there were a few dying embers in the stove. Stroking up the ashes he threw some sods of turf onto the heat and opened up the damper. He sat in front of the fire as he waited for the kettle to boil and found his thoughts automatically reverting to Eve.

Eve had visited the farm every day since his return and he was aware that she was clearly disappointed with his attitude or lack of it. He had not as much as hugged her since they had been reunited, he just hadn't been able, and he knew that she could not understand this at all. She made several attempts to get close to him but Tommie could not bear to feel the breath of another human near his own body. He could not explain any of this to her. He needed her, perhaps now more than ever, and he loved her with all his heart but he was incapable of any physical contact. He told her that he had been depressed in prison and, because of his mild heart attack, he wanted to take things easy for a while. She hadn't been happy but had no choice but to be content for now.

As Tommie poured the boiling water into the mug he wondered if he would ever be able to hold her to him again. He wanted to, more than anything, wanted to lose himself in the softness that she oozed but was unable to. If he wasn't careful he'd end up losing her again and that was the last thing he wanted. Maybe if he managed a full night's sleep he might have more will, more energy but Ger was still haunting him and sleep still evading him.

Tommie was dreading the very thoughts of Christmas that year but it turned out to be a very quiet affair. Everyone had collected at the Manor, just in time for dinner, and spent the afternoon around the log fire in the parlour, conversing as they drank wine and whiskey. By eight o'clock that evening Tommie had been more than a little intoxicated and had wandered back to his own cottage alone. Eve had expressed a desire to accompany him but he had told her, in the nicest possible way, that he did not want company. He knew that he had hurt her feelings but he couldn't help it. She would be expecting him to take her in his arms and make love to her and he couldn't. It wasn't that he didn't want to! Lord no! His body definitely craved the excitement that had once been theirs. His mind, however, broke down every time he thought of the intimacy she expected and he trembled inside.

When he finally fell asleep, that Christmas night, he had the worst of all nightmares. Not only was Ger before him, his leering face screaming through the darkness, but three other inmates accompanied him and they were all trying to rape him. The images were so clear in his mind that he awoke screaming and swore on Stephen's day that he would seek help early in the New Year. He had to get his life back together or else he'd end up in an asylum. Besides he needed to give Eve the life she deserved after all he had put her through.

Kitty arranged a party for New Years Eve and she was hoping that it would turn out to be the party of all parties. Robbie and Rosie had promised to come from Meath while Sylvie and Ben had already made the trip across from England. Kitty longed for a special family gathering and put her heart and soul into organising the event. So many things had haunted them over the last few years but now, thank God, it looked as if life had finally turned around and everything was going to come right. The New Year was certainly a cause of celebration and Kitty wanted all her family around to help her celebrate the occasion.

Rosie called to see Tommie at his cottage as soon as she arrived home and was a little disillusioned with his mood. She recognised the same apathy that she herself had experienced on her release from hospital and she feared for her brother.

"How are you coping since you got home?" she decided not to make any reference to his black mood. She remembered

214

all too clearly how Kitty had grated along her nerves with her questions.

"Alright, I suppose" Tommie looked at her and realised she was happy. It was written all over her face and he was delighted for her. "I have good days and bad but the farm keeps me on my toes. How about you? Everything working out with you and Robbie?"

"Oh Tommie, I've never been happier. No matter what anyone says I never stopped loving that man and I owe him my life. I can't believe that he has completely forgiven me for the errors of my youth and since I left Dalesport my worries have disappeared. Meath is such a lovely county and the neighbours are all so friendly. You should come up and visit and bring Eve with you."

"Maybe I will in the New Year" he looked at the floor as he spoke.

"She's a lovely girl, Tommie, and she adores you."

"I know!" Why did he feel so guilty?

"I presume she is coming to the party tonight!"

"I suppose!" He had no real interest in the party at all as he didn't feel strong enough to cope with all the laughter. "I was actually thinking of giving it a miss myself."

"You can't do that" she was clearly shocked. "Kitty has gone to so much trouble to get us all together and she will be disappointed.

"I don't feel up to it," he still couldn't look at her. "All I want at the moment is a little peace and quiet. Can you understand that?"

"Of course I can understand, Tommie. I felt like that when I came home first. I wanted everyone to just leave me alone. I longed to crawl into a quiet little corner and stay there forever but let me tell you it does you no good at all. You will only end up becoming more depressed. You need to mix with people, start living again. You need your family around you. And believe me when I tell you that I know exactly what I am talking about!"

"And I will start living again, Rosie, but not tonight." He looked at her as he spoke and prayed that she would not give him the third degree. Rosie always had the knack of getting him to do things that he had no desire to do and he really didn't want to go to the Manor that evening.

"It's up to yourself" she surprised him with her answer. "But it still might be better if you come along tonight."

She had only departed about half an hour when Kitty and Sylvie appeared on his hearth.

"What's this I hear about you not wanting to come to the party?" Kitty held her hands on her hips as she spoke and Tommie thought that she would have made a great sergeant major.

"Be God it didn't take Rosie long to get home and tell you, did it?" He tried to look carefree.

"She is a little concerned about you, that's all. Will you please come, Tommie?" Kitty would beg if she had to.

"To be perfectly honest I'm not in the mood, Kitty" he was not to be swayed. "I'd only ruin your party with my dour face."

"But you have to come" Sylvie echoed Kitty's feelings. "Eve will be disappointed, we all will, if you don't."

"She'll get over it, you all will!" he couldn't believe he had said that and the look of horror in Kitty's face made him wish that he hadn't.

"Tommie Bordoni, what has got into you at all" Kitty still had her hands on her hips. "That woman worked like a Trojan to get you released from prison so the least you might do is come along and spend the evening with her. She loves you so much and I for one hope that you are not going to give her the run around again."

"I love her too, Kitty" his voice had softened now. "But I'm just not in the mood for partying. Give Eve my apologies, will you?"

"Ah come on Tommie, you have to come" Sylvie tried again but no amount of coaxing on her part could persuade him to change his mind.

As they walked back to the Manor, completely defeated, they began to wonder what was up with him. "Maybe Robbie might be able to get him to come" Sylvie suggested. "I know that the pair of them became pretty close over the years."

"No" Kitty finally accepted her brother's decision. "You know Tommie as well as I do and when he makes up his mind about something no amount of persuasion will change it for him. Let him sit on his own in the cottage, if that's what he wants. We'll enjoy the party without him." Still she worried about him as they crossed the old stile. He seemed to prefer his own company these days and it was looking like prison life had marred him for good. She would call up to him later on when things had quieted and have a chat with him. Maybe he would tell her exactly what was on his mind.

Bill dropped into the cottage at around six that evening, a bottle of whiskey clutched carefully under his arm and a huge smile plastered across his handsome face. As soon as he looked at Tommie he sensed that something was wrong. Tommie was clearly down in the dumps.

"Why the big long face?" he surveyed him and twisted his face in an attempt to make him smile.

"Don't know to be honest!" Tommie winced at the face. "I just feel a little down tonight."

"Well, tonight of all nights is no time to be down. Maybe a glass of this might help cheer you up!" Bill opened the whiskey and searched the dresser for two glasses. Handing Tommie a very generous measure he smiled.

"Slainte, me ole pal" he rose his glass. "We've been through some tough times together but we have always manage to come out smiling. You'll smile again too as soon as the lovely Eve gets her hands on you!"

"I hope so, Bill, I hope so!" Tommie was not as confident.

"Any plans for New Years Eve celebrations?"

"Not really! Kitty is having a family get together up at the Manor but to be honest I don't feel like going."

"God Almighty, sure you may go anyway!" Bill could not get over the change in his friend. "New Years is not for sitting at home alone. I'm taking Sadie out to dinner and then we are heading to an ole dance in Ballyhale. Would you fancy coming along?"

"Jesus, no!" Tommie actually managed a smile at the thought. "I'm sure Sadie would love to see me there ruining her evening. I'm really glad that it all worked out for you Bill. You were so young when you married her and I don't mind admitting that I for one was a little skeptical. I honestly didn't think that you two would last as long as this. Especially when you were such a ladies man."

"God, I was, wasn't I?" Bill drank some of the whiskey and made a face at the taste. "I had my fair pick of women alright! But you know yourself what it's like when the right woman comes along. You just keep looking at her beauty and fail to notice anyone else. I wouldn't swap Sadie for all the women in the Ukraine!"

"It's a pity it took me so long to recognise the right woman!" Tommie was becoming depressed again.

"All that is behind you now" Bill raised his glass again. "1995 is going to be your year. I can just feel it in my bones. You and Eve will marry and I will do the honours of being your best man!"

"I hope so, Bill, I really hope so!"

Eve arrived at the Manor at five to nine, totally oblivious to the fact that Tommie would not be attending the party. She was dressed in a red, off the shoulder dress and had her hair neatly piled on top of her head. The high heel shoes were killing her but she looked amazing and prayed that Tommie would appreciate the effort she had gone to. As soon as she entered the overly decorated hallway Kitty greeted her warmly.

"Eve, delighted you could come. You look fantastic! Are the kids with you?"

"No, I'm afraid not" Eve was looking towards the room with the noise. "Jack has a bad cold so the other two volunteered to stay behind and look after him. To be honest I think that they were too shy to come. They don't know anyone here. Anyway, I was looking forward to some time alone with Tommie. Is he in the parlour?"

"Oh, Eve, I'm afraid he's not here!" Kitty could have cried when she witnessed the disappointment on her face. "I can't understand him at all. I so wanted all the family here tonight. I practically begged him to come but he refused."

"Oh!" It was all she could mutter as the smile left her beautiful face. "And I was so looking forward to seeing him."

"Maybe he'll realise what he is missing, change his mind and come along later." Kitty was hopelessly trying to cheer her up. She hated to see the girl disappointed again. "In the meantime we might as well try to enjoy ourselves. Here, have a glass of wine and go along to the parlour. Rosie and Kitty are in there and the kids are somewhere about."

Eve took the glass of wine and slowly wandered towards the parlour. She could hear the singing as she made her way down to the hall and prayed for the will to join in. However, she knew that the evening had suddenly lost it's sparkle now. She had wanted so much to see Tommie and try and figure out why he no longer wanted her near him. She meant to get to the bottom of it before the sun arose on another year but how on earth was it going to be possible when he wasn't even here?

"Hi Eve, come on in" Sylvie greeted her warmly as she entered the room. "Have you a drink?"

"Yes, Kitty gave me one" Eve decided to shrug her despondency and try and enjoy herself. After all one year had just ended and they were about to enter a new one and Kitty had gone to so much trouble to make the night a special one for them all. Fuck Tommie, she wasn't going to let him ruin her night.

Full of resolve she looked around and attempted to join in with the singing. Sarah was playing Christmas carols on the piano while the rest of the family sang along. Kevin was talking to Robbie near the fireplace while Jack sat on the couch with his girlfriend. Ben was pouring wine for Jake, the farmhand and all of a sudden Eve felt almost like an intruder. It would have been different if Tommie had been there but his absence caused her to stick out like a sore thumb.

In order to feel more comfortable Eve swallowed back the wine in her glass and nodded at Slyvie for a refill. Four glasses of wine later she almost felt giddy but had to admit that she no longer felt like an outsider. And Tommie's family were all so nice! Oh, if only he had come along!

An hour later Eve was definitely feeling drunk and needed a strong cup of black coffee. Rising from her seat near Rosie she prayed that she would not stumble in her heels. She'd never wear them again as long as she lived. As she made her way slowly to the kitchen she wondered why on earth she had gone to so much trouble to get ready. She recalled her excitement as she has made her way to the Manor but now Tommie would never even see her!

She found Kitty in the kitchen, still busy attending to the food and she was so intent on what she was doing that she never even looked up. Eve noticed the stove burning cheerily in the centre of the room and the Christmas lights twinkling brightly. All of a sudden she was overcome by a dizzy spell and knew that she had to sit before she fell. Making her way towards Harrison's chair she placed her head in her hands and, as the heat rushed through her weary body, she felt desolate. Desolate and so alone! Suddenly she started to sob.

Startled, Kitty looked up and immediately rushed to her side.

"Whatever is the matter, Eve?" She had come to adore this woman and hated to see her so distressed.

"Ah, it's nothing Kitty, don't mind me, I'll be okay in a moment or two." She knew that the wine was not helping but she did feel so low.

"Ah come on now! You can tell me. It's to do with Tommie, isn't it?" Kitty knew how disappointed she had been when her brother had not showed up. She still couldn't understand him; he could have made the effort for Eve's sake. They were supposed to be in love after all and Kitty remembered how important New Years Eve had been to her and Mick.

Eve was silent for a few moments and then slowly lifted her head and dried her eyes. Looking into Kitty's kind and gentle face she suddenly felt the need to talk and who better to talk to than Kitty!

"You're right, Kitty, it is because of Tommie that I am so unhappy. I came here tonight full of joy and expectation and he never even showed up. I don't know what is wrong with him since he came home from that prison. He's a changed man! He seems so distant and I can't reach him at all no matter how hard I try. I'm beginning to think that he doesn't want me anymore."

"Don't be silly, Eve, of course he wants you. For God's sake he loves you! He needs time that's all. He's been through a hell of a lot."

"Oh, I understand all that! Prison is not a nice place to be and it's bound to have affected him. But he's not the only one who has been affected by it all! We've all been through the mill over the last few months but we got through it, didn't we?" The sorrow in his voice caused her to stop for a moment. "I was so looking forward to getting him out of that prison. I counted the hours until he would be a free man again. You see I thought that things would really start to improve as soon as he came home but they haven't. I need him so much, Kitty. I want to hold him and comfort him and tell him that everything is okay but he won't let me."

"What do you mean?" Kitty did not fully understand.

"He won't let me touch him. Every time I try to get near him he seems to move away and it hurts a lot. Maybe he doesn't love me anymore, maybe that's what's wrong!" She released a big sob at this point and Kitty was alarmed.

"You mean you haven't, you know, since he came home?"

"No, we haven't even kissed. Can you believe that?"

"Jesus, Eve, this is more serious than I thought. Maybe he thinks that you don't love him now that he has been in prison."

"For Christ sakes, Kitty, he knows that I love him." She knew that this was not the problem.

"Have you told him as much lately? As you said prison is not a nice place and it can do strange things to a man. Maybe he just needs to hear those words from your lips."

Eve was silent for a moment as she pondered what Kitty had just said. Surely be to God Tommie did not need to hear her say that she loved him? He must know in his heart just how much she actually adored him! Still, he had been through his fair share of stress and, as Kitty had said, prison does strange things to a man. Maybe his self-confidence had been shattered somewhere along the way!

"Perhaps you are right." She finally spoke. "Perhaps he does need to hear me utter those words again. First thing tomorrow I'll go to the cottage and tell him."

"If I were you I wouldn't wait until tomorrow." Kitty was excited now, confident that this could have a very romantic ending after all. "It's New Years Eve, a night for a new start. Go over there this minute and tell him exactly how you feel. It will cheer him up and by the looks of you it will do wonders for you too!"

"He mightn't let me in" Eve was not as confident as Kitty.

"No problem, I have a key to the cottage. Hold on and I'll give it to you."

She left the food for a moment and went over to the china teapot on the dresser. After rummaging around inside for a few minutes she eventually managed to locate the key.

"Here it is!" she handed it triumphantly to Eve.

"Do you really think this is a good idea?" Eve was a little anxious and wondered if Tommie might be angered by her intrusion.

"Of course it is! You have the key so go and let yourself in. Tell him how much you love him and see what happens! He will both throw his arms around you and tell you that he loves you too or kick you out. One way or the other you will know where you stand. Good luck, Eve, and remember, you are to come back here if Tommie loses the cool. Don't go wandering home alone in a state." She kissed her before she left and as she turned her attention to her pastries again she prayed that she had done the right thing.

Eve grabbed her coat and scarf and, listening to one last bar of ' Silent night', stepped out into the cold, still night. The moon was high and lit her way as she walked across the fields. She was full of determination but as she neared the cottage she was overcome with a sudden anxiety attack. Pausing near the old lime trees she took a few moments to steady herself. What was wrong with her? Why was she feeling so nervous? This was Tommie she was meeting, for God's sake, Tommie whom she had loved all her life. After all that they had endured together why should she be afraid of him now?

The light was on in the front room, she could see it's orange tint through the crack in the window curtains, and as she turned the key in the lock she heard a dog howl in the distance.

Slowly she entered the cosy cottage and found him sitting at the open fire, an empty bottle of whiskey at his side. He was genuinely surprised to see her.

"How did you get in?" He did not even greet her. Did he not want her there?

"Kitty gave me a key." Her voice was mellow. "I hope you don't mind. It's just that you weren't at the party and I wanted to see you."

"The reason that I did not go to the party was because I did not feel like company today. I thought I explained all that to Kitty earlier. She should have known better than to go handing out my key!" He was looking rather cruelly at her and she was startled. This was not the Tommie that she knew and loved!

"Will I go then?" She didn't want to but was suddenly feeling very uncomfortable. She had also noticed that he was a little drunk and she had never seen him like that before.

"No, you might as well stay now that you are here. Grab that bottle on the kitchen dresser and get yourself a glass. The New Year will be in shortly so we might as well toast it together."

Eve did as she was bid and, although she had no gra for the whiskey, poured herself a healthy amount. She spluttered as it hit the back of her throat and wondered how anyone could drink the stuff.

"That Paddy there is hard on the body." He laughed at her, breaking the awful silence that had developed and reminded her of the man she loved. "I used always wonder why my father used to drink so much of it. It was his favourite tipple, you know. Now I know why! It certainly helps a man forget."

"Forget what, Tommie? What are you trying to forget?" She looked into his eyes and could sense the awful hurt that was breeding there. Surely be to God he was not trying to forget her? Her stomach actually felt sick at the very thought.

"What do you think I'm trying to forget, Eve?" His patience was limited. "I'm trying to forget the terrible year that I have had. I am trying to forget the pain that I have caused and the fact that I actually killed a man. But most of all I am trying to forget the absolute horrors of that cold, damp prison." He drank from his glass and she noticed that he was unable to look at her as he spoke.

"Was it really awful in there?" She knew that it was, it was a stupid question to ask, but she desperately needed to continue the conversation. Needed to know if he still wanted her.

He turned and looked strangely at her for a moment, causing her heart to jump. "You'll never know how bad it was there, Eve. No one could unless they had first hand experience of it. It has to be the worst place on earth and the last that God made!"

"Do you want to talk about it?" She prayed that he would start to open up to her at last, start to trust her again.

"No!" His answer was definite and dulled her spirits. "I want to try and put the whole thing behind me and talking about it is not going to help matters. Now look, it's a minute to midnight. Raise your glass and welcome in the New Year."

"Let's hope it's a better one than the last one." She lifted her glass and as the clock struck the midnight hour she automatically leaned over to kiss him. "Happy New Year, Tommie" she whispered as she got close.

"We'll be having none of that." He could feel her warm breath on her face and suddenly froze within. As the terror gripped him small beads of sweat began to form on his brow.

"Why not?" She was angry at his rejection and needed to know the reason for it. "Why do you not want to kiss me anymore?"

"I don't want to kiss anyone anymore." He looked so fierce that she could feel her heart pound uncontrollably against her rib cage.

"Why not? You have to at least tell me that much! Do you not love me? Is that it? Have you stopped loving me, Tommie?" The truth needed to come out here but she wondered how she would cope with a negative answer.

He looked at her for a moment and was deeply saddened by the heartache that was so clearly written all over her face. He knew that he was being cruel to her and he wondered exactly how much more pain was he going to cause this woman.

"I do love you Eve, you must know that! I have always loved you" he finally spoke. "But I just can't touch you."

"Why not? Tell me, Tommie. Why can't you touch me? Is it because you do not find me attractive anymore?" The tears began to form in her eyes and added to his grief.

"Don't be silly, Eve. You're a beautiful woman. Any man would be honoured to have you by his side."

"Well then, what's wrong? Tell me!" She was shouting at this stage, her emotions running riot. "Don't you think that I have a right to know?"

"I can't tell you. You will just have to trust me on this one." He bowed his head for a moment and wished that she would go away.

"That's not a good enough answer, for God's sake." She intended to get to the bottom of this if it killed her. "We were going to get married, weren't we? I love you Tommie, I can't bear what you are doing to us, please talk to me."

"Eve, you don't know what you are saying here at all! You can't marry me now. You wouldn't even love me if you knew the truth." He hung his head in shame and wished that he could die.

"Well then, tell me what the truth is and let me make up my own mind. Don't you think that I have a right to know and you have a right to tell me? After all we have been through surely I can cope with the truth!" What was causing him such anguish? Surely it could not be that bad? "Oh, Tommie, please, please trust me. I have worked so hard to get you out of prison. I was looking forward to the future and it breaks my heart that we cannot be together. I need you more than anything else in this world."

"Oh, Eve!" The hot tears stung his eyes and spilt down his face. She was afraid to reach out to him but needed to offer him comfort. She took his hand and was delighted when he did not pull away.

"Please, Tommie, tell me what is bothering you. It will do you good to get it out of you system and surely be to God we have been through enough together to sort this one out!" She gazed into his eyes and he was indeed comforted by the love that shone from her.

Tommie sighed heavily as he contemplated his choices and was aware that if he did not let Eve know what was bothering him he might lose her altogether. He didn't want that, not after all the grief that he had experienced to get her.

Sighing again he eventually looked at her and licked his lips. She did have a right to know and he definitely needed to get it off his chest. If she left, so be it! Anything had to be better than the way things were at the moment.

"I'm not a real man anymore!" He almost whispered as the awful truth was uttered.

"Don't be silly, how can you say that? Of course you are a real man." She did not fully grasp what it was he was implying. "You look real enough to me anyway!"

"No, Eve, you don't understand, you can't even try to understand! Something happened to me in that prison. Something really awful and I simply can't tell you what it was."

"Tommie, you know that you can tell me, you can tell me anything. Please try. Were you beaten up?"

"No, it was worse than that, Eve, far worse. I could have coped with a beating but this?" He rubbed his eyes and fought to hold back the fresh fall of tears that were developing. "This is far worse than anything that you could possibly imagine!"

"Tell me what happened" she was insistent and not about to give up. "I can deal with it and help you through it. After all, that is what I am here for!"

"Oh, darling" he willed himself to continue. "I was raped! I was raped in the prison." He stared at her for a moment awaiting her reaction and the tears continued to fall. What would she think of him now?

"Raped?" She couldn't fathom it at all. "What do you mean raped?"

"A cell mate raped me, Eve. He had only come into the prison that day and he was put in my cell. He was a queer and he raped me." He rubbed his face with his hand and he bowed his head. "It was the most painful experience of my life and certainly the most degrading. That was why I suffered that stupid heart attack. So what do you think of me now?"

"Oh, my poor, poor darling." It was all that she could utter but as she took him in her arms and he placed his head against her shoulder there were no need for any more words. Tommie cried until he felt his heart would crack and Eve's spirit was broken as she witnessed his sadness.

Within minutes she also began to cry at the horrific thought of his ordeal and she pulled him closer and cradled him to her.

It took over half an hour for both of them to compose themselves and it was Tommie who spoke first. He harboured no regrets at telling her now. He had needed to get it off his chest and suddenly felt as if a weight had been lifted from his shoulders. Now he wanted to know what she would do, needed to sense her reaction.

"Well, what do you think of me now?" He repeated his last words as he dried his eyes and she slowly released him.

"Oh, Tommie! I don't know what to say! I'm so sorry that this had to happen to you. It must have been awful! That animal deserves to be put down. He is only scum of the earth but the entire façade was completely out of your hands. My only regret here is that you did not tell me all this sooner. It might have saved a lot of heartache. But tell me, how did you think that this was going to change the way I feel about you? Do you not realise yet just how much you mean to me? I love you more than anything in this world and I'm going to love you no matter what. You are a victim in all of this and there was nothing you could do to save yourself. You will have to try and put it behind you and get on with your life."

"I know, I know but it is not going to be easy. I can still feel him crawling on my skin and I wake up sweating at night from the nightmares. I can't even let you near me for God's sake. Every time I feel your warm breath on my body I am reminded of him and I freeze!"

"And I thought that you didn't want me anymore. I don't know what I would have done if that had been the case." She leaned towards him, relieved that he still cared for her.

"I never wanted you to find out, that was the last thing on earth I was wishing for! I thought that once you knew you would hate me. But to tell you the truth I am glad now that I told you. Oh Eve, I do love you too and I wish that I could make love to you again."

"And you will Tommie, you will, I promise you that." She took his hand and held it within her own. "We will just have to take things one step at a time. We'll go slow, I have the rest of my life to wait for you, and if that does not work out for us then we will seek professional help."

"I'd prefer not to have to. I don't want anyone else to find out about this. Promise me that you won't breathe a word to Kitty or to anyone."

"Of course I won't, it's our secret and we'll work something out together. I'm confident of that! Maybe you could can start by giving me a hug!"

Tommie actually managed a weak smile as he took her to him and held her in his arms. As their closeness became more demanding she could feel his body shake. He really was in a bad state and she grieved for him. But she was going to be strong and get him through this. She had no choice and he needed her! Before long they would be enjoying each other again; if their love stayed strong everything would turn right again. Her New Years resolution was decided there and then, she would do all that she could to mould Tommie back into the man that he once was. Still holding onto him she whispered into his ear. "What would you say if I stayed with you tonight?"

"What do you mean?" He was a little startled for a moment and automatically released her.

"Just for the company, nothing else! I know that you can't make love to me yet and I don't expect you to but we could sleep in each others arms and feel secure."

"I suppose it is worth a try!" He definitely could see no harm in it and hoped that it might help ward off any nightmares that might develop.

"Joe and Pete can look after Jack. I think that you need me more tonight than he does. And Tommie."

"What?" He was feeling happier already.

"Happy New Year."

"Happy New Year, Eve." He whispered his reply and finally admitted that he could see some light at the end of the long dark tunnel.

They remained by the fire, drinking the whiskey and chatting about old times until well after two o'clock. When they did actually retire both were exhausted and fell asleep wrapped around each other. For the first time in ages Tommie experienced a full night's sleep and had no nightmares.

CHAPTER TWENTY NINE

After New Years Eve, Eve spent nearly every second night at the cottage and by the end of February she was beginning to notice a big improvement in Tommie. He seemed to be more cheerful and content and, as he began to be return to his former self, she felt that his ordeal was already starting to fade into the past. She was happy to take things slowly and was very surprised on that day when he actually pulled her to him and kissed her passionately on the mouth. They had not yet made love but she felt that he was nearing that goal. She had decided to let him make the first move because she had no desire to pressurise him into anything that he might later regret. He would come to her when he was ready, of that she was confident, and she was willing to wait!

March that year was a cold and dreary month. The winter fires continued to burn and everyone was praying that the long evenings would soon bring a bit of warm sunshine. The cattle were still in the sheds as the fields were too wet and soggy and no one wanted a mess on their hands. The daffodils had budded but had not yet displayed their welcome yellow trumpet although the snowdrops had already blossomed and died.

On St Patricks day, the seventeenth of March, Tommie had taken Eve and Jack to the grand parade in O' Connell Street. It had been a great day, he knew that she had enjoyed it as much as Jack, and they had eaten in McDonalds before taking the train home. Jack was thrilled with his adventure and as Tommie looked at him he finally admitted to himself that he was his. No amount of blood tests could alter his opinion.

Eve left an exhausted Jack to Joe at eight o' clock that evening and made her way to Dalesport Farm with Tommie. He held her hand as they walked and talked non-stop about the parade. It really had cheered him up to leave the farm for the day and she promised herself that they would do it more often in the future.

As soon as they reached the cottage Tommie set about lighting the fire and was glad to be in out of the biting winds. The kitchen was cold and as he waited for the fire to throw out it's heat he opened a nice bottle of white wine. Then they sat, content in one another's company, and savoured the sweet taste as they both stared into the growing amber flames.

After he had polished off the third glass of the wine Tommie began to feel relaxed and happy. The room had now warmed considerably and as he looked across at Eve he was reminded again of exactly how beautiful she really was. Her skin glowed from the light of the flames and her sweet smile caused his heart to sing. He knew that he was indeed a very fortunate man to have her by his side, hadn't she stuck with him through thick and thin, and he loved her more than life itself. Perhaps it was time to show her that love again! He felt that he was ready and so, without hesitation, he gently moved closer to her and kissed her passionately on the mouth.

As he tasted her sweet lips he was overcome with his old longings and he prayed that nothing would stop him. He didn't need any flashback to remind him of his horrendous nightmares and he was glad that they had suddenly begun to frequent him less and less as one month rolled into the next. Eve became excited as his hand wandered underneath her jumper and she silently hoped that he would not stop.

But Tommie had no intention what so ever of stopping. The ghosts that had been haunting him were suddenly at peace and as he fondled her breasts he was happier than he had been in a long time. Within minutes he was undressing her and as he entered her he felt that he was home again. He was delighted afterwards and realised that finally he had become the man that she deserved. They spent the entire night making love and when the sun was high in the sky they both fell into an exhausted sleep.

It was noon before either of them awoke and Tommie was the first to stir. He lay still for several minutes just looking at her face. She was so beautiful and sweet and she had made him whole again. She was his saviour and he knew that he wanted to spend the rest of his life with her. She would make him happy, of that he was confident and without her everything would become meaningless. Enough time had already been wasted and he would waste no more! Without giving the matter a second thought he gently pushed her in the bed and awoke her. She sat up wearily and rubbed her eyes but as she noticed him staring lovingly at her she smiled and felt good.

"Eve." He was whispering softly. "Are you properly awake? There is something that I need to ask you."

"What is it, Tommie?" He wasn't having any regrets about last night, was he? "What's so important that you have to awaken me out of my peaceful dream to tell me?"

"Don't look so frightened!" He couldn't help but laugh at her cute startled face. "I was wondering if you would do the honours of becoming my wife."

"Oh Tommie, you know how I feel about that, don't you? I would be delighted to become your wife, isn't it all I have dreamed about since that first night that you asked me to dance at Ballyhale!" She threw her arms around him, relieved by his question and overcome by the change in his spirit, and kissed him.

"I want to get married as soon as possible. I want to have lots more babies with you. We'll give Jack a few sisters. What do you think?" He sounded excited now, reminding her of the original man that she had fallen in love with.

"I think that would be wonderful. How about a summer wedding? The first of June has always appealed to me. We'll keep it simple. Just family members and a few friends."

"Yes, and we'll have the reception at the Manor. That place could do with a bit of shaking up."

"Oh, I can't wait to tell Kitty. I'm going to get her to be my maid of honour. And I'll ask Sarah to be my bridesmaid."

"Yeah and I'll get Bill to be Groomsman and Joe to be best man. We'll make it a day to remember."

"It'll be the best day ever! We've both waited so long for this to happen."

"Would you like to live here or at the Manor? You know Rosie signed it over to me after she left for Meath. She figured that since it had belonged to my father I should have the right to live there. She wanted nothing more to do with it." His mind was definitely racing ahead now, the horrors of his past forgotten.

"Well, I've kinda got used to this old cottage. And anyway it would be a shame to hunt Kitty out of the Manor after all the years that she has spent there."

"I was hoping that you would say that. The boys won't mind living here will they?"

"Jack will be delighted, you already know that he adores you. As for Joe and Pete, sure they won't be coming along. Both of them are old enough to run the farm by themselves. I'm going to sign it over to them. They will make a go of it and sure if they don't we can always help them out, can't we?"

"You have it all worked out haven't you." He smiled a smile of sheer contentment as he ruffled her hair.

"As I have already told you it's what I've always wanted and God knows I have had plenty of time to think about it!"

"It's what I've always wanted too but it took me a little longer to realise it. Oh, Eve, thank God I have finally come to my senses!" He kissed her again and knew that the future was indeed looking good. Harrison's heir was finally about to become a married man and he had absolutely no regrets. He had managed to survive the hardest of all ordeals that would ever be thrown at him and he hoped that his father would indeed be proud of him. As he looked towards the ceiling he wondered if Harrison was actually smiling down at him. He felt that he was because at that particular moment in time he felt closer to him that he had ever felt before.

THE END

ISBN 1425130054-2